The Mojave Gimmick

The Slater Ibáñez Books

That First Heady Burn
True Vermilion
The Dark Shill
A Stack of Sawbucks
The Hillside Roble
The Peroxide Pomp
The Incidental Twin
Brawl in Bardo
The Window-Shade Job
The Convenient Patsy
The Artisanal Grifter
Shrink in the Shadows
Project Chartreuse
From a Desert Playa
The Tired Canary
A Desperate Frame-up
Trail of the Blue Agave
The Saucer-Heads
The Satin Squeeze Play
Chiseler in Jade
The Eagle and the Weasel
The Mojave Gimmick

Subscribe to the Slater
Ibáñez Books newsletter:
slaternews.dagmarmiura.com

The Mojave Gimmick

The Mojave Gimmick

George Bixley

Published by Dagmar Miura
Los Angeles
www.dagmarmiura.com

The Mojave Gimmick

First published 2024

ISBN: 979-8-89195-041-2

ONE

SLATER KIND OF HATED Labor Day, with its melancholy vibe, the tacit message that summer was over. LA never got that cold, but Labor Day still meant the end of the warm weather, the days growing shorter. He didn't have any work on right now, and it felt like he was pissing the day away, working on pruning the foliage in the side yard, doing fiddly little maintenance jobs around the house, tightening loose hinges and swapping out lightbulbs for the warmer ones that Pike liked.

He hated when Pike wasn't around, and he'd been away for a while. The guy worked for the feds, and his department had loaned him to some team or task force, something to do with bikers. The idiot was actually riding around on a motorcycle. Slater hated that too. It seemed so damn risky.

Standing in the kitchen on the top floor, he heard the garage door roll up. That had to be Pike. No one else had an opener. Heading down the stairs, he stepped into the garage as the door rolled down again. Pike climbed off his bike and pulled off his helmet. The guy was thick and had lush dark hair that had grown way too long. He used to cut it, and shave, but for the biker persona he'd grown it out, and let his beard grow wild. The whole look was unctuous and grubby and rough.

Embracing him, Slater mashed their mouths together, and ran his hands over his back, squeezing him through his leather jacket. Eventually he pulled away.

"Are you back to stay?"

"Unfortunately not," Pike said. "It's just for the night. I didn't want to miss Doris's barbecue."

Slater mouthed his neck, and ground his burgeoning woody into his thigh, and spoke in his ear. "I sense a biker uprising."

Pike chuckled. "Let's go upstairs."

The bedrooms were on the middle floor, and they slept in the one facing the street. Pike tossed his jacket on the armchair and soon had his clothes off. Once Slater had ditched his jeans, he pushed Pike back onto the bed and climbed up, straddling him, mouthing his neck and his chest and squeezing his cock.

Pike ran his hands into Slater's hair, then squeezed his shoulders. "You need to fuck me."

Once he'd grabbed the lube from the bedside drawer, he pushed Pike's knees apart and moved closer, pressing into him, starting slow.

Wincing, Pike massaged his biceps, and tilted his

head back, and soon got into it. Slater leaned in and buried his nose in his long hair as he pounded him, inhaling the scent of his sweat. Shifting upright, his hands on Pike's waist, he strained into him as he came.

"Stay there." Pike stroked himself until Slater batted his hand away and took over. A moment later Pike climaxed, a shudder running through his body.

Once he'd pulled back, Slater stretched out next to him, catching his breath. "I missed you so hard."

"I hate being away from here. Away from you."

"What exactly are you doing with the bikers?"

"I can't really talk about it," Pike said.

"You think I'm going to let it slip when I'm gossiping across the back fence? I know the stakes."

He interlaced their fingers and squeezed his hand. "I know you can keep your mouth shut. It's one of your highly developed skills. Sometimes I don't even know what's going on in our own narrative complex."

"I'm working on that." Slater took a breath. "It has to be guns or dope. That's what bikers do."

"It's mostly drugs. They're manufacturing a fuck-ton of meth."

"Are you posing as a buyer? What's your alias?"

"You already know that."

"Seth Pine?" Slater said. "I love that guy."

"Seth has a network of low-level penny-ante dealers under him," Pike said. "They're selling product around Southern California. A couple of hours ago I had several pounds of it in my saddlebags."

Slater sat up and straddled him, massaging his chest. "So you're a macher, not just a small-time buyer. That's actually hot. Where did you take all that meth?"

"To my network of low-level penny-ante drug dealers."

"Bullshit."

He laughed, flashing that beautiful smile. "Some of my colleagues are going to check into it."

"You should clean up to go to Doris's."

"I wish I could," Pike said. "Unfortunately I need to stay in character."

Climbing off him, Slater padded into the bathroom and turned on the shower. Pike joined him, and was still washing his hair after Slater had toweled off and walked out. He put on a clean shirt and jeans, and when Pike came out he pulled on the same grubby denim he'd rode up in.

They trooped down to the garage and climbed in the Continental, a classic 1970s model. It was big and unwieldy sometimes but Slater loved driving it, loved the cloudy-blue paint job and the cherry interior. As Pike climbed in he lifted the pink pastry box off the passenger seat, briefly opening the lid.

"You've been to the deli. Doris is going to love these."

Slater backed into the street and waited for the door to roll down, frowning at the sight of Pike's bulky motorcycle in the other bay, then drove to hilly Mount Washington. It wasn't far, on the opposite side of Elysian Park and the stadium. Doris's Buick was in the driveway in front of her bungalow, but there was no sign of her stupid boyfriend's stupid doll car. That was a relief.

It felt warmer here as they climbed out, and Pike handed him the pastry box as they walked to the side gate and into the backyard. The plantings looked tight,

Slater decided, surveying the space. They should—he'd put in the time on the yard this summer. The roses had stopped blooming for the season, and the beds of ornamentals seemed content. The buckwheat was still thriving, and looked wild and chaotic, but it wasn't overstepping its edges yet.

Doris had already laid stuff out on the patio table: corn chips and a bowl of guac with plastic wrap on it, a stack of glasses, a pitcher of lemonade, and a bucket with beer bottles on ice.

Doris stepped out the back door of the house and greeted them. Petite, she had some gray in her dark hair, today wearing plaid pants and a summery white blouse. As Slater leaned in to kiss her, she embraced him, then pulled back and planted her palms on his cheeks.

"My handsome son."

"You don't need to be pawing the merchandise, woman."

Doris laughed. "What's in the box?"

"Just some snack treats from the deli."

She opened the top and peered inside. "Ooh, black-and-white cookies. What a treat."

Once she'd embraced Pike, she pulled back and grasped his forearms. "Your hair is so long. You're really letting it all hang out."

"It's not like I'm having a psychotic break," he said. "It's for work."

"That sounds exciting. Come and sit." Doris looped an arm through his and led them over to the patio table.

Pike took the chair opposite her, and grabbed a beer, and twisted off the cap. Once Slater sat down, he poured lemonade for her, and a glass for himself.

"Are you off the sauce?" Doris said.

"I have no reason to do that." He frowned. "I'm not drinking because I'm driving."

She held up a palm. "Just asking."

"Your yard looks amazing," Pike said, and gestured to it with his bottle.

"That's the long-term dividend of encouraging this one to study horticulture."

"Interesting choice of words from the puppeteer," Slater said. "I remember standing there with my degree in hand and thinking, *How did this happen?*"

Doris laughed. "I wasn't pulling your strings. I knew you'd be good at it."

"He's very good at it," Pike said, "based on the state of your landscaping."

She raised her eyebrows. "I suppose you can't talk about the work you're doing."

"All I can say is that it's easier for people to relate to you when you look like them."

"I can handle the clothes," Slater said, "but I hate that he's riding a motorcycle."

"So it's about biker gangs."

"We call them motorcycle clubs," Pike said, "and no comment."

Slater gestured toward him. "With the biker clothes and the beard it feels like Purim. I was about to bust out the hamantaschen."

"I was thinking I kind of like this look," Pike said. "I might have to keep it going after this project. Let my hair get even longer." He held Slater's gaze and raised his eyebrows. "I'll have to buy a hairbrush, and pomade, and a bunch of pricey hair products."

"You're torturing him," Doris said, and chuckled. "Long hair is a lot of work."

"I've been finding hair everywhere," Slater said. "Rosa said there was so much of it around the house, it burned out the motor in the vacuum."

Pike laughed, his tone deep. "That is such a lie."

"I signed up for a drip-dry pit bull," Slater said, frowning at him, "and I wound up with an Afghan hound."

"Part of making a relationship work is being flexible," Doris said. "Your father and I got through our disagreements with humor. Do you remember that? He laughed a lot."

"You both did. The house was always full of that. I used to wonder if there was a nitrous leak somewhere." Slater sat up. "We're not really in a mere relationship, by the way. What we have is a narrative complex. It extends light-years in multiple dimensions, its curling tendrils seen and unseen."

"So I've heard." She eyed Pike. "You should get some scrunchies. They'll change your life."

"At least I have a way to stop him from borrowing my car," Slater said. "I just hide the keys under the soap."

"Do not listen to him," Pike said. "I still take showers."

Slater threw up a hand. "And lo, maybe Yahweh really is a merciful god."

"You look fine, sweetie," Doris said. "I love you just the way you are, and so does my cranky son."

Slater stifled a scoff. He wasn't sure why either one of them was so chummy. It felt like they were up to something.

TWO

"I DON'T WANT TO JINX it," Slater said, "and accidentally summon him, but where's that old guy who's been mooching off you?"

"Albert is with his kids today. And he contributes plenty."

"At least he has some common sense to leave once in a while, not skulking around here all the time."

"He has his own house," Doris said.

"So he says. Maybe he really sleeps in his car. Are you sure he's not chiseling? I mean, does he steal?"

"You need to accept that he's around," Doris said, "and that I want him around. You need to make peace with it."

"If he ever lays a finger on you, I'll make sure he winds up in pieces."

She raised her eyebrows. "He's not that man, and

neither are you."

From the side of the house came the sound of the gate opening, and Conrad walked in. Built thick, he was wearing chinos and a Hawaiian shirt with a palm tree print, his dark hair slicked back. In one hand was a six-pack of cans. He called a greeting, a goofy smile on his face.

"What's he doing here?" Slater said.

"I told you I was inviting him."

"I guess I forgot. My mind tends to block out traumatic information."

"Be civil," she said under her breath.

Conrad was his ex, and he hated that the guy had become friendly with Doris. It made no sense, but there wasn't much he could do about it. Walking over, Conrad greeted them with loud bro bluster, and set the cans on the table. It was some kind of hard seltzer.

"I like the shirt, detective," Pike said.

"It seemed appropriate. It's my day off." He swirled a palm toward Pike. "It feels like you've loosened up a little."

"It's for work."

"No plus-one?" Doris said.

"I'm rolling stag today."

"What happened to that twink with the hot pants?" Slater said.

Doris's brow furrowed. "Do people still wear hot pants?"

"They're called booty shorts now," Pike said, and eyed Conrad. "His name was Sullivan."

"That's right." Slater jutted his chin. "Did you break something?"

"Sweet Sullivan has chosen to flit off among the

blossoms," Conrad said.

Slater scoffed. "He dumped you because you wouldn't buy him enough stuff, Daddy."

"It wasn't like that," Conrad said, and chuckled.

"So now you're just living the quiet desperation of an aging train wreck."

He put his hands on his hips. "If you're concerned about train wrecks, you should take a closer look at the hot mess you see in the mirror every morning."

"I want to say knock it off, both of you," Doris said, "but then there's actually significant information embedded in the smack talk." She eyed Conrad. "Why don't you sit down? In a minute I'll get you to help with the grill."

Conrad took a chair and reached for a bottle of beer.

"The detective job seems to suit you," Doris said. "I'd say this is what success looks like."

Slater folded his arms. The guy did look good. By comparison Slater really was a train wreck. Success for him was any day he made it home without getting shot or thrown in the hoosegow. Maybe that's why Doris liked this yutz, and liked Pike. They were both better versions of anything he could ever be.

They talked and drank, and eventually Doris put Pike and Conrad to work on food prep at the barbecue, using her classroom skills to make them think they'd actually volunteered. The pair of them collaborated on grilling like it was an intricate special op. It was actually entertaining to watch them as he chatted with Doris, but it made him feel a little odd, seeing the camaraderie between them.

Soon they brought over a platter of burgers and

corn on the cob, nicely blackened from the grill.

"The burgers are all plant-based," Doris said, "so no one needs to have a vegan meltdown."

"I'm the only vegan here," Slater said, his tone intent, "and I don't do meltdowns."

She pulled the plastic wrap off a serving bowl and set it in the middle of the table. "The macaroni salad is made with fake mayo, so you can eat that too."

Once they'd gotten into it, Pike gestured with his fork. "Thanks for feeding us. It's all delicious. Classic Labor Day."

"It makes me sad that summer's over," Doris said.

Conrad was loading his burger. "I know—I'm not looking forward to the dark days ahead. Driving to work in the dark, driving home in the dark."

"At least when you're suffering in the depths of winter, eventually you get the solstice," Slater said. "The days start to get longer. It reminds you that the world will wake up again. Life will come back." He eyed Pike. "Remember Persephone? She'll keep her promise to return from Hades and green things up."

"My son, the philosopher," Doris said.

Pike scoffed and pushed his hair back. "You are such Angelenos. It's still hot as hell out, and even in February it's going to be seventy degrees every day." He waved at the garden. "I know for a fact those roses will be blooming."

"I guess it's relative," Doris said. "The days get so short, and the low winter sun is awfully depressing." She looked to Slater. "Pike said you were overseas. Why was that, and why haven't I heard anything about it?"

"It wasn't planned. It was just a couple days. I was following a lead in a case." He frowned at Pike. "You big gossip."

"I just laid out the facts as I understand them," Pike said.

"I have to get the details from somewhere," Doris said, "if you don't volunteer them."

Pike set down his burger. "He was in Europe, and he came back with a suitcase full of new clothes."

"So what?" Slater said. "I'm allowed to buy clothes. I found some sales."

Doris furrowed her brow. "That does not sound like you."

"What was in the suitcase?" Conrad said.

"An Italian suit, and linen capri pants. A billowy cotton shirt with no buttons, open down to here." Pike tapped his belly. "The kind of thing you'd wear on the beach in Saint-Tropez. And get this: sandals."

"I've never seen you in capris," Doris said. "Were you sober when you bought all this?"

"Even more interesting," Pike said, "the tags were cut out of everything."

"I didn't want to pay duty on them at customs." Slater waved a hand. "No tags makes them look used."

"It's also what spies do," Conrad said, "to make their origins harder to trace."

Slater scoffed. "I'm not smart enough to be a spy."

"You're sneaky enough, though," Pike said.

Conrad cackled and reached over to tap his beer bottle against Pike's. "Preach, brother."

"Spread out," Slater said through his teeth.

The conversation moved on as they ate, and then got into the pastries, and later on they helped Doris clean up. After Conrad left, Doris walked them to the gate.

Leaning in, Slater kissed her. "Love you."

She held his gaze. "Next time, tell me when you're going abroad."

———◆———

TWILIGHT WAS SETTING IN as Slater drove back to Echo Park, both of them riding in contented silence, full up on barbecue fare. He nosed the Continental into the garage and killed the engine.

When they got upstairs, Pike stretched out on the bed. "I'm wiped out."

Slater put his hands on his hips. "I get it. Doris is a handful."

"It's not that. I've been working a lot."

"I want to maul you right now, but you look like you need to sleep."

"I'm never too tired to be assaulted by you, forty-niner. Are you sure you're up for it again?"

"You're the one who rode off on your hog and cut off my sex supply. You need to put out, longhair."

Pike raised his eyebrows. "I guess it's not like you'd be able to find anyone else to fuck, in a city of ten million people."

"I know you hate that." Slater took a breath. "You know I'm no damn good."

"It's about the double standard. You can do it, but if I did, you'd go ballistic."

He sat on the bed. "It's not about my heart. You're the only man in it." Leaning in, he punched his shoulder. "It's all about Pike." And louder, "You."

Pike reached for the back of his neck, and pulled

him down, and met his mouth. Scrabbling for his fly, Slater pulled out Pike's junk, already getting hard, then unbuttoned his own fly, and stroked them together. Pike came first, and then Slater did, relishing Pike's insistent mouth.

He rolled onto his side and had barely caught his breath when Pike's breathing became regular—he was already asleep. Slater watched him for a while, mesmerized by his serene expression, the beauty of his face despite all the hair.

Eventually he got up and trudged upstairs to the kitchen, where he pulled the fifth of bourbon from the cupboard. Compared to the decent stuff Pike bought, this was just cheap-ass applejack, but it did the job. He poured out his ration, half an inch in the bottom of a tumbler, then added a little bonus. He needed it after dealing with Doris and his ex.

Taking a slurp, he closed his eyes to relish the burn. He didn't need this stuff, not really, despite Doris's passive-aggressive prodding about drying out, but he wasn't sure if he'd be able to sleep without it.

Tumbler in hand, he walked through the big empty room to the French doors that led to the deck, not bothering to turn on the lights. Most people who saw this room advised him to fill it up with furniture, but it already had a sofa and chairs and a TV in one corner, and he liked it empty, liked the feeling of simplicity. Their narrative complex needed uncluttered space to unfold.

Standing at the glass he looked out at the lights on the hillside and the distant towers of the Financial District. He took another slurp, coughing at the delicious fumes. Soon it would take the edge off, lift the weight of all this, the seething metropolis, the constant grind.

THREE

When Slater woke in the morning, he could hear Pike's voice, upstairs in the kitchen. He rolled out of bed and pulled on a pair of boxer shorts and a T-shirt, then trudged up. Pike was on a call, the phone pressed to his ear with his shoulder as he spread peanut butter on half a bagel. He was listening to somebody talk, intermittently interjecting "Uh-huh."

"Seriously?" he said. "What are they cutting it with?"

Slater poured himself a mug of coffee from the carafe, and leaned back on the counter, sipping at the steaming java until he ended the call.

"News about the dope?"

"Quality control issues," Pike said. "I'm going to have to bring it up with the manufacturer."

"I thought the cartels manufactured the meth, and the bikers sold it for them."

"That's what makes these guys interesting. They're stepping onto cartel turf." He frowned. "You shouldn't be asking me about that."

"If I have to get beard burn from your hippie persona, it only makes sense that I want background on why I'm being subjected to it." Slater gestured to the other half of the bagel. "Are you going to eat that?"

Pike chuckled. "I'll toast it for you."

After they'd eaten, Pike pulled on his leather jacket, then embraced him, and explored his mouth. He squeezed Slater in a tight hug before he stepped back, and they both went down to the garage. Pike grabbed his helmet and climbed on his bike. It was a big machine, with lots of chrome and a black leather seat, the gas tank trimmed in lemon-yellow stripes.

"Listen, don't split the lanes," Slater said. "It's not worth it. Some idiot teenager will lane-change and put you in a Mojave overcoat."

"You sound like my mother." Pike frowned. "What the hell is a Mojave overcoat?"

"A tree suit." He waved his arm. "You know—a wooden box they put you in that gets planted in the ground."

"Why is it named after the Mojave?"

Slater put his hands on his hips. "I didn't invent the English language, toots. Probably because it's a rough place. A Mojave how-do is a shotgun blast, and Mojave lightning is homemade moonshine, and a guy who's a Mojave 9 is an LA 6."

"You mean how attractive someone is?" Pike laughed. "That's so mean. There has to be hot people out there."

"There are. They're called Mojave 9s. But they don't moisturize or cut their hair." Slater jabbed a finger at him. "Just be careful on that damn thing."

"I love you, forty-niner," he said, and pulled on his helmet.

"Forever."

Slater slapped the button for the garage door, and Pike started the engine. As he watched him ride off, he felt a lump in his throat, and tried to push it out of his mind as the door rolled down. Trudging up the stairs, he got dressed, pulling on yesterday's jeans and a collared shirt.

He was still buttoning it when the doorbell sounded. It couldn't be Pike, he thought, trotting down the stairs, as he'd use his garage door opener if he'd forgotten something. When he pulled open the door, a guy was standing in front of it. His eyes concealed by wrap-around sunglasses, he had long brown hair and a bandana tied around his head. He was wearing a sleeveless plaid shirt and a leather vest, exposing his tanned arms and their great musculature. Parked behind him, in front of the garage door, was a big old motorcycle.

"What do you need, Butch?" Slater said.

The last thing he remembered was the guy cocking his head to one side, looking at him the way a dog did when it was trying to figure out what you were saying.

———·———

THAT WAS THE CONTINENTAL, Slater knew, as he started to regain consciousness. The familiar cloudy-blue color was in the periphery. He was in a chair, he decided, sitting next to its rear quarter panel. His jaw hurt, and he couldn't move his hands. As his mind got clearer, he twisted his arm. There was a band around each wrist, secured to the back of the chair. Not handcuffs. They felt like zip ties.

Eventually he felt lucid enough to lift his head. That guy was here, standing in front of him, his sunglasses up on his head now.

"Wakey, wakey." He leaned in and slapped him hard.

It stung but it did perk him up, the impact sparking a surge of adrenaline.

"Knock it off," Slater snapped, then waggled his jaw. "Did you deck me?"

"It was more of a stun-gun type situation. You weren't out for very long."

"Why am I tied to a chair?"

The guy wound up and slapped him again, hard enough to turn his head. "You're going to answer my questions."

"You haven't asked me anything yet. You know that, don't you? I'm not actually able to read your mind."

He slapped him again with his other hand.

Slater took a deep breath and met his gaze. "I get it. You're a tough guy. You know what you're doing. Message received. Christ, it's like a gun show up in here."

His brow furrowed. "How do you know I'm packing?"

"I mean your arms, man. You must lift. If I had biceps like that, I'd rip the sleeves off my shirt too."

He raised his eyebrows. "It's a total turn-on. If you're going to keep me tied up, you should at least go down on me."

"Do you not realize that I'm the one in charge? This isn't a sex thing."

"It easily could be, Butch. You just have to pop a couple little buttons." Slater thrust his crotch upward. "I'll settle for a tuggie."

The guy huffed. "What's the unlock code to your phone?"

It wasn't in his pocket where he kept it, Slater realized, and the guy was holding a phone. "Why would I tell you that?"

Reaching behind his back, he pulled out an ugly black handgun and waggled it at him. It was one of the compact Glocks.

"Because otherwise I'll be giving you some lead supplements."

"You shouldn't be using lead ammo. That stuff is toxic. Stainless steel does the same job, and it doesn't even cost more."

"The code," he said, raising his voice.

Slater sighed. "It's one-one-two, one-one-two."

That wasn't his unlock code—it would launch software from his Russian tech vendor, Svetlana, that would wipe the device of her illicit apps and everything else. It would also alert Max, his business partner, that he'd wiped the phone, and where it had been at the time.

The guy stood staring at the screen. "What just happened?"

"What are you talking about?"

"It went blank. And now it says 'Welcome to your

new phone.'" He turned the screen toward him.

"What did you do to it?" Slater demanded. "You broke my phone, you big mook. What did you do?"

"Fuck," he roared, and hurled the device overhand toward the side of the garage. It struck the workbench with a sickening *snap* and dropped to the floor. Breathing hard, the guy leveled his weapon at him.

"Easy, baby," Slater said. "Are you a juicehead? That felt like some serious roid rage."

"Just shut the fuck up and let me think."

"What were you looking for on my phone? You can ask me. I'm sitting right here. Clearly I'm not going anywhere."

"Why did Pine stay here last night?"

"Seth Pine?" Slater said. "That's what this is about? I should have known. The motorcycle, and the bad haircut. You kind of look like him."

"Who's house is this?" he said, raising his voice.

"It's my house, dumbass. Pine comes around here to get sex from me."

His eyebrows shot up. "Pine is a 'mo? That's all this is?"

"You make it sound simple. It's not. Pine and I are embroiled in a multidimensional narrative complex."

"The fuck is that?" he shouted.

"It's like what squares call a relationship, but deeper. More complicated. Operating on more levels."

"You're not some kind of cop?"

"Do I look like some kind of cop?" Slater scoffed. "I work for an insurance company. Listen, Butch, if you grease me, Pine will come for you. He'll see your bike roll up on my doorbell camera, and he'll see your face. You can't really erase those recordings. It's all cloud-based."

There was no camera out there, but he was counting on the fact that this guy wasn't too bright. Slater watched him as he knotted his brow. He could see the wheels turning.

"Seth is pretty into me," Slater said. "I'm thinking he'll croak you as payback. But if you leave things the way they are now, with me still breathing, you'll have his respect for being smart enough not to overreact."

The guy studied him for a minute. "If I cut you loose, what are you going to do?"

"Take a deep breath and appreciate how sweet it is to be alive."

"You can't come at me."

"That would be suicide, Butch. You're the one with the heater." Slater raised his eyebrows, watching as he tucked the weapon into his belt in the small of his back. "We could mess around. That's still on the table. The way your jeans fit implies you're stacked."

He frowned. "I've got a girlfriend."

"She doesn't have to hear about it. I know how to keep my mouth shut."

From his pants he produced a pocket knife, and pulled it open as he stepped behind the chair, crouching to cut the zip ties. "You are such a weirdo."

"So I'm told."

As his hands came free, Slater winced at the pain of the circulation suddenly returning. The guy stepped back, watching him. Slater rubbed his wrists, then rose, unsteady at first, and planted his feet apart, taking deep breaths.

"Are you going to call the cops?"

"I can't. You busted my phone." Slater gestured toward the workbench. "Besides, you didn't really do anything, except get my engine revved up." He grabbed his crotch. "You're really just going to leave me hanging?"

The guy scoffed, and walked to the doorway into the little foyer at the bottom of the stairs, and out the front door. Slater heard the bike start up. It was a lot louder than Pike's. It revved a few times and then faded away.

The patio chair had been next to the wall, and he'd moved it here, but nothing else looked disturbed. Stepping over to the workbench, he scooped up his phone. The screen was cracked from side to side, a spiderweb pattern in the glass, and when he pressed the button it wouldn't power on.

He tucked it in his pocket anyway and hit the button to roll up the garage door. As it rose, he saw Max walking up, in the middle of the street. A beefy guy with mousy brown hair, he was wearing a gray suit without a necktie. He'd drawn his sidearm, holding it down at his thigh, a grim expression on his face.

"All clear," Slater said, and held up his palms. "You got here fast."

"I was at my place." Max lifted the side of his jacket to holster his weapon. "It's literally on the other side of the four level. What happened?"

Slater explained it in broad strokes.

"You definitely look like you've been worked over," Max said, then pulled out his phone and glanced at the screen. "This might be the Russian."

"She'll be looking for an explanation."

"I get it. I'm on the family plan." Max picked up

the call and listened for a second. "He had to wipe it. I'm with him now. I'll put him on."

When Slater took the phone, Svetlana said, "Things are OK, yes?"

"All clear."

That specific phrase told her that he wasn't under duress. Not that it would matter much to her—if he was in a bind, she'd take steps to distance herself from him, wipe his accounts and any trace of his access to them, and move on.

"I'll need to get a new phone," he said. "After I wiped it, mine got smashed."

"It's good that you're OK. Come over when you have the new one. We'll make you whole again."

He handed the phone to Max. "I feel like I should buy you lunch or something, after you hustled over here."

"I've got stuff to do today, so rain check." Max waved an arm. "Showing up is part of the deal."

It was for him too, a part of the rapport they'd built. He'd saved the guy's neck before, and Max had done the same for him.

"Well, I owe you one."

"Back at you, buddy," he said, and walked down the block.

Stepping into the garage, Slater hit the button to close the door, then trudged up the stairs. His back hurt too. Maybe he'd fallen when that idiot zapped him. Sometimes he wondered why he'd bought a place with all these goddamn stairs. At the time he'd needed the space for Pike, room for things to evolve, but why hadn't he looked for that on one level?

In the bathroom he found the ibuprofen bottle,

and shook some into his mouth, then peered at himself in the mirror. When he lifted his chin he could see two red welts on the side of his neck. He had no memory of that happening. He knew he'd passed out, but that idiot must have punched him too, otherwise his jaw wouldn't hurt.

Trotting down to the garage again, he backed the Continental into the street and drove downtown. He knew a phone store on Broadway, and pulled into a street space just past it. Climbing out, he took a minute to look up at the street tree he'd parked next to. He'd never noticed it before. There wasn't room for many of them in this dense neighborhood. The city called them fern pines but they were really some kind of podocarp. They planted them because they were hardy and needed zero maintenance once they were limbed up high enough.

Why was he staring at this damn tree? Maybe he was still a little punch-drunk. Taking a breath, he walked back to the store.

Half an hour later he had a new phone, repopulated from the cloud backup with his contacts and all the other bullshit, at least the legit stuff. The clerk even agreed to recycle his busted phone. Walking out to the street, he scrolled through his contacts to find Hopkins, one of Pike's work colleagues, and dialed his cell number, glad that he picked up.

"I'm near your office," Slater said. "Can you meet me for a minute?"

Hopkins didn't question him, and didn't hesitate. "Sure. There's a coffee place on Main."

FOUR

THERE WAS NO STREET parking in the Civic Center, so Slater nosed the Continental into a structure, then walked the half block to the coffeehouse. As he stepped in he saw Hopkins sitting at a table against the wall. A chunky guy with his Black hair in shaggy curls, today he was wearing a dark jacket.

Slater went to the counter, and returned a minute later with a paper cup in hand, and sat opposite the guy.

"What's going on?" Hopkins said, furrowing his brow.

"You know that Pike's on loan to some task force. He's off with the bikers. I have no way to contact him."

"Pike told you that? He's actually on vacation. He

27

went to Tahiti. He told me he needed a break from his crazy life." He raised his eyebrows. "I guess that means you."

"Are you fucking kidding me?" Slater demanded.

Hopkins guffawed, his head tilting back. "I'm just messing with you. I know what he's doing."

"Something came up about his case. I need to talk to him."

"What came up?"

"Are you involved in it?"

"Tangentially. I'm working on background support. I can get a message to Pike."

"I want to talk to him myself," Slater said. "I just need five minutes on the phone."

"You can't call him. Nobody can. His own phone stays in a drawer, and the one for the undercover job is off-limits. It might get searched by his targets."

"But there's a way, isn't there?"

"I really shouldn't share that."

Slater studied his face. "One of my vendors says, 'Two people can keep a secret, if one of them is dead.'"

"My point exactly."

"I'm not going to blow his cover. You know I'm smarter than that."

Hopkins lowered his voice. "If it was anyone else, Slater."

"Just spill it."

"You have to be extremely careful. If his targets figure out who he really is, things will get ugly."

"I know my way around lowlifes. Most people put me in that category."

He nodded. "I get that. You and Pike are like cops and robbers."

Slater frowned. "I'm not a crook."

"You can bump into Pike if you make it look like a chance meeting. He goes to a diner for breakfast on certain days. Whatever you do, don't use his name. You have to follow his lead—if he acts like he doesn't know you, you have to do that too."

"What days does he go in?"

"It changes," Hopkins said, "but one of the days is tomorrow."

"Will anyone else be there to connect with him?"

"It's possible, but unlikely. It's a standing backup mechanism. We don't use it for regular meetings. Only contingencies."

"Where's the diner?"

"Oh, baby." He sat back. "You've got some driving to do. It's way out in the Mojave."

Hopkins explained where the place was, and insisted he didn't write it down, and store it only in his head. They walked out together, and Slater went back to the Continental, and headed to Glendale. The afternoon traffic on the freeway was already sluggish.

Pulling up in front of Svetlana's building, he looked over the plantings out front. The ivy covered most of the long low structure now, concealing its age and shabbiness. There was a front door here, but it likely hadn't been used in years, and he walked around to the alley and the way in. Once he'd pressed the bell next to the back door, he looked up into the camera mounted overhead.

It used to take a minute for somebody to check the camera, but she'd converted it to automated facial recognition, and Slater was on her list of known faces, so the door lock clicked open almost instantly. He stepped in and stood in the little anteroom as Svetlana's tech scanned him. A moment later the inner door lock snapped open.

The workshop had high narrow windows, and workbenches littered with wire and circuit boards and plastic components. It always smelled like machine oil and solder. Perched on a stool in front of a computer screen, Svetlana was wearing a red and yellow blouse, the floral print distorted by her ample frame, and had her hair pinned back. She swiveled toward him and waved a piece of paper.

"Jury duty."

Slater had to laugh. "You got summoned."

"I have been a citizen of this country for less than ten minutes, and already I'm expected to do this," she said, her Slavic accent flattening the vowels.

He put his hands on his hips. "A lawyer I know told me you can just throw those away. They don't go after people because they can't prove you actually received it."

"But it will still be on record, and if I have some other legal problems, ignoring this summons would compound them."

"That actually makes sense. My mother said if you really don't want to do it, tell them you get your news from extreme sources. Far left or far right. If you go right, though, you have to dress the part. A dark-blue suit."

Svetlana frowned. "They will ask me where I get my news?"

"Mostly it's just sitting around waiting for a couple days, but if you get interviewed for a jury, your news sources are the way they assess how crazy you are. You can also tell them you can't afford to be away from your business. Use the phrase 'financial hardship.' It might work."

"This sounds like sage advice." She sat up straighter. "You have a new cell phone."

Slater dug it out, and unlocked it, and handed it over. Once she'd connected it to a cable, Svetlana peered at her monitor and tapped at the keyboard. He couldn't see her screen because it had a directional privacy filter, so he stood nearby and looked around the room. Sometimes she had people working in here, but today she was alone.

The woman specialized in stealthy software, and he wondered if she had more insight into him than just what he did with her apps. She could easily location-track him, and monitor his calls, and read his texts, and he'd never know. But it didn't really matter—he knew what her motivations were, and if she were monitoring him, it would only be to protect her business. Unlike the legal part of the tech industry, she wouldn't be selling his history and his habits and his movements to data brokers.

It took a while, but eventually she unplugged the phone and handed it back to him.

"Everything should work the same as before."

"What do I owe you?" Slater said.

She waved a hand. "Included with your subscription. Also, I have some new products. Facial recognition. I can monitor the web for pictures and video of you. Only a small increase in your subscription price."

"Interesting," Slater said. "It's all automated, I'm thinking."

"The task is too massive for me to do with my

own software," Svetlana said. "I have a trusted provider with the capability to monitor media and social media sites. Based in a place that doesn't regulate facial recognition."

"Can you monitor other people besides me?"

"Of course. Send me photos."

Pulling out his phone, he found a picture of Pike, and one of Conrad, and one of Andy, and texted them to her.

"I don't get service in here," he said, "but they'll come through once I'm outside."

"My building is radio shielded."

"Do you need a photo of me?"

"I know what you look like." She raised her eyebrows. "I also have new vehicle tracking devices if you need them. Much improved battery time. Up to ten days."

"I can always use those," he said, tucking his phone away.

Heaving herself off the stool, Svetlana chuckled. "You go through them like other people go through cigarettes."

Pausing farther down the workbench, she picked up a black plastic box. "How many do you need? Right now I have four."

"I'll take them all."

She scooped them up and walked back to her computer, then took a minute to scan the bar-code label on each of them with a wand, peering at her screen.

"They are connected to your account now." She peeled off the labels and handed him one of the boxes. It was smaller than a cell phone but thicker, and had rounded corners, with one side studded with magnetic ribs. The plastic housing wasn't smooth and shiny like the ones she'd sold him before.

"It's a lot smaller than the previous iteration," Slater said, turning it over in his hands.

"Better radios, smaller battery."

"I like the matte surface."

"No reflection makes it harder to notice."

"What's the damage?"

"Two dollars each," she said. "Special price for a good customer, seven dollars total."

Digging out his wad, Slater peeled off the C-notes and set them on the counter. Once she'd loaded the trackers into a paper bag, she counted the cash, and tucked it into her bra, then handed him the bag.

"*Spasiba*," Slater said.

Responding with a few words in Russian that he couldn't parse, she added, "You should go to Russia someday. It's a beautiful country."

"I wish I had the time."

"You could bring my brother back with you."

"He's still in the far east?"

"He's spending another winter in Siberia."

"Like Raskolnikov," Slater said.

Her eyebrows shot up. "You know Dostoevsky?"

"I didn't actually read the book. It came up in a case."

"Well, Raskolnikov was sent to a gulag. Igor is much more foolish. He's there by choice."

———·———

THE SUN WAS LOW in the sky as Slater negotiated the sea of brake lights in the stop-and-go traffic on the freeway. Eventually he exited in his own neighborhood, and pulled into his garage, and trudged up to the top floor. The lounge furniture was in a corner of the big room past the kitchen, and he sat on the sofa to pull off his boots and socks, then squeezed the fake turf between his toes. Meant for outdoors, it felt like real Bermuda grass. Pike had chosen a swatch of this to put under the coffee table instead of an area rug. It was a little odd, but he loved that about Pike, loved his unexpected eccentricities.

Thinking about Pike made his heart ache. He'd been with him yesterday, so he could probably take a night off, and keep it in his pants for a change. Pike hated that he hooked up with other people. But he was the one who'd left him for the bikers—it was his own damn fault.

Stretching out, he opened the hookup app, and scrolled through the images of nearby buff torsos and dick pics. A message popped up:

Sup?

Slater checked his profile. Just a couple of miles away, the guy had a salt-and-pepper beard, and in several of the images he was wearing a leather biker jacket and chaps. He messaged back:

I like the look. Fuck me. My place. No drugs.

His response came a moment later:

Should I bring gear?

Slater wrote back:

Minimize that. But you have to wear the chaps.

He sent his address, and went downstairs to the bedroom, and changed into a tight white T-shirt. When the guy arrived, he trotted down and pulled open the door. His beard looked darker than in his photos, and it was neatly trimmed. He was wearing the leather jacket and the chaps.

He cracked a smile. "Nice place."

"Nice chaps. I'm getting chubby just looking at you. What's your name?"

"How's Mike?"

"That works."

Slater led the way up to his bedroom. Mike stepped close, squeezing his arms, then his shoulders. Leaning in, he kissed him, probing with his tongue, and Slater went with it. Even though the guy was too insistent, it was hot.

Stepping back, Mike barked a command. "Clothes off."

Slater started to undress, and ditched his jeans, and once he was naked, grabbed his burgeoning woody.

"Hands off that." Mike stepped close, and grabbed him, stroking him until he was hard.

Stepping back, he pulled off his jacket, then the chaps and his jeans. Slater stepped close, and grabbed his cock and squeezed it, then ground his own into his thigh.

"You have to put the chaps back on," Slater said.

The guy frowned but grabbed them off the floor and deftly zipped them on. Pushing Slater onto the bed, he climbed on top of him, mouthing his neck and his jaw, then sat up and squeezed their cocks together. Eventually he found the lube and reached between his legs, pressing into him with a thumb, then shifting closer, and penetrated him. Slater grimaced as he started to pound him, and folded his hands behind his head. Straining deeper, Mike grunted as he came, his face contorting.

Pulling back, he took hold of Slater's cock and stroked him, holding his gaze. A minute later Slater climaxed, an electric spasm racking his body. Mike stretched out beside him as he caught his breath. Resting a hand on his thigh, Slater caressed the leather.

He'd started to drift off when Mike spoke.

"I'm the top," he said. "You talked to me like you're the top."

Slater looked at him. "What did I do?"

"You told me to put the chaps on. Like you were in charge. It was rude."

He took a breath. The processing, the jabbering. Guys always saved this bullshit for after the main event, after they'd got what they wanted. He hated this part. Digging deep, he pulled up an expression he'd learned by rote, back when he was a teenager, from one of the many shrinks Doris had sent him to.

"I apologize for my impulsive behavior. What can I do to make things right?"

"It doesn't matter that it was impulsive," Mike said. "It's about respect."

Reciting those words usually had the power to mollify people, but not this time. "It sounds like this isn't fixable, Mike. That means you need to hit the bricks."

He sat up. "Fuck that."

"You don't really want to be here, do you? What

with all the disrespect in the air?"

He scoffed and got up, scooping his shirt from the floor and pulling it on. It took him a minute to get out of the chaps and into his jeans, and he folded the leggings over his shoulder.

"I've got lots of b-boys. You wouldn't even make the first string," Mike said, and walked out.

Once he'd heard the front door close, he grabbed his phone and took a minute to block the guy on the hookup app, so that he wouldn't inadvertently hit him up again. Doing this meant he didn't have to waste any brain cells storing the details or even remembering anything about it.

He got up and went down to bolt the front door, then trudged up to the kitchen. It wasn't that late, but he needed to get up early. He grabbed the fifth from the kitchen cupboard and poured his ration, then slurped at the glass.

The warm glow would spread from his belly, and calm things down, smooth over the rough parts—the biker with the stun gun, the hassle of replacing his phone, the performative poseur who craved respect.

"Idiots," he muttered, and pushed it out of his mind. He took another slurp, willing the golden elixir to obliterate all the bullshit.

FIVE

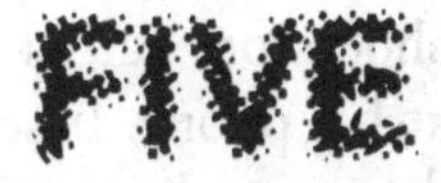

Later knew there'd be morning traffic, and he got up early for the long drive, timing his arrival for the window that Hopkins said Pike would be at the diner. Once he'd showered and pulled on his jeans and ate some leftovers out of a plastic container in the icebox, he went down to the garage, and fired up the Continental, and headed to the freeway.

Rolling east on the 10, the Continental rode smooth, content to be moving at highway speed. There were some slowdowns around the big interchanges, like there always were, but in an hour he was through the sprawl of the metropolis, then in the Colorado Desert, and he left the freeway to head up into the high desert.

The southern end of the Mojave was a little

wetter and felt lush compared to the wildlands farther north. It always felt good to come out here—the place was straightforward, up-front about what it was, devoid of hidden motives.

As he rolled into the small town near the national park, he watched for the diner along the highway. Hopkins had insisted that he set the navigation to take him to the shoe store across the road, in case someone looked at his phone. It seemed excessively cautious, as nobody gave a damn what Slater was up to, but he did it anyway. When the navigation told him to turn left to the shoes, he spotted the diner on the right, set back beyond a service road.

Pulling into the lot, he had to grin—the familiar bike with the yellow trim was parked at one side. He climbed out and stretched after the long drive, turning his face to the warm sun. The air felt dry, and it had that heady dusty desert smell.

On the way to the front door, he paused to look over the Joshua tree that grew at the side of the lot, protected by a ring of rocks around the base. They were endangered, so it was easier to pave around it than to get a permit to cut it down. With spiky and cartoonish limbs, its blades were an idiosyncratic shade of blue-green, with a black dot near the tip of each.

One of his profs had explained that these had evolved symbiotically with giant sloths. Those had gone extinct twelve thousand years ago, probably because of people, but somehow these things had carried on. In another century, she said, human activity would likely send these into oblivion too. But for now, just for a moment, he could admire it.

As he walked into the diner, he scanned the space. The booths and tables were half occupied with desert-rat types, most of them clad in work clothes. Pike was sitting at the counter along the side of the room. Slater sat on the stool next to him and flipped over the coffee cup.

Pike had sensed him somehow, maybe glancing over at his boots, and he spoke quietly, not looking at him or turning his head.

"I don't know you, stranger, so don't touch me. Why are you here?"

The server stepped over to fill his cup from the bulbous carafe. "What can I get you?"

"Oatmeal, and hold the milk."

Once the server had stepped away, he spoke.

"It's too late for the stranger jazz. One of your biker pals tailed you to LA. He tased me, and zip-tied me to that patio chair in the garage, and interrogated me."

"Fucking hell." Pike eyed him. "Are you OK?"

"I'm fine—I can handle all that. But I knew you'd want to hear about it."

"What did he look like?"

"A little paunchy," Slater said. "Lots of hair. He had on a leather vest."

"That describes all of them. Was he wearing the club colors?"

"I think so. It's hard to tell how old he was. Maybe forties."

"Desert rats don't moisturize."

Slater waited while the server set down his oatmeal. "His jacket had a patch that said 6."

"That means he's an enforcer. Did he have a dark

beard with a red strip on either side?"

"That's the guy."

"It sounds like Lenny," Pike said. "He's a block-head."

"I kind of got that vibe. He tried to get into my phone, but he couldn't."

"Good. What did you tell him?"

"I said it was my house, and we were sleeping together. Nothing more. The idiot didn't ask about Doris's place—all he knew was where your ride had spent the night."

"So he wasn't actually tailing me. He has a tracker on my bike."

"You need to find it," Slater said.

"Just let me think."

Pike sipped at his coffee as Slater dug into his oatmeal. He was mostly through it when the door swung open, and a familiar voice called out, "Yo, Pine."

Slater swiveled on his stool to watch the guy approach. "If it isn't old Slappy."

Standing next to them, Lenny pushed his sunglasses up onto his forehead, and frowned. "That's not my name."

"How do you know Lenny?" Pike demanded.

"This guy knocked me out and tied me up in my own damn garage," Slater said. "It was pretty kinky."

"It was not." Lenny huffed and jabbed a finger at him. "You are a sex maniac."

Pike stood up, and dug out a wad of cash, and dropped some bills on the counter.

"Outside," he snapped, jutting his chin at Lenny, and followed him out to the parking lot.

Slater slurped at the dregs of his lukewarm java, and dropped a twenty for his own meal, then walked outside. They were standing at the side of the lot, near the big black bike that was parked next to Pike's.

"You tailed me to his place?" Pike demanded. "Why the fuck are you shagging me?"

Lenny threw up his hands. "What's going down is big doings, man. We can't trust anybody."

Stepping closer, Pike smacked his chest with both palms, shoving the guy hard. Lenny stumbled backward.

"Stay the fuck away from my people. You want to know something about me, you talk to me." Pike pounded the side of his fist on his own chest.

Slater had never seen Pike in this persona. The guy could be intimidating, and Lenny looked cowed.

"How do you know this guy anyway?" Lenny stood taller. "He lives in a new house, and drives a spiffy car. Who the fuck is he?"

"To you, he's nobody." Pike stepped up to him and pushed his shoulder with the heel of his palm.

"Quit your shoving," Lenny said, stumbling back.

"That's not quite accurate," Slater said. "I actually retail your product. My niche market is club guys."

Lenny frowned at him. "You told me you worked in insurance."

"That's my day job. Product sales is a side hustle. Your last shipment had some serious quality issues, by the way."

Pike jutted his chin. "You don't need to be talking about that."

"Why didn't you tell me you were hustling?" Lenny said.

"I didn't know who the fuck you were when you jumped me." Slater raised his voice. "Busting into my place with a stun gun and waving a heater at me. And why is that any of your damn business? I don't work for you."

Lenny threw up his hands. "Either way, *mee*-mo wants to talk to you."

"The fuck is *mee*-mo?"

"It's spelled like *memo*, but it's Mexican, so it's *mee*-mo. He's the boss."

"Why?" Pike gestured to him. "Slater is strictly small-time. A nickel rat. He's not important."

"I don't know why. I showed him your picture. Memo said, 'Bring him out.'"

"Why did you take a picture of me?" Slater demanded.

"I'm just glad I saw your bike here," Lenny said. "It means I don't have to go back to the city to pick him up. I was about to rent a van."

"Fuck that," Slater said. "Nobody picks me up." He jabbed a finger at Lenny. "And fuck you."

Ignoring him, Lenny eyed Pike. "You'll bring him out, yeah?"

Stepping over to the motorcycle, Lenny pulled on his helmet, a black dome without the face shield, and connected the chin strap as he straddled the bike. It had much fatter tires than Pike's, and the front rim was black instead of metallic. Lenny jumped on the pedal to kick-start the loud engine. That meant it was carbureted. It had to be older than Pike's bike, with its starter button. A fuel-injected ride was a lot easier to get running.

Slater folded his arms as Lenny pulled out and

rolled toward the highway. "Are you burned?"

"If they knew who I was, I'd already be dead." He pushed his hair back as they watched Lenny turn onto the road.

"Do these guys do that?"

"It's likely. Several people in their orbit have gone missing." Pike took a breath. "Whatever this is, it's not about me. Something else is going on, and it's about you."

"I guess I'm coming with you."

"Why did I tell you about any of this? It's my career, Slater. You're putting my op at risk, and you're putting me at risk."

"It would have happened anyway, no matter what you told me. That biker trash dragged me into it when he zip-tied me to a chair and slapped me around."

"It's my own damn fault," Pike said. "I should have stayed away."

"How could you? Our narrative complex is addictive. Its gravity extends in all directions through time and space. Stronger than the willpower of any lone individual. Like the best dope ever." He stepped in front of him, and grabbed his biceps, and kissed his neck. "I'm coming with you," he whispered, digging his nose into Pike's sweaty hair. He grabbed his butt and pulled him close. "I'm coming with you. You hear that?"

Pike sighed and mouthed his jaw.

"I'm coming with you."

Eventually Pike pulled back. "We should go."

"So is there any way to communicate privately with the real Pike besides coming out here?"

"You can text my regular phone. I won't be able

to check it very often. I have to ride into the city to access it." He pulled his sunglasses on. "Let's roll. You can follow me."

Slater fired up the Continental and watched as Pike pulled on his helmet, and started his bike without jumping on it like Lenny had. He kicked up the stand and rode out of the lot.

Shifting into gear, Slater followed him onto the highway, then onto the road that led north to Landers. Eventually he turned off the pavement, and they traveled a couple of miles on dirt roads.

Pike stopped in front of a gate in a chain-link fence topped with coils of razor wire. Wooden slats threaded vertically into the chain-link made it mostly opaque, and the fence ran a long way in both directions. There were other building sites in view in the dusty landscape, but none of them were nearby.

Pulling off his helmet, Pike waved to the camera mounted on top of the fence, and a minute later the gate rolled open. Slater followed him a short distance inside the fence. Pike parked his bike on the dirt, and set it on its stand, and climbed off.

As he got out, Slater looked around. There were a trio of wooden buildings that looked like they'd been here a while, and a construction trailer on tires with a jack stand at each corner. Farther back he could see the top of a tall shed. Sided with white-painted metal sheeting, it had an arcing peaked roof, and no windows, and a double-high garage door. That was the kind of structure people used to store heavy equipment, big trucks and graders and loaders.

There was just one other bike parked here in front, with the black front rim, a half-helmet hanging from the handlebar—Lenny's ride. He knew there were other people here, Memo at least, but they must park farther inside.

"We should wait here," Pike said. "They don't want people just wandering around."

"That looks like a bunkhouse." He gestured to the largest of the wooden buildings, a long low structure.

"It's where the guys sleep when they're up here working."

"Is Lenny the only punch dummy?"

"He's the only one that I've met," Pike said. "The other guys are cooks. That's what's happening in the big shed."

"You all sleep here?"

"I'm staying in San Bernardino. I come up for business."

"Christ, man, if I'm caught up in this now, I need to know your backstory."

"I guess you're right." He folded his arms. "Seth Pine is a truck driver. Currently he's out on disability. Seth doesn't look injured because he's not. He filed a fake claim."

"Plus he's a gangbanger now," Slater said, "along with these yahoos."

Pike spoke intently. "Incorrect. Did you not notice that I'm not wearing the club's colors?"

"I thought maybe you were on probation."

"I'm not a candidate for membership. I'm an external contractor. A buyer and distributor."

"Why don't they have people in the club to do distribution?"

Glancing toward the structures, Pike lowered his voice. "Memo is ambitious, and club growth is slow."

He jutted his chin at the yard. "How many people would seriously want to be part of this? Memo wants to expand the business more quickly than the club. He decided to work outside the traditional structures of the industry."

"I guess that's what they call the wisdom of the market."

In the distance someone called out, "Yo, Yella."

It was a guy walking between the buildings, dressed like Lenny. Pike raised a hand in greeting.

"Did he call you yellow?" Slater said.

"It's just a nickname."

"Because your bike has yellow trim. He looked kind of foxy. Are you fucking any of these lowlifes?"

"If I were, I wouldn't have had to come back to you," Pike said, "and get you mixed up in this."

"I get it. You just can't stay away from this old foot-long." He briefly grabbed his crotch.

Pike scoffed. "You wish that's what was in your pants."

"You love it. You know it, and I know it."

Reaching for his face, Pike caressed his cheek with a thumb. "Either that, or you're just the most convenient come-dump."

"Whatever keeps you coming back, petal."

He kissed him, and got lost in his mouth, until Pike pulled back.

"Heads up."

SIX

SLATER FOLLOWED HIS GAZE to the guy walking over from the trailer. In his fifties, maybe, he had longish black hair, and a short beard, and dark sunglasses like all of them. This had to be Memo. Lenny followed a few paces behind him. Memo looked Latin, with a deep desert tan, his face lined by age and maybe a hard life. Wearing jeans and a baggy plaid shirt, he grinned as he stepped up.

"So it's true," he said. "You're a man's man, Pine. Is this your boyfriend?"

"Why would you ask me that?" Pike demanded.

"Well, you just had your tongue down his throat."

"What the fuck business is it of yours?" He jutted his chin. "Who are you sleeping with? Show me some pictures."

Memo laughed. "Just chill. I don't care who you're boning."

"Are you the guy in charge?" Slater said.

"Might be. Who are you, exactly?"

"You already know that, big guy, or you wouldn't have told your ape to pick me up."

Lenny scowled. "I'm not an ape."

Slater jutted his chin at him. "Cool it, baby."

Briefly raising a hand, Memo glanced at Lenny. That was enough to shut him up. He pushed his sunglasses up onto his forehead and looked back to Slater. "I guess that's fair. I do know who you are, Ibáñez." Stepping closer, he extended a hand, and Slater shook it. "I'm Memo. Thanks for coming out."

He waved an arm. "I didn't feel like I had much choice."

Memo chuckled and looked him up and down. "I'd offer you a taste of our product, to be hospitable, but I see you're already tweaking."

Glancing at Slater, Pike said, "Are you sure about that?"

"You should know what your bindle men are up to, Yella," Memo said. "I've seen it enough that I can tell."

Slater was stone sober, except for caffeine, but he knew he might come across as a little impatient, like tweakers were. He didn't bother to correct the guy, as it didn't really matter.

"What do you want with him anyway?" Pike said.

Memo rolled his shoulders. "I guess I can't say I invited you up for the view. There's nothing out here but rocks and sand."

"You're wrong about that," Slater said, glancing

around. "The forbs greened up with the monsoon rain, and look at all the creosote bush."

"The locals call them greasewoods."

"Same thing."

"I hate those damn things. In summer they grow a million little fuzzy white balls." Memo held up a thumb and finger. "Like this. They blow around, and get into every fricking crack and corner."

"Those are the seeds."

"That seems like a waste. There's too many of them. They're not all going to grow into trees, are they? Why do they have to make so much of the stuff?"

"It's a survival strategy," Slater said. "It doesn't work like your market economics, where you manufacture crap and sell it all as soon as possible. Some desert seeds are playing the long game. They disperse through time as well as space. They'll be dormant in the soil for years until the conditions are right to sprout. If the ones that grew last year get wiped out for some reason, the species still has more chances next year."

"It's starting to sound like public television up in here," Lenny said.

"I'm just saying." Slater gestured to the landscape. "The Mojave isn't empty. There's a fuck-ton of life all around you." He raised his voice. "So wake up."

Memo frowned. "Thanks for your insights."

"Why am I here?" Slater demanded.

"You sound steamed. Come in out of the sun. You need to drink water when you're on the ice. You guys always forget that." He waved to Lenny. "First, though, Lenny's going to check you out. Pine knows the drill."

Pike sighed, and moved his feet apart, and extended his arms. Stepping over, Lenny gave him a thorough frisk, then checked Slater. He wasn't shy about digging into his crotch and massaging his junk. Eventually Lenny stepped back.

"Nobody's armed."

Memo waved for them to follow, and Lenny walked away, toward the production shed. The trailer looked so mundane, considering how illegal this enterprise was, and Memo led them up the trio of metal stairs and inside. It was set up as an office, and Memo sat behind the desk, and waved to the chair in front. Slater dropped into it, and Pike sat in the one at the side of the desk, under a window. It actually felt comfortable in here with the air conditioner running.

"I wanted to talk to you because there's a guy you should meet," Memo said, leaning back in his chair. "He might have a gig for you."

"I already have a day job," Slater said. "I sell to club rats on the side, but it's small volume, and trusted clientele. I don't need to be doing any more than that. It's too risky for me."

"It's not about my business. It's about his. The guy's name is Brian. He's based in LA like you."

"Dude—you don't know me."

Memo made a languorous gesture. "I know you look Latin, but you're more Anglo than Latin. Brian is the same. Kind of assimilated. A *pocho*. I get it a lot too. I'm a brown guy, and my name is Latin, but I grew up with all the white folks in the trashy part of Portland."

"Now that we've established everyone's ethnicity," Slater said, "why do you want me to work for your friend when you and I have never fricking met?"

The door swung open, and a guy stepped in, then stopped short, eyeing Slater and Pike. He had a dark beard and shaggy hair past his ears, wearing a leather vest with the gang colors, and holding a half-size baking sheet, like a trainee server in a low-rent noodle joint.

"Should I come back?" he said.

"These two know what we're doing here," Memo said. "What have you got?"

The guy stepped over and set the tray on the desk. Its contents looked like the rubble of a shattered car window, like chunks of cloudy safety glass. Memo sat up and studied it, then tapped one of the chunks with the end of a Sharpie until it crumbled. He pressed a finger on the resultant dust and then licked it.

"Looks good to me," he said finally. Eyeing Pike, he raised his eyebrows. "Anybody want a taste?"

"No," Pike said flatly.

He looked to Slater. "I know you don't need any more."

When he gestured, the guy who'd brought it lifted the tray and walked out.

"How did you know my name?" Slater said.

"I'm not used to working with outsiders. This approach is new for me."

"That's not an answer."

Memo laughed. "Lenny took your photo yesterday. I ran it through a facial recognition site. It came up with your name and that you're an insurance industry gumshoe. I didn't actually know you were grinding for us too."

"If you don't care who Pine is sleeping with, why

go to all that trouble?"

"I need to know who gets close to my business, and why they're around, and what they want."

"OK." Slater watched him for a moment. "That actually rings true."

Memo raised his eyebrows. "So what do you want?"

"From you, nothing. From him, it's all about the gravy."

"Meaning what?"

He gestured to Pike. "Look at him—it's all gravy. Then you dig under the gravy and there's more gravy."

Memo frowned. "You make him sound like Thanksgiving dinner."

"To spell it out, then, he's got a warm throat to shove my dick into."

"You don't need to be crass," Pike said.

Shifting in his chair, Memo chuckled. "One of the names that came up connected to you was Marisol Hart. Remember her?"

"Sure. I heard that's not her name anymore. She changed it when she got married."

"I'm told you worked for her."

"Not for very long. It was a contract job."

"Well, her ex-husband does some accounting for me."

"That doesn't surprise me," Slater said. "That nebbishy moron is shady as fuck."

"Abner said the same thing about you. He said you were smart and did what needed to be done, not necessarily according to John Law's standards." Memo sat up. "If you're already hustling my product, what harm is there in talking to one of my friends?"

"What kind of business is Brian in?"

"You can talk to him about it." Picking up his phone, Memo tapped at it, and wrote on a yellow sticky note with the Sharpie, then held it up, stuck to his index finger.

Rising, Slater took it. "I'll call him if I have time."

Memo flashed a wry grin, holding his gaze. "I'm not asking."

The guy knew he didn't need to drop an explicit threat, knew that Slater understood who he was, knew what he was capable of.

He took a breath and gestured with the sticky note. "Got it. I'll call him today."

"That's what I'm talking about." Memo rose and clapped his shoulder. "Check your navigation app. From here sometimes it's faster to go the back way. Up around Big Bear and through Victorville. If you like the empty desert so much, you'll love that drive." He looked to Pike. "Do we need to talk?"

"Hell, yeah, we do," Pike said, on his feet now too. "You've got production problems."

Memo jutted his chin. "Says who?"

"Half the meth-heads in LA." He gestured to Slater. "Let me get rid of him first."

Pike followed him out of the trailer. As they walked toward the Continental, he spoke in a low voice.

"Do not work for his friends."

"It didn't sound like I had a choice," Slater said.

"You have to talk to him, but don't take it any farther. Blow him off. Tell him you can't do whatever it is."

"I still don't get why Memo wants me involved."

They stopped next to the Continental, and Pike pushed his hair back.

"You're a loose thread. Everybody is either inside or outside the operation. Outsiders are a risk because you can't control them. Memo knows you're close to his business because you're sleeping with me. It's safer for him if you're also working for somebody in his network."

"Do you know this Brian guy?"

"Never heard of him."

"Memo's not what I expected," Slater said. "I assume drug dealers are stupid, but he's not."

"He did manage to muscle in on cartel market share without getting croaked. At least not yet. That makes him more dangerous than most." Pike glanced back toward the trailer. "I need to talk to the guy." He jabbed a finger at Slater. "Do not come back here."

"This whole dick-swagger thing is putting lead in the pencil, Seth. I like the butch boss persona."

Pike ran a hand through his hair and took a breath. "Forty-niner, you have to go."

Under it all the guy was stressed out, Slater realized.

"Have I put you in danger?"

"I put myself in danger by coming home, and now I've put you in danger." Pike eyed the trailer and spoke in a calmer tone. "To be honest, your story about being a low-level dealer probably helped me. It fleshes out my identity, and gives me some credibility. I know they bought it, but I fricking hate that Memo wants to use you."

"I'm not about to be used." Slater raised his eyebrows. "Take Lenny's tracker off your damn bike."

Pike grabbed his shoulders, and kissed him, lingering in it a moment before he pulled back. He swatted him on the butt and walked away.

As he climbed into the Continental, he watched Pike walk back to the trailer. The guy was so damn hot, he could hardly stand it. And for some inexplicable reason, he wanted to be with Slater.

Thinking about it, nobody else was in sight, and the only camera he could see was aimed outside, watching anything that approached the gate. Svetlana's vehicle trackers were still tucked in beside the spare tire. He got out of the car again and opened the trunk, grabbing one of the trackers. Clicking on the tiny recessed power switch, he walked over to Lenny's bike.

There were lots of metal parts on this big machine. The exhaust pipe would get too hot, and melt the housing and fry the electronics, but inside it was a horizonal brace that ran to the rear wheel. He didn't bother to wipe his prints off the device—if Lenny found it, he wasn't going to turn it over to the cops. These guys could check facial recognition databases, but fingerprint records were harder to get, mostly limited to law enforcement.

The magnetic ribs easily adhered to the strut, and Slater stepped back to look it over. It was pretty obvious if you were looking for it. Lenny might notice the addition, even though it was tucked in the shadows, but it was worth a shot.

Looking around again to make sure nobody was watching him, Slater climbed into his car. The navigation app said the Victorville route would take half an hour longer—he'd drive back the way he came.

Once he'd rolled out through the gate, he drove slowly on the washboarded dirt road, and eventually got back to the pavement. An hour later, when he was on the 10 in the Inland Empire, he dialed the number on the sticky note.

"Is this Brian?" Slater said when a man's voice answered. "A mutual acquaintance told me to reach out."

"Memo said he had a guy," Brian said. "I'm glad you called."

"It didn't seem like a good idea to say no to Memo."

"Yeah, he's definitely that guy. Can we meet this evening?"

"I have an office in Downtown LA."

"Can you come to my neighborhood? There's a restaurant called Cebolla. It's in South Gate or Downey. Not far off the freeway."

"You're not sure what town it's in?" Slater demanded.

"They kind of meet around there. You can only tell by looking at the street signs." He raised his voice. "It doesn't matter what the fuck town it's in. Just look up the name of the place."

The line went dead, and Slater glanced at the screen. He really had hung up on him. This was going to be interesting.

SEVEN

T RAFFIC WAS STARTING TO slow down for the afternoon when Slater got into the jumble of interchanges in East LA, and eventually he nosed the Continental into his garage. Upstairs he pulled his boots off, and stretched out on his bed, and set an alarm for later on.

There was a new alert from Svetlana's software, he saw: "распоз." That was new. When he tapped through, he found a news article about a house fire and a missing person in Westlake. He scrolled through the text, and when he got to the photos, he saw what had triggered the alert. Standing on the street in front of the torched building, at a little podium with an array of media microphones, was a cop with buzzed hair. Slater didn't recognize the guy, but from his age and the load of bling on his uniform, he ranked up in the department. Behind him stood a line of several people in suits, wearing dour expressions. One of them was Conrad. This was Svetlana's new facial recognition monitoring. Scanning the article, Conrad wasn't mentioned by name, but the software had spotted his face. He couldn't care less about the case Conrad was on, but at least he knew the monitoring actually worked.

Sometime later, waking before his alarm rang, he forced himself to sit up. Outside, the gray of twilight had set in. Even though he'd been up early, it felt bleak to wake up at this time of day. Once he'd pulled his boots on, he backed out of his garage, and waited for the door to roll down, and followed the navigation to the 710.

The place was on an old retail strip, he saw, as he exited the freeway and turned onto the boulevard. The storefronts hadn't been updated since they were built, maybe in the 1960s. Even though it hadn't gentrified, it was still functional, with signs for a dental clinic, an eyewear store, a panadería. They were all shut for the night, but the restaurant looked open, and he pulled into the lot behind it.

As he walked in through the back door he looked the place over. It had a high ceiling, with tables and booths around the sides, and lots of floor space. That was a dance floor, he decided, with a setup for a band at the back, a keyboard stand and a drum kit and music stands.

The place wasn't busy, with a few couples and families at the tables. A guy waved at him from a booth. Slater stepped over and slid in across from him.

Like Memo said, Brian looked Latin, his dark

hair past his ears and tucked back. In his thirties, he was clean-shaven and wearing a neatly pressed dress shirt. Basically fuckable, Slater decided.

Brian flashed a fake smile as Slater sat, then gestured to the room. "It turns into a bar later on. People come to dance."

A woman stepped up, wearing a black shirt and a little apron around her waist, her hair bundled tightly behind her head.

"Bring us some salsa and chips," Brian said, then raised his voice. "And don't keep me waiting. I know it's quiet in here right now."

"Got it." She looked to Slater.

"Can you do java?"

"Sure," she said, and stepped away.

"Do you come in here very often?" Slater said.

"It's one of my places. Not for the bar, but in the daytime. I come for lunch."

"Why would you treat the server like trash if you're going to be in here again?"

"You have to keep people on their toes," Brian said. "Otherwise you become the trash. If she knows I expect a certain level of service, I can ease off, and I'll get better treatment. Usually I only have to do it once."

"You don't think it might go the other way? You'll get bad service?"

"If that happens, I can escalate, and get her canned." He scoffed. "Do you live under a rock? When you're nice to people, they take advantage of you, and fuck you over."

Watching him talk, Slater thought about that. In any given situation Slater was usually the asshole, so if he'd perceived it in this guy, it meant he was way over the top. He shifted in his seat.

"So how do you know Memo?"

Brian held his gaze. "We have a shared interest in motorcycles."

People did that when they really wanted you to believe them, that intent wide-eyed look. Usually it meant they were lying hard.

"What do you ride?"

"A Sportster," Brian said. "I don't get to use it much. You know bikes?"

"Not really. Do you work with Memo?"

"I know what he does. I'm not involved in that. I run a vehicle-rental business. It's right up the road."

"What is it that you think I can help you with?"

He raised his eyebrows. "Find my wife."

"She's missing?"

"Not the kind of missing where I'd go to the cops. But she takes off for days at a time. I want to know what she's doing."

"Did you ask her?"

He huffed. "If I did that, it would look like I didn't trust her."

"Clearly you don't."

"Wouldn't you want to know what your wife was doing all day?" Brian demanded.

"I'm on dick, brother."

"Your husband, then, or whatever. It's a simple surveillance job."

"It sounds more like a window-shade job. Creeping around and peeping into bedrooms." Slater shook his head. "It's messy. I don't do that."

"You're making a lot of assumptions. I don't actually know what she's doing, or where."

"Are you angling for a divorce?"

He sat back. "I'd never do that. We just got back from a trip to Paris. We're closer than ever."

The server set down a couple of bowls of salsa, and chips, and a mug of coffee. Brian didn't acknowledge her or even glance up.

"Thanks," Slater said as she turned away.

"Listen," Brian said. "I know what Memo does, and the risks he takes, but this isn't like that. It's a legit job. He said you do gumheel work anyway."

Slater slurped at his joe. "I already told you I don't do boy-girl stuff."

"It's not that," he said intently. "I'll pay you what you ask. And think of the rep you'll build with Memo. He'll feel like the hero because he introduced us, and helped us both out. It might make things easier for you down the road when you have to negotiate with him." Brian grabbed a corn chip and gestured with it. "Or whatever it is you do with him. He's not a man's man too, is he?"

"Not that I know of, but then most straight guys will bend that way after a couple of tequila shots in a dark room."

Brian guffawed, tossing his head back. "You're cocky. I like that."

"Two grand to start," Slater said. "Cash only."

"Fine." Carefully wiping his fingers on a napkin, he dug in his pants and pulled out a thick bankroll, then peeled off the C-notes and set the wad on the table.

Slater tucked the bills away and pulled out his phone. "What's her name?"

"Thorpe. Janine Thorpe. I can text you a photo."

As he reached for his phone, Slater thumb-typed a note with the name. A moment later a message popped up, and he studied the image. It was a head-shot. Thorpe had Black hair styled in little twists, gold jewelry around her neck, and a blank stare. At the side of the image were the remnants of some lettering that had been cropped out.

"This is from an ID card," Slater said.

"From her job. She works for a brokerage house. Their office is in Downtown LA, but she works remotely most of the time. It's called Sobinère."

"That sounds French."

"It's Swiss," Brian said.

"It's a financial brokerage?"

"What other kind is there? They buy and sell stocks and other money-type stuff. I don't understand it very well."

"Can you spell it?" he said, and thumb-typed as he recited it. "What does Thorpe drive?"

"A silver G-Wagen."

"Gross."

"Not a fan of the Benzes?"

Slater looked up at him. "I'm Jewish," he said sharply.

He frowned. "OK, then. I'll send you a photo of the plate."

"When does she typically disappear?"

"Thursday is a good bet," Brian said. "That's why I wanted to meet tonight. In the past she's told me Thursday is an office day, but then she's not in the office."

"You checked?"

"I was downtown one time, and dropped in unannounced to take her to lunch. They said she was working remotely that day, but she wasn't—I knew she wasn't. That's when I started to get suspicious."

"I'll need your home address," Slater said, "if that's where the G-Wagen will be parked tonight."

Brian dug into the salsa with a corn chip. "You're going to put a tracker on it?"

"Do you know what plausible deniability is?" Slater sat back. "If you don't know how I do my thing, your wife's lawyers and the cops can't make you tell them."

"Fine," he said, and recited the address. "Thorpe parks in the driveway next to my rig. There's a gate."

"What do you drive?"

"A Range Rover. It's dark green."

Slater scoffed. "Of course you do. I'm thinking tonight you forget to close the gate."

"I can do that."

"What else can you tell me about Thorpe? You have kids?"

"It's just her and me." Brian took a breath. "She's no-nonsense. I guess that's the banker type. She likes expensive stuff. Jewelry and spa treatments and vacations."

"And Aryan cars," Slater said. "What else? What does Thorpe do in her free time?"

"She spends lots and lots of time at the gym. And she sees ghosts. They visit her at night sometimes."

"Interesting. Do they give her stock tips?"

Brian chuckled. "She doesn't talk about it much with me. She saves that for other ghost people. I know it's odd."

Sliding off the bench, Slater tucked his phone away as he stood up. "Can you pay for this?" He waved at the coffee cup. "I'll be in touch."

He saw the server standing behind the register, and dug out a twenty, and palmed it. He paused at the counter and spoke to her.

"Numb-nuts is going to cover the bill," he said, "but this is for you. Because he's an asshole."

She took the bill and grinned. "Thanks."

In the parking lot, Slater flicked on his headlights and drove back to his house. Climbing the stairs, he walked through the kitchen and dropped onto the sofa, pulling off his boots and socks, and set them on the fake grass. He stretched out and got comfortable and thought it through.

He was getting soft—he'd let Brian talk him into doing what was likely a boy-girl job, even though he fricking hated those. Pike didn't want him working for the guy either. It hadn't been a tough sell, he had to admit, as he didn't have anything else on right now, and without the distraction of Pike's presence, the work would be a relief.

Eventually he decided it was late enough to go put a tracker on the G-Wagen. Brian wouldn't hassle him if he was awake and spotted him, and Thorpe was likely asleep already, since she had a regular nine-to-six.

Down in the garage he walked back to his gear safe and got it unlocked. It was really a gun safe, disguised as a basic sheet-metal office cabinet but built with heavy steel, and a four-point lock, and bolted to the floor. He didn't have any firearms, but it worked just as well to store all his illicit tech. Any junkie who broke in to steal copper wire and tools wouldn't waste time trying to get into it.

Pulling the signal jammer off its charger, he locked the cabinet again, then took the squat box to the trunk of the Continental and tucked it into his canvas satchel. Even though he was colluding with Brian, he wasn't about to let himself be recorded. Most security cameras were wireless, and this box would knock anything nearby offline.

Fishing out a couple of the new vehicle trackers from the gap next to the spare tire, he put them into the satchel, then slammed the trunk and set the bag on the floor of the passenger side.

The drive to South Gate went fast as the freeways were moving at this hour. The dark suburban street was lined with bungalows, and he slowed down as he rolled past the address Brian had given him. As promised the G-Wagen was parked next to the Rover, in the driveway in front of the garage, and the gate was rolled open. Even if it were closed it wasn't much of a security measure, as the fence along the sidewalk was just a few feet high—he could easily step over it.

Slater circled the block and parked at the curb, a few doors down and facing the place, then sat to watch for a minute. There was nothing happening, no signs of life, so he reached into the back seat and grabbed a pair of black latex gloves from the box he kept there, and wriggled his hands into them. From the glove box he took the stealthy glasses Svetlana had sold him, and clicked on the power switch, and pulled them on. In the frames were little infrared and ultraviolet lamps that generated glare to mess with security cameras, even though the human eye wouldn't notice any visible light.

Once he'd found his blue ball cap on the back seat, and pulled it low over his brow, he lifted his satchel, and flipped it open, and switched on the signal jammer. It had a bright blue indicator lamp when it was powered up, and he folded the satchel closed and climbed out. He was on the clock now. Even late at night you couldn't disrupt everybody's Wi-Fi and cell connectivity for very long before they started to freak out.

Slinging the satchel onto his shoulder, he strode over to the driveway. The house had a doorbell camera, and another one on the eaves, aimed toward the street. He knew that model—it was consumer gear that worked with Wi-Fi and cloud storage. It wasn't recording him right now because of the jammer. The light on the doorbell camera confirmed that, its indicator light strobing orange as it tried in vain to reconnect.

Slater squatted at the rear tire of the G-Wagen and fished a tracker out of his bag. With a latex-clad fingernail he found the little power switch and clicked it on, then reached up into the wheel well. Moving it around, eventually he felt a satisfying tug as the magnets adhered to a piece of steel.

Rising, he looked around. Nobody was watching him, and the indicator light on the camera on the eaves was slowly strobing orange. The signal jammer had knocked it offline too. Walking around to the Land Rover, he squatted next to the rear tire. There was lots of steel under this vehicle, and the tracker instantly found purchase.

As he strode back to the Continental, he switched off the signal jammer, extinguishing its brilliant blue light. Svetlana had built it to be obnoxiously bright so that it wouldn't get forgotten and attract attention—it was extremely illegal to mess with radio signals.

Once he got back to his house, he went upstairs to the sofa again, and dug out his phone, and checked Svetlana's app. Three trackers were active now. The map for the one on Lenny's bike showed it was up in the high desert, within a wide green circle of uncertainty. The tracker used Wi-Fi and cell signals to calculate its location, rather than GPS, which was more precise but took a lot more battery power. Out in the desert there were fewer reference signals, but it was still accurate enough to show Lenny's bike was in the general vicinity of Memo's place. The location circle for the G-Wagen and the one for the Land Rover were much smaller, both overlapping in the same spot, where he'd left them in South Gate.

He was too tired for a hookup, he decided, setting the phone on the faux grass. Without sex the only other thing to do was get fucked up. Forcing himself off the sofa, he went to the kitchen and poured out his ration from the fifth, scowling at it. This is what his booze rules dictated, but it was hardly even a dribble. He'd been on the road half the fricking day, and he'd basically been abandoned—he deserved a little more. Tipping the bottle, he poured out a few more fingers.

As he slurped at the tumbler, he closed his eyes to relish the burn, then poured another slug. Walking back into the big room, he killed the lights, then went out onto the deck to look at the city lights. It felt chilly out, and he could hear the dull roar of it all. The Mojave was so quiet by comparison. Out there you could hear the wind in the creosotes and the yuccas. Here it was the grind of the metropolis, and it never stopped. He took another slurp. This place was completely relentless.

EIGHT

WHEN SLATER WOKE, IT was still early, and he threw off the covers and swung his feet to the floor so that he wouldn't drift off again. His head hurt, but it wasn't a full-blown katzenjammer. He took some deep breaths to dispel the achy brain fog, then got dressed, and trudged up the stairs.

Briefly staring at the coffeemaker, he decided not to bother with it. He could get java out somewhere. Pike knew better how to operate the thing anyway. He could get it to work himself, but right now it would take too much brainpower.

Grabbing some fruit and bread, he went out on the deck and sat at the patio table to munch on it. The sun felt great, and the air was warm and dry. It had to be the Santa Ana wind. People complained about the dust and the pollen that blew down from the Mojave, and it did tend to get people more riled up than usual, but at least it was a reprieve from the imminent cold weather.

Once he was lucid enough, he checked on his vehicle trackers. Brian's had moved to a boulevard in Downey, not far from his house. Zooming in, it looked like a commercial strip, and the green circle was on a car lot. That must be his business. The street view showed a chain-link fence with a small structure inside.

Thorpe's vehicle had moved too, not long ago, down the 710 to Long Beach. He knew that neighborhood—Bixby Knolls. It was suburbia, near the boundary where it changed from middle-class to low-income. When you crossed a specific boulevard, the tony brewpubs and coffeehouses gave way to dollar stores and drive-through fast food.

The software had good precision on the G-Wagen, with a circle that covered just a couple of houses. The street view showed bungalows with middle-class front lawns—they weren't fenced off like they were in poorer neighborhoods. It wouldn't take him long to get there.

Back inside he found the ibuprofen bottle in the bathroom, and popped a couple, then trudged down to the garage, and backed the Continental into the street. Turning onto Sunset, he stopped in front of a coffee place. There were no open parking spots, so he double-parked in the bicycle lane, and left his hazard lights flashing as he hustled inside.

Walking out a minute later with a paper cup of java in hand, he stepped in front of his grille as a cyclist pulled up and stopped next to the front fender on the driver's side. He was wearing a bicycle helmet and mirrored sunglasses.

"You're blocking the bike lane," he shouted.

"I'm about to move it."

The guy banged on the hood of the Continental with a gloved fist, then stood up on his pedals. Setting his cup on the hood, Slater stepped in front of the bike before he could get it rolling. When he grabbed the handlebars, the bike stopped abruptly. Slater straddled the front wheel and delivered a rapid kovac, slapping his face left and right. The impact was tempered by the side straps of the idiot's helmet.

"Why do you make me do this to you?" Slater demanded.

"Stop that, you psycho." The guy slapped at him and tried to push him off.

"You're going to make me crack you, aren't you." Slater slapped him again. "Why do you make me do it?"

Shoving hard with both hands, the guy shifted his ride backward, and stumbled, and the bike fell into the street. An SUV in the travel lane laid on its horn as it roared by.

The cyclist picked up his bike and shouted, "Asshole."

"Keep moving, or I'll break you in half," Slater said through his teeth.

He climbed on and pedaled away, riding as close as he could to the parked cars next to the bike lane. Slater had to scoff. As if he'd run the guy down at this point. The Santa Anas made people a little nuts, but not to that extreme.

Grabbing his coffee, he got behind the wheel, waiting for a break in the traffic, and pulled a fast U-turn. Once he was on the freeway, through the congestion of Downtown and on the way to Long Beach, he checked the tracking app a few times to make sure the G-Wagen hadn't moved. Pulling onto the narrow street, he spotted Thorpe's vehicle parked in a driveway in front of a ranch-style house fronted with tan stucco.

Once he'd turned around, he pulled to the curb farther up the block, and thumb-typed a note of the address. There were no front fences, and most of the yards still had turf like a golf course. Only one front yard up the block had dryland plantings. That was another measure of means in a neighborhood—it took resources to replace the grassy lawns.

Slater cracked the windows and got comfortable. He was close enough that he didn't need to pull out the binoculars, he decided. Before long Thorpe appeared from the front door to the house, stepping into the driveway. Her hair looked longer now than in her ID photo, the cut a little less conservative, but it was her. Curvy and tall, she was wearing stretchy pants and a black athletic top with pink sleeves.

A guy stepped out behind her and twisted a key to lock the door. He was dark, and totally bald, and wearing office clothes. The fit of his shirt showed he was buff.

The pair of them embraced, lingering in a kiss. Thorpe obviously wasn't shy about being seen—although this far from South Gate, it was unlikely anyone would recognize her. Eventually they broke it up, and Thorpe climbed into the G-Wagen, and backed into the street. As she drove off, the guy walked out to the curb and climbed into a boxy iridescent-green Soul. He drove this way, past Slater, not even glancing at him as he went by.

He sat thinking about it for a minute. Thorpe had come here for a hookup. This really was a window-shade job. He should bail on it. He knew that. But then he'd have to give Brian his money back, and that two grand felt good in his pocket. As he considered his next move, he checked the tracking app, and absently watched the location circle for Thorpe's vehicle hop through the neighborhood.

The movement stopped, and the green circle shrank as the software got more confident about its location. Slater zoomed in on the map. The G-Wagen was in the parking lot of a strip mall not far from here. Looking at the street view, he could read the names of the stores. It seemed unlikely that Thorpe had gone into the cigar lounge, or the box-and-ship, but there was also a pancake house.

This whole thing felt messed up. Slater took a breath. Fuck it, he decided, and started the engine, and drove the few blocks. The G-Wagen was in the lot, and there was no sign of the fugly green Soul. When he walked in, he found Thorpe sitting alone at a booth at the window.

Sliding in across from her, he said, "Mind if I join you?"

Thorpe frowned. "What? No." And then louder, "I mean, yes, I mind."

"You sound confused," Slater said. "I hope you don't do your stock trades that way. Although I'd be a little distracted too if I'd just hooked up with the guy with the Soul. He's a total smoke-show. I bet he's stacked."

"The fuck are you?" she demanded.

"An observer of human nature."

"Did Brian send you to spy on me?"

The server stepped over with a plate and set it in front of Thorpe. She had the coffee pot in her other hand, and Slater turned his cup over.

"What can I get you?" she said as she poured.

"Just the java is fine."

Once she'd stepped away, he saw that Thorpe's expression had shifted. Her eyes had gone dead, the initial surprise and anger replaced by indifference.

"You're one of Memo's goons, aren't you." She reached for the syrup bottle. "You look like one of Memo's goons. I know Brian sent you. Well, you can watch me eat, if you really want to, but it might get a little dull. I shall be consuming this short stack."

Slater watched as she dug into her pancakes.

"So why the baldy? Does Brian not put out enough?"

She briefly glanced up. "I'm actually ignoring you. Did you not pick up on that?"

She really was unruffled about being confronted, he decided. It wasn't an act. That meant she'd been in similar situations, knew the drill, knew how to handle him. This was a bona fide lowlife.

"Are you planning to divorce him?" Slater said. "I thought the Paris trip went really well." When she didn't acknowledge that, he raised his voice. "Sing, sister."

Thorpe gestured with her fork. "You know nothing, thug."

"It must have been romantic, though. The city of lights."

On the tabletop her phone buzzed, and she picked it up, tilting it away from him as she tapped in the unlock code with her thumb. Why did people think that if you couldn't see the screen you couldn't figure out the numbers? There were only a few of them, and they were always in the same layout. From Slater's perspective the sequence was obvious, and he spent a second committing the digits to memory.

Once she set the phone down again, Slater spoke. "So what's up with the ghosts?"

Thorpe scowled at him. "Did Brian tell you about that? Why would he do that? He's such a big mouth."

Finally a reaction. "Are they the spirits of anyone you knew in life, or just randos who come to hassle you?"

She took a breath. "Have you ever seen a ghost?"

"Negative."

"It's not like the Halloween stories. Ghosts are like guides. They're not here to scare people—they give advice, and warnings, and sometimes reveal hidden truths."

"What hidden truths have they told you?"

"Be wary of Memo, for one."

"I could have told you that without supernatural input," Slater said. "How well do you know Memo?"

"Brian deals with him, not me."

That made it sound like a business relationship. It made sense that they weren't just biking friends—why would a gangbanger hang out with a civilian? It made much more sense that they were working together.

As she set down her fork, Thorpe met his gaze. "Spirit contact is just one of those things. You can't understand it if you haven't experienced it."

"That sounds like hipster bullshit. 'You wouldn't understand how we do things.'"

"It's not bullshit. It's called the mystic's dilemma, and it's been around since ancient times. How do we bring transcendent experiences back into ordinary reality?" She shook her head. "Basic people just aren't going to be able to understand extraordinary stuff."

"You can't really deny that you're a hipster elitist when you call other people basic," Slater said.

She raised her eyebrows. "You want basic? Take a good look at Brian. Ask him about the badger game." She dabbed her lips with a napkin and shifted sideways on the bench. "I need to get to the gym."

"I'm pretty sure you can just walk into those places whenever."

"Not when you have an appointment with a personal trainer." She flashed a thin smile. "Marcus doesn't like to be kept waiting."

Slater sat and sipped his coffee as she walked out. He could see the G-Wagen from here, and he watched her climb in and drive away.

Something didn't wash. Thorpe wasn't that surprised to see him, and she had the serenity of a lowlife. It wasn't what you'd expect from a civilian white-collar desk jockey. Most significant, she'd implied that Brian was working with Memo. These two weren't just dope pushers for Memo either—it felt like there was more to it, like they were running bunco, running a gimmick. If Brian ran a legit business too, maybe he was laundering Memo's drug earnings for him.

Digging out his phone, he texted his operative Andy:

Can I swing by? It's work.

He hated that the guy gatekept him like this, insisted that he request permission to go over there. They used to have a groove, him and Andy, but then that bland twink Kyle had somehow tricked him into marrying him, and now he had to check in just to go over to talk.

Rising, he tucked his phone away, and stopped at the register.

"What's the damage?"

The server tapped at the machine. "Two coffees and the short stack, correct?"

He had to chuckle. Thorpe had made him pay for her breakfast. Props to her for chutzpah.

Once he'd paid, he got on the freeway, and headed to Downtown LA. He parked in the surface lot behind Andy's building, then walked around to the entrance on Broadway.

It took Andy a minute to answer when he knocked, as he didn't move all that fast, but eventually he pulled the door open. Wiry, with a mess of brown hair, Andy was wearing his usual boxers and a T-shirt. He cracked that beautiful smile as he waved him in. Slater admired his butt as he followed him inside.

It was always cold in here. Even on cool days Andy blasted the air conditioning as his CP made his metabolism run hot. His loft was mostly one room, with big multipane windows that dated to when it had been a textile warehouse a century ago. His desk and an array of computer monitors sat under them, in the corner, not far from his bed.

As Andy dropped into his gaming chair, Slater stood facing him.

"Where's spouse B?" Slater said. "I can tell he hasn't been here in a while because I can't really smell his cologne. Usually it makes my eyes water and my throat constrict."

"He's doing something with … his dad today."

"That fricking guy. I remember him from your wedding. Great hair, and tits for days, and a real bad attitude."

"You basically assaulted him."

"I thought he was a crasher," Slater said. "Did Kyle need to pick up a trust-fund payment today?"

"He's not that guy. You know he's not. If he was an … elitist, he definitely wouldn't be with me."

"You know it's the other way around, right? You're way out of his league. You're the Cadillac and he's the noisy minibike with the two-stroke engine stinking up the neighborhood."

"I think you actually like Kyle. All the … smack talk is just bluster."

"I like the way his pants fit. I won't deny that." Slater put his hands on his hips. "But if I ever see a mark on you, or a single teardrop falls, I will not hesitate to put that sicko to bed with a shovel."

"Right," Andy said, furrowing his brow, "because violence is … the answer."

"Exactly." He gestured widely. "I'm glad you can see that. I was worried that little toothache hypnotized you into believing some alternate version of reality."

"Slater, why are you here?"

He pulled out his phone. "I'm going to text you an address. The guy who lives there is named Brian. I don't know his last name. Does he own the house? Is his wife on the deed? I'll text you her name too. Anything else you can find out about him."

"I'll get on it today."

Once he'd sent the details, he looked up and tucked his phone away. "So I guess I'm not allowed to suggest a hookup, even though your bed is right here."

Andy's random muscle movements intensified a little, and he waved a hand. "You're starting to catch on."

Slater watched him for a moment. "Bye, beautiful."

NINE

WALKING AROUND TO THE parking lot, Slater climbed in the Continental, and drove the few blocks to the Fashion District, and parked in the surface lot across the street from his office. Hustling over in a break in the traffic, he strode through the lobby, where a couple of day laborers were looking over the sticky notes on the wall that listed gigs in the garment factories upstairs, and rode up to the ninth floor.

Built for white-collar work in the 1920s, today the building was all small-scale clothing production, except for their small suite, with a front office and one each for him and for Max. As he twisted his key in the deadbolt, he admired their names emblazoned on the door:

SLATER IBÁÑEZ
MAXIMILLIAN CONROY
INVESTIGATIONS

The lights were off, and he stuck his head into Max's office to make sure he was alone. Their operative Etta had decorated the place, warm yellow for Max's walls, taupe in the front office, and in Slater's a shade of turquoise. It was an upgrade from the utilitarian space it had been before, as she'd brought in art deco furniture and light fixtures that gave the place a classic vibe. Etta worked at the reception desk sometimes, and it had a computer and a landline that nobody ever used, plus a little plaster statue of Rey Pascual. A skeleton holding a scythe and wearing a crown, it had been a gift from the woman who sold him pupusas. Even though it was incongruous with the clean deco lines, Rey had become the de facto office mascot.

In his own office he dropped into his desk chair and peered at the computer screen, pulling up the history for the tracker on Thorpe's G-Wagen. After she'd left the pancake house this morning, she'd driven to the Financial District. The tracker had then gone offline at an office tower. That meant she'd parked where there was no cell connectivity, likely in the building's underground garage.

Thorpe had said she was going to the gym, and looking at the map of the building where she'd parked, he saw the tenants were mostly lawyers and bankers, but on the mezzanine level was a gym. When he looked up the brokerage where she worked, its offices were a block away in another tower. It made sense that she'd picked one near her workplace.

Tapping the number into his phone, he got the gym's front desk.

"I'm at Sobinère, and I'm doing Janine Thorpe's calendar," Slater said. "I know she's training today with Marcus. Is it at 11 or 11:30?"

"Give me a second," the woman's voice said, and then, "It was actually at 10:30. She has a standing appointment at the same time Tuesday to Saturday."

"Got it." Glancing at the screen, he tapped it to end the call.

Leaning back in his chair, he thought about it for a minute. With just a little more effort he could get a lot more insight into what she and Brian were up to. Most of what he needed was already lined up. He texted Etta:

Are you back at school yet? I've got some work.

Her reply came soon after:

At the office? I can come by on my lunch break.

It wasn't far for her, as the middle school where she taught was right across the tracks in East LA. He wrote back:

I'm here.

A moment later, Etta sent a second text:

School went back weeks ago. How did you not notice that? Morning traffic gets insane from the day it starts.

He scoffed and swiped it away, then checked on the other trackers. Brian was still at his business, but the one on Lenny's bike had moved—he was in LA.

Zooming in on the map, it was parked in the structure for the central market, right downtown. What was that knuckle-dragger doing here?

Locking his computer with a keystroke, he flicked off the lights and twisted his key to set the bolt as he left. In the elevator on the way down, he texted Etta:

Change of plans. Meet me at the central market.

A few minutes later he nosed the Continental into the structure next door and found a space. Once he was in the big market hall, he walked around, scanning the crowd. The place was busy and noisy with people looking for lunch. Not that long ago it had been an actual food market, with produce stalls and bulk dry goods, but it had become almost entirely eateries, most of them trendy and overpriced.

First he walked around the Hill Street side, then over toward Broadway, stepping around the lines of bodies waiting to order grub. Finally he spotted Lenny, sitting alone at a table, looking at his phone. Still wearing his club vest, his arms were bare, his sunglasses shoved up into his hair. He didn't have any food, but there was a book on the table in front of him, a paperback with a red and yellow cover. That seemed odd. He'd be surprised if the guy was even literate.

There were tables a few steps higher up, and Slater sat at one that gave him a view of Lenny. The guy might spot him if he looked around, but right now he was focused on his phone.

His own phone buzzed in his pants, and he pulled it out to find a text from Etta:

Where you at?

He typed a terse reply:

Broadway side. By the pizza stand.

A minute later Etta walked up and beamed at him. Curvy, she kept her black hair butched short, today wearing her work drag, a natty tweed vest over a dress shirt and dark pants.

Etta pulled out the chair opposite and sat, handing him one of the golden half moon–shaped pastries she had in hand, wrapped in a swatch of thin waxy paper.

"It's pai fala," she said. "From a stand up there. The dude is actually from Samoa. He knows some of my people."

"It looks like a meat pie."

"It's got coconut and pineapple in it. No dairy—I asked."

She bit into hers, and Slater took a bite of the one she'd given him. It was sweet and gooey and delicious.

"Not as good as my grandmother's," Etta said, studying the contents, "but definitely authentic."

"It's fricking amazing. You've been holding out on me."

"So why are we here?"

"I'm multitasking," Slater said. "I saw that my target had come in." He jutted his chin toward Lenny. "The guy on his own with the hair and the leather vest. He's obviously not here to eat. That means he's meeting somebody. I'm waiting to see who."

"He looks like a biker."

"He's totally a biker."

"Those guys are scary. Lots of them are white supremacists." Etta crumpled up her pastry wrapper and looked at him again. "He's playing the tourist."

"Why do you say that?"

"The book on the table. I can't read the title from here, but I know that color scheme. It's a series. Travel guides." She sat back. "So what's the job?"

"I need to get into a phone. I know the unlock code, and I know it's going to be unattended in a locker at a gym tomorrow morning."

"So you want me to go after it. Why can't you do it?"

"I can't really be stealthy in the women's changing room," Slater said. "Bring it out for a couple minutes, and I'll install surveillance software on it, and then you put it back. The problem is, that locker is going to be locked."

"People usually bring their own padlocks to the gym," Etta said. "Do you have a way to get through one of those without being noticed?"

"It's probably an upscale gym, considering where it is, and she goes there every day. I'm thinking they'll have a dedicated locker for her."

"Is it far?" She raised her eyebrows. "I can go scope it out today, maybe set up a trial membership. That way I can easily access the place tomorrow."

Slater nodded. "That would be great. If you can take a picture of the lockers, we can figure out how to get into them."

"What time is your target supposed to get there?"

"She has an appointment with a trainer at 10:30, but you'd have to be there before that to see which locker she's using."

"That works. I can take time tomorrow. I'm not in the classroom."

"There's his date," Slater said, looking over at Lenny. A guy set a paper coffee cup on the table and sat opposite him. Lanky, with his dark hair cut short, he was wearing a tan summer suit.

Etta was watching too, he realized. She hadn't turned her head but was looking at them side-eye. It was a great technique—from a distance it would appear that she was looking at Slater, and only one of them was facing Lenny.

"That guy is no biker," Etta said. "With the suit he looks more like a desk jockey."

"What does that tell you?"

She watched them a while longer. "Earnest talk, no humor. They're not friends. It's a business meeting."

"That sounds right."

A minute later Lenny and the other man stood up and did a fist bump.

"The guy in the suit took the book," Etta said.

"So it's some kind of handoff. Dope or cash. Do you have time for a quick tail?"

"It might cut into my gym excursion. And I really should get back to work."

"Just find out where the suit goes from here," Slater said. "You don't have to invest the whole day."

"Why can't you do it?"

"I need to talk to the biker."

Lenny and the suit were still chatting, standing on either side of the table.

"What do I do if he makes me?"

"Dazzle him with your people skills," Slater said. "I know you have those. It's why they let you teach teenagers."

The suit strode away, and Lenny sat down again to look at his phone.

"It's an easy tail," Etta said. "Nobody else is dressed like that."

They both got up, and Etta headed after the suit. Slater went down the steps, dodging the people in the aisle, and stepped up to Lenny's table.

"What are you doing here?" Slater said. "I thought you were a desert rat."

Lenny looked up at him. "I know you. You're Pine's squeeze."

"Am I? Or is he my squeeze? You know I owe you a knuckle sandwich."

"I was just doing my job." His eyes flicked over him. "You need to let it go."

Slater forced a laugh. "I know that, man."

"Why are you in here?"

"This isn't far from my place. You know where that is—it's where you tased me." He gestured at the market hall. "There's a fuck-ton of food here. Did you eat yet? Let me buy you lunch."

Lenny frowned. "Why?"

"We have mutual acquaintances, and it seems like we're working for the same guy." He threw up his hands. "It's just lunch, toots. I'm not trying to sell you anything."

He looked around. "I came in here because I had a meeting. It doesn't really feel like my kind of place. More like somebody in a white apron will try to grate cheese onto my food."

"Not everything is upscale. You can get tacos or a burger. This place is for everybody."

"It feels like there's a lot of Mexicans." He met

Slater's gaze. "Nothing personal."

"I'm not Mexican."

"You're buying?" Lenny said as he stood up.

They walked around the hall, and Lenny stopped at a burrito place, and Slater paid after he ordered. The guy might not be comfortable with people he perceived to be Mexicans, but he had no bias against Mexican food.

"I'll catch up," Slater said. "There's nothing for me to eat here."

"Why not? It smells amazing."

"I'm vegan."

"You really are an LA boy. I didn't go upstairs in your house, but I assume you have a sound-bath vortex area, and a Zen room?"

"Funny." As he walked away, his phone buzzed in his jeans, and he pulled it out to check. It was a text from Etta:

> Silver Lexus. It was in the garage next door. Bumper sticker says Taiwan something.

A subsequent text had a photo of the car's rear plate, and the next one was an image of the bumper sticker, with TAIWAN in orange letters above some Chinese characters. He had to grin. She must have taken these surreptitiously as the guy was getting into his car. Etta really had a knack for this work.

Slater stood in the line at the udon stand and zoomed in on the bumper sticker. The guy in the suit could definitely be Taiwanese. He ran the image through a language site, and it translated the characters as "Taiwan Resource Center." That wasn't especially informative, he decided, and tucked the phone away.

By the time he was at the front of the line, Lenny had joined him, burrito in hand. The counter guy had his hair in a great pomp, his apron a muddled patchwork of food stains. Slater eyed his pecs as he ordered and paid.

"I can't believe that's what a bowl of vegan soup costs," Lenny said. "It feels like a clip joint. Or is that what people actually shell out for rabbit food?"

"Like I said, there's something for everybody."

Folding his arms, Slater watched the counter guy dipping the mesh basket of noodles into the boiling water. His pants were pleasingly tight.

Sensing his gaze, the guy turned to him and frowned. "Is everything OK?"

Slater jutted his chin. "I was looking at your ass."

The guy laughed. "I've never actually had an objective view of it."

"You don't have to be modest. It's worth looking at."

"Good to know." A minute later he set the bowl in front of him. "I should get your number."

Slater raised his eyebrows. "Are you planning to write it down?"

Grinning, he pulled out his phone. "Fire away," he said, and thumb-typed as Slater recited it.

Carrying his food to a table nearby, Slater pulled the cover off the bowl as Lenny sat opposite and started to unwrap his burrito.

"You make it look easy," Lenny said. "I could talk to a hundred women like that before one would even crack a smile, never mind ask for my damn phone number."

"I find that hard to believe. You've got the body,

and I bet you can lay the mack down." He gestured to a stall nearby that had bottles and taps. "Want a beer?"

"I don't drink."

"Are you working the steps?" Slater said, and snapped his chopsticks apart.

"I'm supposed to be. When I have time." He bit into the burrito and spoke with his mouth half full. "Are you in program?"

"Nope. Still a drunk."

"I know Pine drinks. I kind of like that guy. He's a hard-ass but he's easy to talk to."

Slater jabbed his chopsticks at him. "You need to keep your paws off him."

"I don't want to fuck the guy." Lenny scowled. "Jesus, man. I had enough of that bullshit in stir."

"You were sent up?"

"Not for long. I behaved myself and got out in three. And here I am, back in the life, running a racket. Like I didn't learn my lesson."

"You're on the outside and you're sober," Slater said. "That sounds like the good life."

He slurped up the last of his noodles as Lenny balled up his burrito wrapper.

"Maybe you can help me with something," Lenny said. "I don't really know the city, and I hate being here on my own."

"You need a tour guide?"

"No, man. I need backup. I have a meeting at somebody's store."

That was scut work, and not the kind of thing he'd usually do. He could easily say no, like Pike told him to, but he didn't. It felt like he was too immersed in this to just let it go. They made a plan to meet later, and eventually Lenny rose, and scanned the hall.

"Where's the parking lot? I got turned around."

"Halfway along that side." Slater pointed it out, then watched him walk away.

TEN

PULLING OUT HIS PHONE, Slater called Etta, glad that she picked up.

"You totally did it," he said. "You got the guy's tag."

"You're welcome. You have to pay me. A hundo for my time."

"You know I will."

"That gym is fricking expensive, but I'm set up for tomorrow. You were right about the private lockers. Nobody brings their own padlock—it's too upscale. The locks are built into the locker doors. Everything's made out of redwood."

"My target tends toward bougie," Slater said.

"I'm going to send you a bunch of pictures of the locks. They have little wheels to dial in each number. The woman who showed me around told me they also have a master key in case you forget your combination."

"Good intel. I'll let you know what I come up with."

"You'll talk to the Russian?" Etta said.

"Somebody else. The spike man."

"What does that mean?"

"A lock person. Somebody who knows about keys and alarms and all that."

"I'm going to need to meet him too."

"You will," Slater said, and ended the call.

He hadn't talked to the spike man in a while, and he had to dig through his contacts to find him. Eventually he found the number and texted:

Are you around?

His reply came a moment later:

You know where to find me. Here till dark.

Rising, Slater walked into the parking structure and nosed the Continental out onto Hill Street. The navigation sent him on the 110 and then on the boulevard to Hyde Park.

The street was an odd stretch of several blocks where compact hundred-year-old houses were interspersed with light industrial spaces, all of them backing onto a rail line that cut through the city grid on a diagonal. On this block was a carpet installer, a body shop, and a gray building marked only by the hazardous materials diamond, with an A in place of the numbers. That meant artists, not dangerous chemicals. They were likely attracted here because the rent was cheap, but it didn't bode well for the future. The next step was gentrification—rich idiots moving in, attracted by the bohemian arty vibe, and then pricing everyone else out.

When he parked at the curb he sat for a minute to check the place out. It looked different now, but this was the right one, he decided. The spike man had no signage out front, just a metal fence with sharp pickets along the sidewalk, backed by corrugated steel to block the view. The part of the building inside that was visible over the fence showed that it had been painted white, and it looked a lot cleaner.

When he got out he saw there was a scraggly eucalyptus on the verge. He'd never seen one so distressed and stunted. They tended to get massive, and this one looked miserable here. Why would anyone have planted it on a narrow curb strip?

Grabbing his satchel, he looped it onto his shoulder as he went to the gate in the fence, then pressed the bell. A minute later the guy rolled it open a few feet. Flashing a smile, he greeted Slater by name, and waved him in. He had to study the guy's face for a second. It was the same person, but there was a lot more mileage on him. He'd cut his hair to a thin layer of fuzz, and it had some gray in it now.

"You chopped off your dreads," Slater said, as the spike man rolled the gate closed.

"Do you have any idea how much work Black hair is? Half my income went to my loctician."

"Ouch."

"Poverty is just an excuse. To be honest, I had to. I started losing it on top."

Slater frowned and peered at his head. "I guess that happens."

He laughed. "You're not getting any younger either, Ibáñez."

The spike man walked toward the building. It must have been a garage at one time. Both big doors had been boarded up and stuccoed over, but their recessed outlines were still visible.

Slater paused in front of the entrance. In the adjacent patch of dirt was a lush coyote brush.

"This looks great."

"I'm trying to glow the place up a little. Just for my own sanity. The woman at the nursery said it would grow fine in the shade."

"It'll grow anywhere," Slater said. "It's really hardy. Just don't baby it."

He frowned. "How would I do that?"

"Don't water it. Let nature do that when it rains. It's a native—it can handle it."

"Good to know," he said, and stepped inside.

There actually were windows, he saw, even though the structure looked like a monolith from the outside. Ancient and filmy, they were high up on the side that faced the tracks. The space had workbenches and cabinets like a car repair place, and a gas welding kit parked by the back door, and a long table in the middle covered with metal parts. A cluttered desk sat farther back. The tools on the wall rack were inscrutable—most of them were small, more precise than landscaping gear or what a handyman would use. This guy was probably a licensed locksmith.

"Let me show you some pictures." Slater dug out his phone, and pulled up Etta's locker-room photos, and handed it to him.

The spike man swiped through them. "Somebody's

been hanging out at that fancy gym."

"On Fig. You know the place?"

"It's a chain. I never went in one, but I know these locks." He handed the phone back and met his gaze. "I'm thinking you want to open a locker without causing a ruckus."

"Can you sell me a skeleton key?"

"They're different at each outlet, so no. But I can sell you a spike. Using it will look suspicious if anyone's watching, but it's quiet."

"Will it bust the lock?" Slater said.

"It damages the cylinder, but the combination will still work. It won't be noticeable until the next time someone tries to use the universal key."

Slater nodded. "That works."

The spike man went over to a wall unit and pulled open a drawer, then another, and eventually dug out a tool. It looked like a mini tire wrench with a sharply pointed end. Judging by the color, it was made of brass.

Stepping over to the long table, the spike man picked up a lock mechanism, then set it in the vise mounted on the workbench nearby. He tightened the vise with the keyhole facing out, the way it would be positioned on a door.

"You have to push in with some force." He pressed the tool into the lock, then pounded the opposite end with the heel of his palm. "Then you twist it clockwise if the bolt is on the left, counterclockwise if it's on the right. You try."

Slater took the tool from him, and shoved it into the lock, and gave it a twist. He could feel the metal parts inside grind against it. Eventually he pulled it out again.

"It seems straightforward. What do I owe you for this?"

"Let's say three dollars."

He dug out his wad, and peeled off the C-notes, and handed them over. Flipping open his satchel, he tucked the tool inside.

The spike man flashed a smile. "That was easy."

"I hope it works."

"It will. I built that tool myself."

The guy walked him out to the gate, and Slater checked the time as he climbed into the Continental. He needed to hustle—he was meeting Lenny soon.

———◆———

BACK IN HIS OWN neighborhood, as Slater slowed down to turn onto his street, he realized the motorcycle making the same turn in front of him was Lenny— he knew those bare arms and the half helmet.

His stance on the bike was louche, not at all the way Pike rode, and it made him look kind of hot. Following him up the street, Slater hit the button for the garage door and nosed in. As he stepped out of the car he waved Lenny inside, then hit the wall button to roll the door down.

Lenny parked next to him, and killed the noisy engine, and set the bike on its side stand.

"I noticed this beauty when I was here before," Lenny said, pulling off his helmet and waving at the Continental.

"When you zip-tied me to that chair and trashed my phone," Slater said.

He frowned. "I'm pretty sure that phone was already busted when I got hold of it."

Slater had to chuckle. "Fair enough."

"So are you a car whack?"

"In a way. I don't have the time or the smarts to maintain it myself, but I love driving it."

Lenny pulled one of the black leather saddlebags off his bike and gestured with it. "Let's roll."

"That looks empty," Slater said. "I assumed this was a product delivery."

"I'm picking up cash."

"What kind of store is it, and who are you meeting?"

"It's a woo-woo type deal."

Slater put his hands on his hips. "The fuck is that supposed to mean?"

"They teach yoga. I've never been to the place, but I've met the boss. Her name is Chara. Apparently she always wears white."

"You have to leave your heater here."

Lenny frowned. "No way."

"I'm not coming with you if you're armed. Plus you'll do a lot less time if you get popped."

"I'm not going to get popped."

"I have a gun safe."

"Fuck me," Lenny muttered, and pulled his handgun out of his waistband. "Where is it?"

"Is that a 27? That's a lot of gun." He walked over to his gear cabinet.

"It's actually pretty small."

"Large caliber, though. That means business."

Once he got the cabinet open, Lenny set the weapon on a shelf. "There's no guns in here. What is all this stuff?"

"Valuable electronics." Slater locked it again, and

they climbed into the Continental, and he hit the button to roll up the garage door.

"So where is this place?"

"West Hollywood." Lenny recited the address. "Is that far?"

Pulling out his phone, Slater punched it into the navigation. "Forty minutes."

"Why do you use the map? You don't know how to get to that part of town?"

"It knows about traffic," Slater said, and backed into the street. "It sends me a different way every time. Even just to go downtown."

"I don't know. I'd hate to be that dependent on technology."

"Like your motorcycle? Without that technology you'd have a three-day hike back to Landers."

Once the door was all the way down, Slater drove up the block and headed to the yoga studio. The place was on a busy boulevard, and he pulled around the corner and parked at a meter on the side street. Climbing out, they walked back to the place, Lenny with his saddlebag in hand. The last gray glimmer of twilight was fading in the west.

The front door was flanked by tall wooden boxes planted with horsetail. He knew why a landscaper would think it fit with yoga, because it looked like bamboo, and bamboo was vaguely Asian, like yoga was. But it was stupid to plant it here. It hogged up the water and needed way too much attention.

He followed Lenny inside. This was a foyer, with a bench along the wall made of dull dark wood and a set of tall shelves at one side, crowded with shoes. Parked on the bench was a woman dressed in stretchy black pants and a sports top. She was pulling off her tennis shoes.

Her eyes flicked over Lenny. "You have to take your boots off. The studio is just inside that door."

"Where's the office?" Lenny said.

"I think it's a different entrance." She gestured to the door to the street. "Around the side."

Slater followed him back out to the sidewalk. Along the side of the building was a breezeway, gated but not locked, and they walked to the end. The lone door here had no markings, and Lenny tried the handle, pulling it open and then stepping inside.

The small office had a couple of desks and a hall-way leading deeper into the building. At one of the desks sat a woman, wearing a white robe and a tur-ban, her back to the wall. A ceremonial dagger hung at her side. This was Chara. She sat back in her chair as they stepped in.

"You have something for me," Lenny said.

Chara frowned at him. "Oh, hello."

From the hallway a guy stepped in. Tall and thick, his dark Latin hair was buzzed short, and his face was pocked with the scars of long-ago acne. He was dressed like a customer, baggy cotton pants and a tight gray T-shirt over his bulky torso, but it was obvious that he worked here. He gave them a pointed once-over.

"Why does a yoga studio need a bouncer?" Slater said.

Chara sat up. "Josué is my bodyguard."

"Why does a yoga teacher need a bodyguard?"

She raised her eyebrows. "I'm not a teacher. I'm a

yogini. It's like a guru."

"That's so interesting," Lenny said, and raised his voice. "Where's my money?"

Chara sighed and rolled open her top desk drawer, pulling out a bundle of cash bound with a tan elastic band. It was way thicker than a standard bundle. Most lowlifes were better organized with their cash, sorting it into manageable round numbers.

Stepping close to the desk, Lenny pulled off the elastic band and started to count the bills.

"You're going to do that right here?" Chara said.

Lenny ignored her, and as he worked, Josué moved between her desk and the back door, stepping behind Slater.

Scowling at him, Slater took a few steps into the room. He knew what the guy was doing, but he didn't need the goon standing behind him. Josué folded his beefy arms, and held his gaze, and raised his eyebrows.

Slater looked to Chara and jutted his chin. "Who's responsible for the horsetail out front?"

She frowned. "What are you talking about?"

"The planter boxes at the front door. You should put in native grasses. They'll look vibrant, and they need zero maintenance."

"I have a guy that looks after all that."

"Then he needs to take a good look at himself in the mirror," Slater said, "and admit that he's part of the problem."

She studied him for a moment. "I've actually got more important things to worry about."

"Why do you sell dope if you're selling yoga, anyway? Meth is kind of the opposite of all the wellness jive."

"That's the way the economy works." She shrugged. "You have to diversify. There's some overlap between the two revenue streams."

He scoffed. "Tweakers in yoga pants. You've definitely found a niche."

Lenny shuffled the bundle of bills together, and wrapped the elastic around it again. "This is only twelve. You're four grand short."

Chara waved a hand. "I know. I'll make it up next time."

"I get that you're new at this, so I'm not going to get mad." Lenny braced his hands on the desk and leaned toward her. "But that's not how it works."

Behind him, Josué grabbed Lenny's shoulder and pulled him away from the desk. As Lenny stumbled back, Slater lunged toward them and threw a hard right at Josué's face. He'd been focused on Lenny, not paying attention to Slater, and that gave him the time to put a lot of power into it. His fist connected with the guy's cheek, and his head snapped sideways.

Stepping back, Slater wriggled his fingers. That had hurt. For a second he thought the guy had paused to wind up and punch back, but then Josué sank to his knees, a flailing hand grabbing for the desk and missing it. He slumped against the wall.

Lenny briefly glanced at the guy, then looked to Chara. "Where's the rest?"

Her eyes wide, she was sitting bolt upright now, and didn't answer. Clearly she hadn't expected that.

"Check the safe," Slater said, and gestured to a squat gray box on the floor. "The door's ajar."

Stepping over to it, Lenny crouched and pulled it open. "Ho—what have we here?" He held up a couple of bundles of cash and waggled them at Chara. "These look new."

"Those are twenties," Slater said. "Two of them is four grand."

Lenny eyed him. "How do you know that?"

"The color of the currency strap. They're from the bank."

"Such a lovely shade of pink."

"I'd call it fuchsia," Slater said.

"I'll be taking three of these," Lenny said, and grabbed another. "Two is for your shortfall, and one is a tax for the disrespect."

"That's robbery," Chara snapped.

Lenny cackled as he stood erect. "Go ahead, call the cops. I'd be happy to explain our business relationship to them."

Josué was stirring now, and as he came back to consciousness, he glared at Slater, and started to get up, but his movements were labored.

"I'm going to fucking kill you," he growled.

"You and what army?" Slater waved an arm. "Go ahead—come at me." He eyed Lenny. "We should go. He's not armed right now, but he might have a rod stashed somewhere."

Lenny looked to Chara and spoke intently. "You pay for the product you take. There's no wiggle room, and no deferments." He jabbed a finger at her. "Next time I come in here I'll definitely be packing."

The guard was on his knees now, bracing himself on the frame of the door to the breezeway, murder in his eyes.

Slater stepped toward the hallway. "This way."

"You can't go in there," Chara said, raising her voice.

Ignoring that, Lenny followed him down the short hall and through the door at the end. This was the studio—dozens of people were arrayed around the big room, each of them on a mat, every one of them folded over their knees, foreheads touching the floor, hands limp and resting back by their feet. Dead-ass music was playing at low volume. It sounded like a three-year-old banging on a xylophone.

The only person standing was at the side of the room—a woman in a stretchy black leotard.

"Balasana helps us reconnect with our inner selves," she was saying.

Slater stepped between the mats, aiming for the closed double doors at the back. By his reckoning that's where the foyer with all the shoes was, and beyond that was the street.

The woman in the leotard hissed at them. "This class is closed."

As Slater reached the door to the foyer and pushed it open, Lenny shouted, "Namaste, motherfuckers."

ELEVEN

SECONDS LATER THEY WERE on the sidewalk, and Lenny matched his pace, walking abreast, amped up and strutting. Slater could feel it too, the rush of adrenaline. When they reached the corner, Slater glanced back toward the studio, but there was no sign of the guard.

They got into the Continental, and Slater flicked on the headlights and pulled into the street. The engine roared as he punched the accelerator.

"Why did I let you talk me out of taking my piece?" Lenny demanded.

"I wouldn't be here if you were strapped." He looked left as he turned onto the boulevard. "I don't know you, man. Maybe you're trigger-nuts, and you'd be waving your six-gun around."

"It's a Glock, and I don't cap people for no reason."

"You got your money, plus the stupidity tax, and nobody wound up ventilated. I'd call that a successful transaction."

"You made me look weak."

Slater sighed as he braked for a red light, then eyed him sidelong. "Namaste, motherfuckers?"

He chuckled. "Isn't that what they say in those places?"

"Not usually with that specific phrasing."

"That woman totally disrespected me."

"You said she was a new client. I don't think she was trying to chisel you. It's more like she doesn't understand the relationship. She thinks she's entitled to control the terms."

"Entitled is the word," Lenny said. "When I met her before, it was at a coffee place, and she drove up in a Rolls Royce."

"Seriously?"

"I guess yoga doesn't have the vow of poverty like the Catholics. Is it a little strange that a white woman is wearing a turban and carrying a blade on her hip? That thing looked ornery. Memo said she used to be called Sharon. She's a white girl from Orange County."

"The knife isn't really a weapon. It's part of the religion. She's a Sikh now."

"I'm not buying it. She was one of those peroxide airheads floating around Irvine."

"LA has always been about reinventing yourself," Slater said. "People come here to be whatever they want. They always have."

"Well, she needs to figure out that it's not like dealing with your incense vendor or your yoga-mat supplier. The risk is too high. The rules are different."

"I hear you, brother. I think she got the message."

"I need to get on the road," Lenny said. "I should eat first."

"I could eat."

"Great—let's find someplace with sizzlers. There's plenty of those in the big city."

Slater eyed him sidelong. "I am not taking you to a strip club."

"They're called gentlemen's clubs these days."

"Right, because they're for gentlemen. I thought you weren't into high-tone places." He gestured to a neon sign that said DINER. "This place has decent chow."

Turning onto the side street, he pulled into the lot behind it, and they climbed out. Slater stretched his back, taking a deep breath to dispel the residual adrenaline. It was still warm out, and breezy. He could feel the energy in the air from the Santa Anas.

They went into the place through the back door and waited for the host.

"It looks like the 1970s in here," Lenny said.

"I'm pretty sure that's intentional."

Once they were at a table, a woman with short hair stepped over and greeted them. "Margaritas are two for one right now."

"We don't drink," Slater said. "You can bring me the tofu chili."

"Chili sounds good." Lenny handed her the menu. "Is there one without the tofu?" Once she'd stepped away, he said, "You can drink if you want to."

"I'm not going to do that when you're in program."

When the food came out, they both dug into it.

After a while Lenny set his spoon down. He looked calmer now with some food in his belly.

"I don't want to sound like an ingrate. I mean the whole thing about the rod. I know you saved my neck back there."

Slater met his eye. "You asked for my help. The dustup was part of it."

"A lot of guys wouldn't have done that. They would have let me get beat down, or worse."

"The problem is, then I would have had to go explain that to Memo. I'd have to drive all the way out there, and he'd have so many questions." He shrugged. "Throwing a haymaker was a lot less work."

Lenny chuckled. "He went down like one of those Brazilian soccer players."

"You're into soccer?"

"Not by choice. There's a lot of Mexicans in stir, and they watch all the games."

Slater gestured with his spoon. "The red patches in your beard are pretty unique. Do you go to a salon, or do you touch them up yourself?"

"Are you serious right now?" Lenny demanded. "You think I dye my beard?"

"I'm just messing with you. You don't actually seem like the kind of guy who'd spend time on something like that."

"Mother Nature did this. It's always looked that way. It makes me think I have some Viking ancestry."

"Where were your people from?"

"Landers. I grew up out there. Before that, I've got no idea. Somebody once said Iowa or Indiana or one of those."

"So you're still in your hometown."

"I've never lived anywhere else." He pushed his bowl away. "Not by choice, anyway. My parents are gone. My sister is still around. She's a square, with the job and the kids and the SUV. It's kind of a miracle she turned out normal. Our parents were crazy."

"Everybody says that about their parents."

Lenny raised his eyebrows. "My dad claimed he was the first person sent into space."

"Wasn't that some Russian guy? Or did your dad go on a flying saucer? I know there were UFO conventions out in that part of the desert."

"Did you ever hear about the chimpanzee they sent up before they sent humans? It was part of Project Mercury. It happened just a few months before that Russian went up."

Slater folded his arms. "It sounds familiar."

"My dad said it was really him in that capsule. He was five years old. When he splashed down, they couldn't release the photos of him, because his head got banged up, and he was bleeding a lot, and he looked terrible. So they said it was a chimp, and sent out pictures of that instead. My dad said the head injury was why he was always so moody."

"It seems far-fetched that they'd recruit preschoolers as astronauts."

"His dad was posted on the base where they set up Project Mercury. Holloman in New Mexico. So that makes it kind of believable."

It didn't, Slater thought, watching him talk. Not even a little. But he didn't need to get into it.

"At least I inherited some of the family land," Lenny went on. "My sister got the piece near the highway with the house on it, and I got twenty acres of empty desert. It's not worth anything." He scoffed. "I shouldn't be telling you that."

"Why not? Land ownership is public record anyway."

"Well, I wish I'd never told Memo about it."

"Is that the land where his operation is set up?"

"Memo owns that piece. My place is farther out." Lenny shifted in his seat. "I suppose you want me to buy your dinner, seeing as you saved my neck and all."

"I'm happy to go Dutch," Slater said, and dug out his cash.

Walking out to the car, he could think of a few reasons Memo would be interested in a chunk of remote unoccupied land. He already had his factory set up, but a more isolated place would be useful to conceal stuff—cash or weapons or bodies.

———•———

WHEN THEY GOT BACK to Slater's house, and rolled into the garage, they both climbed out. He went to open the gear cabinet, and pulled the door wide, and gestured to the handgun.

"It's like you're afraid to touch it." Lenny grabbed the rod and tucked it into his waistband, adjusting his shirttail to conceal it.

He closed the cabinet. "I'm not going to put my prints on that thing. I don't know where it's been."

Lenny chuckled and walked over to his bike. He pulled a black leather jacket out of a saddlebag, then took a minute to put it on and zip it up. He had leather leggings too, a little like chaps but baggier, and stepped into them.

"You're OK to ride two hours in the dark?" Slater said.

"I'll be fine, Dad." He pulled on his helmet. "I've got some mad money tucked in my bra in case I break down."

He frowned. "You don't really need a bra. You're kind of flat-chested."

"Fuck you, Ibáñez." He buckled his chin strap.

Slater spread his arms. "Any time."

Watching him get dressed for the road was actually making him a little chubby. He stepped over to the wall to hit the garage door button. Lenny jump-started his bike, making it belch gnarly exhaust, then rode out onto the street. Once the door rolled down, Slater headed up the stairs.

A message had come a while ago from an unknown number, and he read it now:

Where you at?

A second text had come a few minutes later:

Met you at the udon place.

This was the counter guy from the market. Slater sat on the sofa, and pulled off his boots, then stretched out and tapped the number. Lots of people wanted to preapprove a voice call by text first, but if this guy wanted action, he'd pick up.

"Hey, I'm glad you called," he said as he answered. "Do you want to go out for a drink?"

"Not at this time," Slater said. "I can't go out for dinner either, or stroll aimlessly on the beach, or go antiquing in Palm Springs, or whatever it is that you people do. but I'll fuck you, if that's what you want."

"Wow—right to the point. What do you mean by 'you people'?"

"Squares. Civilians. Whatever you call yourselves."

"I noticed that ring on your finger. How does that play into this?"

"I have a hall pass," Slater said.

"I don't meet guys like you very often. I'd like to see you tonight, but I can't really host."

"I can." Slater rattled off his address. "If there's nowhere to park on the street, pull in across the garage door."

Once he'd ended the call, he rubbed his eyes. Maybe he was too tired for this. The gleaming amber elixir was waiting for him too, right over there in the cupboard, ever patient and loyal and at the ready. But it had to be boys before booze. Otherwise things got too muddled, and they'd rob him blind.

He'd drifted off, he realized, roused by the sound of the doorbell. Pushing himself off the sofa, he hustled down to the front door. The guy beamed when he pulled it open. He was wearing a dress shirt and jeans now.

"You know, I don't even know your name."

"It's Slater," he said, and waved him in.

"Goro." As they climbed the stairs, he said, "I like your house. You called me a civilian—are you in the military or something?"

"I'm not." Stepping into the bedroom, Slater stood with his hands on his hips. "So what do you want to do?"

"Do you know how to play blackjack?"

He narrowed his eyes. "Are you fucking kidding me?"

Goro chuckled. "I'm just joking around. Chill." Stepping close, he took hold of his wrists and pulled them onto his shoulders, then squeezed his biceps. "You seem a little tightly wound."

Leaning in, Slater mouthed his neck, and his jaw. He was wearing some kind of musky cologne. Grabbing the sides of his belt, he pulled him close, pressing his burgeoning woody into him.

He sighed and tilted his head back. "You should fuck me."

Slater pulled the guy's shirttails out of his pants, and pulled the shirt off over his head, then unzipped his fly. Goro unbuttoned Slater's shirt and massaged his chest, then kissed him, his mouth warm and intent. A minute later they were both naked.

Dropping onto the bed, Goro pulled him down on top of him, and Slater straddled his pelvis, running his hands over his torso. He squeezed Slater's cock.

"You're ready."

Shifting his knees up, Slater locked their mouths together as he massaged a thumb into him. Moving closer, he pressed into him. Goro gasped and squeezed his eyes shut.

"Don't hurt me."

Slater froze. "You want me to stop?"

He looked at him and grinned. "I'm role-playing here. The ingenue."

Pushing deeper, he worked up to pounding him, looming over the guy, drops of sweat falling out of his hair. Goro bit his lip and then yelped. Slater strained into him as he came, then sank on top of him, burying his nose in his sweaty hair.

When he rolled onto his side, he grabbed Goro's cock and stroked him.

He ran a hand into Slater's hair. "You should smoke me."

"The ingenue knows what he wants."

Goro giggled as Slater shifted down the bed and took him into his mouth. He quickly got hard, and he worked him until the guy climaxed, arching his back.

Stretching out, he closed his eyes, and briefly raised his head when Goro shoved an arm under his neck.

"That was great."

Slater grunted assent.

"I like the paint job in this room. It's kind of lavender."

Here we go, he thought. A chatty one. "Technically it's periwinkle."

"That's a color? I love that name. My brother's name is Kota. Our parents said it was a color. Green. But that's just bogus. That's not what it means. My name too—Goro means 'fifth son.' I only have one older brother. My parents are such airheads."

He didn't respond to that, working to tune him out.

"So why am I a square and a civilian and you're not? You've got this big old house with the periwinkle paint job. That strikes me as a little square. You're not squatting here, are you?"

Slater groaned. "I just meant that I'm a wrong guy. I'm trouble."

"A bad boy."

He met his gaze. "Real bad."

"That's hot."

"Actually it isn't. I hurt people."

Goro caressed his chest. "I guess it works, your brand."

He frowned. "What brand?"

"The look you're working. And then your friend at the market. He's a whole level deeper, with all the hair and the leather. I wondered if he was a method actor, getting into character."

"Are you an actor?"

"Not really. I did some advertising when I was a kid, but I'm not in the game anymore."

Slater listened to him talk for a while. The guy's short attention span soon got the better of him, and he sat up and went to shower. When he came back, he started to pull on his clothes.

"We should do this again," Goro said, scooping up his shirt.

"You've got my number. Maybe we can do a three-way with my boyfriend."

"So that's what the ring is about. What's he like?"

"He's everything," Slater said. "The sun and the moon and the stars. And he's so hot he could set your hair on fire."

Once the guy left, Slater went upstairs, and pulled out the bourbon, and slammed his ration, relishing the fleeting burn. He was resentful at the paucity of it, but no way was he going to overdo it again.

Stretching out on the sofa, he checked his track-ers. The G-Wagen and the Rover were both at the house in South Gate, and Lenny was back in the des-ert already.

That guy was a trip. Slater didn't mind him for some reason. Tonight he hadn't wanted to punch him in the face more than once or twice. Maybe it was because dealing with Lenny was simple—the guy was transparent about his motives, and unlike most people, he wasn't actively trying to manipulate him.

TWELVE

When Slater woke, he forced himself to sit up. The floor felt cold under his feet. He couldn't remember going to bed, but here he was. At least his head didn't hurt. After he'd showered, he went up to the kitchen. The bagels were gone, so he ate the last of the flat bread things Pike had left in the fridge. It was slow going, with a lot of chewing, as it was all dried out.

When he pulled into the surface lot across from his office, he parked next to Max's Challenger, matte gray with dark tinted windows, and grabbed his satchel from the back seat. It was warm and windy again, the Santa Anas still heating things up, subtly stirring the pot. Upstairs the lights were on, and as he stepped in he double-clicked his tongue to greet Rey Pascual, impassively watching the front door with his bony empty eye sockets.

Max was at his desk, wearing his fugly brown suit with a yellow necktie, and Slater stood in his office doorway.

"Have you got a minute?"

Max sat back and waved at the chairs in front of his desk. "Sit down."

"You always have time for me," Slater said as he dropped into a chair. "You're never impatient. I love that."

"Aw." Max furrowed his brow. "I love you too, sweetheart."

"Stop that," he said flatly.

Max laughed. "You and Vanessa are the only people I know who'd bail me out of the clink, no questions asked. I always have time for you two."

"That kind of explains why she puts up with you, even though she's younger and hotter and smarter. You make the time for her."

"You get priority too," Max said. "What would you do if I rolled up on your place at three in the morning, and got you out of bed, and said, 'Hey, buddy, can you get rid of this car? Just don't look in the trunk.'"

Slater pursed his lips. "I'd call Duarte and get an intro to one of those auto wreckers in Sun Valley. I give that guy enough business with the Continental that he'd definitely take my call at that hour. Then I'd swap the plates and drive out there at sunup. Pull the plates and slip the wrecker some lettuce to put it through the crusher. Nobody would be looking in the trunk."

"That's exactly what I mean." Max threw up a

hand. "It's interesting that you had a solution ready without needing to think about it too hard."

"I swim in the cesspool, man."

"Yeah, I'm right there with you." Max sat up. "So what do you need?"

Slater dug out his phone. "Can you run a tag? It's on a Lexus."

Max clicked around, peering at his monitor. "Fire away."

Zooming in on the photo Etta had taken, he recited the plate number as Max pecked at the keyboard with his stubby fingers.

A minute later he looked up. "It's registered to a business. Lau Skilled Importers. The address is in Vernon."

"Can you send me that?" As he stood up, there was a knock at the door. "Have you got a meeting?"

"I'm not expecting anyone."

Slater went to pull it open. The woman standing there greeted him by name and smiled. In her thirties, she was model-thin, and had blond hair that hung to her shoulders. He knew she ran a clothing line in one of the studios down the hall, but he couldn't remember her name.

"Hey, Cassidy." Max had stepped out of his office.

Slater pulled the door wider so she could come in.

"I'm so glad you're both here. There's a bit of an emergency."

"We're not paramedics," Slater said, and frowned.

"It's not that kind of emergency."

"What's going on?" Max said.

She took a breath. "I'm going to try to explain it clearly, even though things are moving fast. Have you been up to the twelfth floor?"

"I didn't even know the building went that high," Slater said.

"One of the factories up there," Cassidy said. "The tenant died. This lawyer came to clear the place out, and when she went in, it turns out it's full of vintage 1970s menswear."

Slater put his hands on his hips. "That does sound like an emergency."

"Right?" she said intently. "I thought of you both. The suits, the shirts. For you, Slater, it's the perfect look to go with your Lincoln."

"How do you know what I drive?"

"It's in the lot all the time. You can't just park a car like that and expect no one to pay attention." She eyed Max. "There's stuff for you too. I talked to the woman. She's there now." Briefly closing her eyes, she inhaled deeply. "And she's willing to let us go through it."

"I don't really need any more clothes," Slater said.

"You're wrong about that." She frowned. "It's a time capsule, Slater, and I know you already like the aesthetic. Your car is mid-seventies."

"It's a '73, and it doesn't require matching outfits."

"We're not in the industry," Max said. "I'd say we're using a different yardstick to assess what we need."

"Boys, listen to me. I know you're probably busy, but fashion is my world. I would not insist on this if it wasn't extremely important."

"When you put it that way," Max said, "it sounds like we pretty much have to go up there."

"You've definitely got me curious too." Slater waved an arm. "Lead on."

They stepped into the hall, and Max bolted the door, and they walked around to the elevator.

"What's your jacket size?" Cassidy said, eyeing Max as they got on.

"I'll have to look at the label in this one."

"It doesn't matter. We can try stuff on." She scoffed as she punched the button marked 12. "Men."

"This one dresses like he doesn't care," Max said, "but he actually knows about clothes. He helped me pick out some suits."

"Not the one he's currently wearing," Slater said. "I won't take the rap for that."

"Why do you know about clothes?"

"It's my birthright," Slater said. "I'm on dick."

She gave him the once-over. "Well, if you're dressing to attract men, we need to up your game."

The elevator lurched to a stop, and she shoved the accordion door aside. Cassidy led them to the end of the hall and stepped into a doorway. It was a lot roomier than their dinky suite, with multipane windows that had a view toward hilly Boyle Heights.

This was definitely a factory, with a trio of sewing machines under the windows, and bolts of fabric propped against the wall. Several rolling racks were loaded with clothes on hangers, and behind them an array of big cardboard boxes sat on the floor, flaps folded open, with more of them on the cutting tables.

Near the door was a desk strewn with file folders and piles of paper, a laptop sitting open at one side. Standing next to it was a woman with short black hair, wearing jeans and a sweatshirt. Pushing sixty, maybe, she had a stack of binders in hand, and set them on the desktop as they came in.

"This is Li-Hua," Cassidy said, and introduced them.

"You're the lawyer?" Max said.

"Guilty." She raised her eyebrows. "I know I don't look like it today. I dressed for manual labor to deal with all this."

"Has this place really been sealed for fifty years?"

Li-Hua chuckled. "It's my uncle's business. He came in every day until recently. He was still producing menswear. But he had a lot of dead stock. All this should have gone to a warehouse fifty years ago. For some reason he left it in these boxes, stacked up in the back." She gestured to the rolling racks. "I've been hanging things up."

"All the dead stock dates to the same era," Cassidy said, "so we think he bought out another manufacturer. Maybe a neighbor that was shutting down."

"Have a look," Li-Hua said, and sat behind the desk. "Let me know if you find anything you want."

"Thank you so much for this opportunity," Cassidy said. "Max, we'll start over here. I've prescreened several garments that should fit you."

Suppressing a smile, Slater went over to one of the racks and started to dig through it. Li-Hua had hung the long-sleeved shirts separate from the dress jackets. The stuff looked new, but it was way out of style, with huge lapels and absurdly wide collars, lots of it in bright vivid colors. The heavy fabric of the jackets felt artificial, he decided. It definitely wasn't wool.

"These prints." Cassidy held up a shirt patterned with orange and yellow diamonds. "Max could wear this, couldn't he?"

"You could totally pull that off," Slater said.

"Are you wearing a gun?" Li-Hua said, swiveling her chair toward them.

Max had taken his jacket off, and his holster was visible over his shirt.

"I've got a permit for it," Max said.

"It's fine." Cassidy waved a hand. "He's a private investigator, not a bandito."

"I don't mind a man with a little firepower," Li-Hua said, and Max laughed.

Slater stifled a scoff. Why did straight women find the guy so compelling? He flicked through more of the shirts. It was amazing that they were in such good shape, considering they'd been sitting in boxes for decades. He looked up when Cassidy let out a little scream.

"Striped pants." Standing over one of the boxes, she held them up. They had broad vertical stripes in gray and black. "They're side-zip. Slater, what's your waist size?"

"I'm not sure I could wear those," he said, but told her anyway.

"You're definitely getting these," Cassidy said. "Your car will have an orgasm."

He chuckled as he stepped over to the next rack. This one was all suits, some two-piece, some with a vest. As he dug through them, Cassidy came over and pulled out one in a shiny red-and-purple plaid.

"Try the jacket," she said.

"It's not really me."

"If you put this on, you'll make it you."

Taking it off the hanger, she handed it to him, and he pulled it on, shrugging his arms into it.

"It fits you perfectly," she said.

"I wish there was a mirror."

She pointed toward the doorway, and he saw there was a full-length one stuck to the wall. Stepping over, he assessed the look. The lapels were huge, and the plaid was broad, but the colors weren't too crazy. It had a sheen to it, but not quite like silk.

"You have to buy this suit." Standing behind him, Cassidy met his gaze in the mirror. "Have to. If you don't, I will, and I'll break into your office and plant it there."

"You're so passionate about menswear," Max said.

"This place is like Christmas morning."

She took the jacket and put it back on the hanger with the pants, then added it to a pile of stuff at the end of one of the cutting tables.

"You've pulled a lot of clothes," Slater said.

"Shirts and sport jackets for Max, and those pants for you, and that suit." Cassidy pulled another suit off the rack and handed him the jacket. "Try it on."

It was heavier than the plaid one, in the fake wool, with a big houndstooth pattern in warm green and brown.

"It seems awfully loud."

She raised her voice. "You'll never have another opportunity like this."

Slater pulled on the jacket, and she whirled her finger in the air. He did a twirl, and rolled his shoulders, then flashed his palms.

"It fits you fine," she said, and added it to the pile.

Back at the rack of shirts, he pulled out a few that looked like they'd fit him, in prints that weren't too crazy-looking, and added them to the pile.

"These are so pristine," he said.

"It's because they're polyester." Cassidy rearranged the shirts he'd brought over, gathering the hanger loops together. "It's a miracle fabric. They called it wash-and-wear because you didn't have to iron it."

"I like that idea," he said. "You know, I'm not even sure I own an iron."

She frowned at him. "Are you sure you're gay?"

Max laughed at that, and she stepped over to another box, and held up a long lime-green garment.

"How do we feel about leisure suits?"

"That looks like a onesie," Slater said. "I love the color, but I can promise you that I'd never wear that."

"I think I've seen enough," Max said. "My vision is going blurry from all the intense colors."

"We found you a couple of things, at least," Cassidy said, and stepped over to the desk. "We've got two suits, maybe five sport jackets, some jeans and shirts. Do you want to look through them?"

"No need," Li-Hua said quickly. "Make me an offer."

"Boys?" Cassidy said, raising her eyebrows.

"Three hundred for the lot," Max said.

Li-Hua waved a hand. "Five and you're out the door."

"How about four?" Max said.

Without hesitating, she nodded. "Sold, to the best-dressed man in town."

"I've got cash." Slater dug out his wad and peeled off the C-notes.

Rising, Li-Hua pocketed the bills. "Take some hangers. They're those cheapo dry-cleaning ones."

Cassidy grabbed a handful, and they gathered up the pile of clothes. Most of it was on hangers, and

Cassidy draped the others over their arms.

Once they were on the elevator, Max said, "You were right. I've never seen anything like that."

"It's good that you did the negotiating," Cassidy said. "I would have offered her a lot more. You just know some retro hipster is going to get wind of this, and buy it all for a few grand, and sell the stuff for fifty times what you paid."

At the office door, Max handed Slater a bundle of the hanger loops, then dug out his keys to unlock the door. Inside they piled it all on the front desk.

"So if wash-and-wear polyester is so amazing," Slater said, "why isn't everybody wearing more of it?"

"Because as a society, we've lost our way," Cassidy said. "There's no imagination anymore. Fun fashion has been relegated to the sidelines." She waved a hand. "There's actually lots of polyester blends these days, so you actually are wearing it. But the colors and the prints from that era ..." She gestured helplessly and shrugged. "It's unsurpassed in all of human history."

"Cassidy, you're a pistol," Max said. He gestured to the pile. "I guess we should thank you for this."

"I'm just glad you got to buy some of it."

Once she'd left, Max lifted a hanger with a blue and white plaid jacket on it. "What's Vanessa going to say?"

"She'll love that," Slater said. "She wants her man to look sharp."

They spent a minute putting everything on the extra hangers. Cassidy had picked out three pairs of pants for him, he found—the striped ones didn't have a fly, instead with a zipper at the hip, and a pair of jeans with big brown felt patches and pockets, and an alarmingly bright red pair, with pockets like jeans. When he touched the fabric, it felt like denim.

"If I wear these, I'll look insane."

Max laughed. "They'd work great if you need to go into the woods during hunting season."

"Can we hang all this in the wardrobe until I can get organized enough to take it to my place?"

They carried it all into Max's office, where a wardrobe sat in the corner beyond the guest chairs. Meant for coats, it wasn't very big, but everything fit.

THIRTEEN

S LATER WENT OVER AND sat at his own desk. A while later he heard keys in the front door, then Etta's voice called out a greeting, and he heard her chatting with Max. She did a lot more work for him than for Slater, and they'd grown comfortable with each other.

Eventually Etta stepped into his office. She was wearing work drag again, a vest and dress pants. As she sat in the chair in front of his desk, she adjusted the little statue next to his monitor. It was a plaster rendition of Pollux, naked and standing with a horse. Slater didn't really need a bunch of tchotchkes around, but it had been a gift from Pike. The corresponding statue of Castor was on his desk.

"The horse wants to see what's going on," Etta said.

"Inanimate objects don't actually have wants and desires."

"In Samoa everything has *mana* in it. Life force. Every tree and rock and horse statue."

Slater frowned. "I thought you were Catholic."

"I'm a lot of things, man." She spread her arms. "I contain multitudes. Just show the horse some respect."

"Thorpe told me she sees ghosts. They tell her stuff, and give her warnings and advice."

"That sounds like white folks' kind of ghosts. In Polynesian culture they're called *aitu,* and you don't want to be taking their advice. They're always bad news."

"Thorpe is actually Black. You'll need to know what she looks like." He dug out his phone and texted her the photo Brian had sent him.

Etta pulled out her own and tapped at the screen. "She's a knockout. It makes me wonder what the rest of the package looks like."

"She's got a solid rack, I'd say, and curves like a mountain road. But it's all toxic under the gravy."

"Hot and dangerous." Etta nodded. "Sounds like my kind of woman."

Lifting the canvas flap of his satchel, Slater pulled out the brass tool, and handed it over to her.

"This is heavy."

"The spike man showed me how to use it. You ram it in the keyhole, then twist it. You have to use some force." Slater explained the technique, then took the tool back and demonstrated it.

Eventually Etta nodded. "I think I've got it."

"We should roll."

They got up, and in the front office Etta picked up her tan carry bag from the desk, and tucked the spike tool into it. She called good-bye to Max, and they rode down to the street, and got in the Continental.

In the Financial District, Slater pulled into the garage under the office building where the gym was. Once he'd killed the engine, he looked at his phone.

"There's no signal down here. I'll have to be upstairs."

"There was a coffee place on the corner," Etta said.

"That works."

They talked through the plan again, then Etta checked her phone.

"It's almost showtime." Grabbing her bag, she climbed out and walked toward the elevators.

He waited a few minutes before he got out and went up to street level, and out through the lobby, and walked to the corner. The coffee place was busy, and he stood in line to order an oat-milk latte, then found a table along the side, away from the window, and sat with his back to the wall.

Looking at the tracking app, he saw the G-Wagen arrive. The location circle went gray as it lost the cell network underground. Thorpe was right on schedule. As he watched, a text from Andy appeared:

I have info for you.

Slater texted back:

I'll be there in a while.

Thinking about it, he sent a second text:

If I'm allowed in, that is.

He knew the guy wouldn't respond to that, and set his phone down, and sipped at his latte. It seemed to take a long time, but eventually Etta appeared from the street, wearing different clothes now, a stretchy black top and leggings.

She sat across from him, flushed and panting, and set a cell phone between them. He had to grin.

"You did it. Is the locker door intact?"

"I'm glad I waited until no one was around," Etta said. "That tool is not subtle, but it worked the way you said it would. There's no visible damage. I couldn't relock it, but that's probably not obvious. The door still closes."

"Give me a second."

Checking his own phone for Thorpe's unlock code, he tapped it in, and the screen resolved into a grid of icons.

"Yes," he hissed, then spent a minute downloading Svetlana's monitoring software, and watched it install itself.

Etta folded her arms. "I dawdled in the locker room until Thorpe came in, but I could see which locker she used without getting made. That woman has an intense aura. I'd say there's no nonsense with her."

"That aligns with what I know about her too," he said, not looking up from the screen.

"Maybe it's the Santa Anas. They kind of put everybody on edge."

Not responding to that, he focused on the phone.

A minute later, Etta spoke. "It feels like it's taking a long time."

"It's almost done. Svetlana's servers are slow. They

must be abroad somewhere."

"Or just extremely encrypted. There's no way Thorpe will notice the software?"

"It runs hidden," Slater said. "I've used it before. Nobody's said anything about it yet."

Finally a bubble appeared on the screen: "To finish and stealth hiding?"

Svetlana spoke better English than that, but he knew she outsourced the coding to the old country, and he knew what it meant. He tapped OK, and the message disappeared. Locking the screen, he handed it to Etta. She rose quickly and palmed the phone.

"Wait for me here. I won't be long."

Slater watched her hustle out, then checked Svetlana's app. A new device was listed. He wanted to read Thorpe's texts and listen to calls, but the hidden software also reported the phone's location, and it was much more precise than the vehicle trackers. Right now it showed a dot on the map right next door—it was definitely working.

It didn't take long for Etta to return, dressed in street clothes again.

"The phone is back where I found it," she said. "In her handbag. I wiped it down, even though I doubt she'll be suspicious about it."

"You're a pro, woman. No nerves at all."

She beamed. "I'll take that as an attagirl. There's no nerves on the outside, at least, but it was stressful. The truly hard part was getting out of the trial membership. I told them the machines were grimy and skeeved me out. They really didn't want to let me leave, but things changed when I started to raise my voice."

"I wish I'd been there to see that."

"You need to pay me."

Slater raised his eyebrows. "Wasn't this a freebie?"

She scoffed. "Including shagging that suit yesterday, let's say four dollars."

"That works for me."

He extended his leg to dig his wad of cash out of his front pocket, but Etta rose and waved a hand.

"Cool it. If you pay me here, it makes me look like a sex worker."

Slater got up. "The look you're working right now is more like a schoolteacher."

"Mission accomplished, then."

He followed her out to the street, and they rode down to the parking garage. In the car Etta pulled the spike tool out of her bag.

"Do you want this back?"

"You have some other use for it?" Slater said.

"I doubt it. It's pretty specific."

"Maybe I'll try to sell it back to the spike man."

————◆————

Slater dropped Etta at her car, across from the office, then cruised to Broadway and parked behind Andy's building. When he knocked on his door, Andy pulled it open and flashed that easy smile.

Dropping into his chair, Andy swiveled toward him.

"You said you had some dope for me," Slater said.

"Your target does own that house, and only … Brian's name is on the deed. I don't think the guy is married to … Thorpe, or anyone else. There's no record of either one of them being … hitched in LA County."

"Could they be married somewhere else?"

"He files his taxes as single. If you're married you're … supposed to declare that."

Slater frowned. "You saw his tax return?"

"No comment."

"That sick little fuck."

"He lied to you?" Andy said.

He gestured helplessly. "I don't know why it even bothers me. Everybody lies to me all the time. It's the default setting."

"Brian also owns a business in … Downey. A rental place."

"I know about that."

"Do you need his photo?"

"Definitely."

Andy swiveled to his computer, and pulled on his black plastic gauntlets. They were an input device that compensated for his lack of fine-motor control.

"I texted it," he said finally, and swiveled toward him again.

"Can you check on another name? It's a business. Lau Skilled Importers. Based in Vernon."

"Send me the name," Andy said. "What do you need to know?"

"Who the fuck they are," he said as he pulled out his phone, "and could they have any connection to the drug trade."

Andy had sent an image—a headshot of Brian, with a blank expression on his face, on a pale-blue background.

"This is his driver's license photo," Slater said. "I'm amazed that you can get these."

"I'm good at what I do. Are you going to … pay me?"

He tucked his phone into his jeans. "Can we roll Brian into Lau Skilled Importers?"

Andy frowned. "I guess so."

"You act like I'm planning to stiff you." He raised his voice. "I've never done that. I always make it rain up in here."

"It's fine, Slater. If you don't … pay up, I know where you live."

He chuckled. "A veiled threat. I like it. It's reassuring that cupcake Kyle hasn't smothered the spark in you."

"I'm my own man, Ibáñez."

"I know." He took a breath. "Bye, beautiful."

Once he was behind the wheel of the Continental, he checked his trackers. Lenny was in Riverside right now. That guy got around. The G-Wagen was still grayed out, last seen in the Financial District, and Thorpe's phone was still at the gym. The Rover was at Brian's truck rental business. He needed to talk to that idiot.

Nosing out onto the street, Slater headed to the freeway and drove to Downey. The gate across the driveway at Brian's business was rolled open, and he pulled into the lot.

As he got out he looked around. The fence was high chain-link, but there was no razor wire, and he could only see one camera, mounted on the building and aimed at the gate. That thing was a bulky antique, so old it might not even be working. It implied there was nothing of value here that wasn't on public display—the vehicles for rent. Those looked like vans and trucks, parked chockablock at the back of the yard, most of them white and unmarked and none of them very new.

Slater walked over to the door of the little building. It was propped open, and he paused outside to listen to the conversation. Brian was talking.

"Fifteen minutes late is late, bruh. I have to charge you. That's just the way it is."

"There was so much traffic."

"We call that life in the city. There's nothing I can do about it. You need to plan your day better."

Standing there, Slater studied the door frame. There was only one slot in the strike plate, like with a bedroom door. That meant there was no deadbolt. Brian really was unconcerned about getting jacked.

A moment later a guy stepped out. With dark hair and a beard, he was wearing the sturdy clothes that people in the trades wore. Glancing at Slater, he scowled and walked away.

As Slater stepped inside he glanced at the mechanism on the door. He was right—the handle had a lock in it but there was no bolt.

This was an office, he saw, looking around, with a short service counter and a desk behind it. Standing at the end of the counter, Brian was wearing a blue dress shirt and dark chinos.

"Was that one of your customers?" Slater said.

"People are so stupid sometimes." He gestured to his chest. "It's almost like I'm wearing a T-shirt that says, 'Go ahead, waste my time.'"

"It looks like you rent vans and box trucks."

"No double axles," Brian said, "no trailers, no refrigeration, nothing over twenty-four feet."

A young guy stepped in the open doorway. Rail thin, his dark hair was styled in a trendy cut.

"You want me to clean that cube van?" he said.

Brian waved an arm. "That's what I'm paying you for, dummy."

He frowned and walked out again.

Slater raised his eyebrows. "What's your staff retention rate like?"

"You don't get to judge me," Brian snapped. "You think I should roll over and get screwed?" He huffed. "So where has Thorpe been? Who's she been seeing?"

"What do you care? You're not married to her."

"How do you know that?" he demanded.

Slater couldn't resist any longer. The guy was just too grating. Stepping to the end of the counter, he slapped him hard, left and right, a rapid kovac.

"Why do you make me do this to you?"

Brian threw his arms up in front of his face and stepped back. Why did white-collar types always do that? It was predictable, and that made it easy to counter. Shoving his arms away, Slater slapped him again.

"Why do you do it?"

"Stop it," Brian shouted, and shoved him off. His face was red. "What is wrong with you?"

Forcing himself to step back, he took a breath. "Why did you lie to me? What's your angle?"

"I didn't think you'd take the job if you thought I had no right to know what she was up to."

"Are you involved with her? As in romance, or sex?"

"Not really."

"So why does she sleep at your house?" Slater said. "Why do you need to keep track of her?"

Tilting his head back, Brian closed his eyes for a moment.

"Sing, brother," Slater snapped.

"We're in business together."

"Why are you in business with someone you don't trust?"

"I know your world is like that too, man. I know you're slinging Memo's ice. Why are you in business with him? It's the same question. You can't trust anyone, upstream or down." He threw up a hand. "Just tell me if she was with someone."

"Why would I tell you anything? You're yanking my chain. I don't know what your motives are."

"I just told you the truth."

"What about the badger game?"

Brian's eyes hardened. "Who told you about that? It was her damn idea."

"What's your version?"

"It didn't work. She'd pick up men, women sometimes, and I'd bust into the room in the middle of them having sex, and try to shake them down. They'd just leave. Nobody was willing to pay. It was a stupid idea."

Watching him talk, he knew exactly why it didn't work. Brian wasn't intimidating—he'd come across like a cranky librarian. They needed somebody like Lenny to get cash out of those saps.

"I don't know why I'm bogged down in this." Slater rubbed his eyes. "I don't owe Memo anything, and I don't do window-shade jobs."

Brian put his hands on his hips. "You seem stressed out. I wish I could do something to reduce your tension."

He glared at him. "Are you fucking kidding me right now?"

"I'm not. I could use a little action myself. I've been in a dry spell."

"So you're a switch hitter. Or were you never actually into Thorpe?"

"What's with the labels?" Brian said.

He pursed his lips and thought about it. "It's not a good idea," he said finally. "I need to keep my dick out of my cases."

"I'm not your case." He threw up a hand. "It's free sex, man."

Slater took a breath. "All right, Brian. I'll fuck you, if that's what you want."

"How hard was that?" He scoffed. "Meet me at my place. I'll finish up here in a minute."

As he walked out, Brian turned to his desk, no longer paying him any attention. Slater pressed the latch on the door as he went past. It was spring-loaded. It wasn't locked right now, so he wasn't completely certain, but he could probably defeat this door with a butter knife.

FOURTEEN

OUT ON THE LOT he climbed into the Continental and nosed through the gate. At Brian's house he parked across the street and killed the engine. In the dark the other night he hadn't noticed the low hedge planted in front of the place. It was some kind of boxwood, and fastidiously groomed, like the topiary in the old Japanese neighborhoods. It looked sharp, but like the Bermuda grass it did nothing for the pollinators, and it smelled like cat piss.

When the Range Rover pulled into the driveway, Slater got out and walked across the street.

"That's quite the old boat," Brian said, eyeing the Continental.

"The preferred term is 'classic.'"

"Do you do the wrenching yourself?"

"I'm not a gearhead," Slater said. "I've got a guy."

Brian went to the side door that faced the driveway and unlocked it. This one at least had a deadbolt. Following him in, Slater looked around. At one side was the living room at the front of the house, and on the other was the kitchen.

There was no alarm tone or panel on the wall. That was typical of lowlifes—they didn't want that kind of attention, security company guards or cops wandering around the place when the alarm went off.

"Can you take off your boots?" Brian said as he closed the door.

Slater sat on a nearby ottoman to untie them, and pulled them off, and set them on the little rug next to the door. Brian had gone into the kitchen, and he was washing his hands in the sink.

Looking into the hallway, Slater saw the closest door was open, and stepped over to it. This was a home office, with two desks facing different walls, two computers, a bookcase, a credenza with a printer on it. Like the front room, everything was tidy, without the piles of stuff lots of people had in their living quarters.

"Where did you go?" Brian called.

Slater went back into the kitchen. It had been renovated recently, with gleaming appliances, and looked clean and uncluttered, like nobody actually used it. The island in the middle had three barstools flanking it. Brian was drying his hands on a towel.

"Aren't you going to show me your Sportster?" Slater said.

He grinned and led him through the kitchen and into the garage. He flicked on a wall switch, flooding the room with extremely bright white light. In the middle of the floor sat a sleek black Harley.

That explained why they parked both cars in the driveway. He'd assumed it was because the garage was hoarded out for storage, like people did, but obviously this bike needed the whole space. There were workbenches and cabinets along the walls, and it all looked hospital clean.

"You could eat off this floor," Slater said.

He laughed. "I like things organized."

"And spotless."

The big red tool chest parked among the cabinets was the same one he had in his own garage, although his was older and grubbier. This had to be a different model. Newer, maybe, as it was deeper, judging by how far it stuck out from the wall.

Slater walked a circle around the bike. The chrome gleamed in the bright light, the way gold and silver did in a jewelry store, and there wasn't a spot of dirt on it.

"I bet it feels amazing to have this kind of power between your legs."

Brian stepped closer. "You have no idea."

"Is it fuel-injected?"

"All the newer bikes are. This one's only a couple of years old."

"Some of Memo's guys are riding carburetor jobs."

"I'm sure they think that's more authentic," Brian said, "and that a machine like this is for weekend riders, not real bikers."

"Isn't that what you are? You're not in Memo's gang or you'd be wearing the colors."

He scowled at him and raised his voice. "I know what I'm doing."

"Don't get steamed. I'm just asking."

Slater stepped close to him, and massaged his shoulders, then put his hands on his neck. Brian caressed his torso as Slater leaned in to nibble his ear.

"Dilettante," he whispered, and mouthed his jaw. "Such a tyro."

Brian pulled back. "Dude—are you deliberately trying to get me riled up?"

"It makes things interesting, don't you think?"

"It makes me want to smack you."

Slater raised his eyebrows. "Bring it. It might be kind of hot."

"You actually want that? Like it's a turn-on?"

"Let's say I'm open to it. We'll see what happens."

"You can't hit me back."

He chuckled. "Deal."

Winding up, Brian slapped him hard enough to turn his head. He could feel the surge of adrenaline, and met his gaze.

"I am going to demolish you."

Brian jutted his chin. "Like the man said, bring it."

Grabbing his face with both hands, Slater met his mouth. Brian was responsive, and firm, and intense.

Eventually the guy pulled back. "Come on."

He led him back into the house, killing the garage lights and pulling the door closed. Farther down the hall, the bedroom Brian went into had a phone stand and a water bottle on one of the night tables and nothing on the other one. It wasn't a shared space— Thorpe slept somewhere else.

Brian unbuttoned his shirt and whipped it off. "What are you waiting for?"

As Slater took off his own and then popped his fly, he watched as Brian carefully draped his shirt and his trousers over the arm of the wing chair. He ditched his jeans, and Brian stepped closer, running his hands over his arms, and his chest, and his sides.

Pushing him onto the bed, Slater straddled him and squeezed his cock. "The greenhorn awakens."

Brian wound up and slapped him, and Slater caught his wrist and flung it away, then leaned in to bury his nose in his hair, and ground his woody into him. Brian mouthed his neck and ran his hands over his shoulder blades.

"Where's the lube?" Slater said.

He gestured to the bedside drawer. "You have to wear a condom."

Grabbing one, he ripped it open, and Brian sat up to roll it on him, then squeezed his cock. Slater pushed him back, then worked his way into him, building up to pounding him. The guy screwed his eyes shut and gritted his teeth, then met his gaze.

"Is that all you got?"

Slater pounded harder, looming over him, then strained into him as he climaxed. Breathing hard, he flopped onto his side, and grabbed Brian's cock. As he explored his mouth, he stroked him, increasing the pace as he felt him getting closer. Brian yelped and pulled away as he came.

Shifting onto his back, Slater folded his arm over his eyes and gradually caught his breath. He felt Brian get up off the bed, and a moment later heard the water go on.

The guy was still in the shower when Slater's phone beeped, somewhere on the floor in the pocket of his jeans, jolting him fully awake. He didn't even have to look—he knew that tone. It was a proximity alert, and it meant one of his trackers was getting close to the location of his phone. It had to be Thorpe.

He got up and started to pull his clothes on. As he was buttoning his shirt, Brian came back.

"What's the rush?"

"I'm concerned that your not-wife might show up."

From the wing chair Brian grabbed his shirt and pulled it on. "She doesn't care who I sleep with."

"So why do you care who she's sleeping with?"

Slater walked out to the kitchen and pulled open the Frigidaire. There was no clutter here either, with all the containers and packages neatly organized. This guy was a total obsessive. The beer looked tempting, but it was too early, he decided. He pulled out a box of orange juice, and found a glass, and poured into it.

The door from the driveway swung open, and Thorpe walked in, and stepped out of her shoes. Stopping short, she scowled at him.

"What are you doing here?"

"Did the spirits not mention I was going to drop by?"

"Why are you in my kitchen, drinking my orange juice?"

"You'll figure it out," Slater said. "Just think of it as a transcendent experience."

Brian walked in, and Thorpe waved her arm. "I knew it. You sent him after me, and blabbed about my personal stuff."

Brian glared at Slater. "You talked to her? Why would you do that? I thought you were a professional."

"Our relationship was based on a lie, toots." Slater gestured with his glass. "That means all bets are off."

"There was also that sheaf of C-notes. Those should have purchased your loyalty." He threw up his hands. "So I didn't tell you all of it. Get over it."

The guy was right, in a way. There was no reason to be upset about the misdirection. Everybody lied to him.

He jutted his chin at Thorpe. "You seem to have a lot of free time. Aren't you supposed to be working for those brokers?"

"Her computer is, at least," Brian said.

Thorpe shot him a look. "Why would you tell him that?"

"It's a flex, not something to be embarrassed about. Besides, who is he going to tell?"

"What is he talking about?" Slater said.

"I am working," she said, and waved a hand. "I've automated a lot of my job using AI tools. My actual office time might be eight or ten hours a week." Her eyes narrowed. "You're not going to rat me out, are you? Or try to use that as leverage?"

"Hey, smoke 'em if you've got 'em," Slater said. "If your corporate masters are too stupid to notice, that's on them."

She nodded. "Honor among thieves. The Italians call it *omertà*. I guess the bikers have it too."

"I'm not a biker. What kind of business do you do with this shvantz? And why do you sleep here if you're not sleeping with him?"

"None of that is any of your damn business." She

gestured to Brian. "Are you sleeping with him? You both look like that. Like you just got busy."

"None of that is any of your damn business," Slater said.

"I hope you've had all your vaccinations."

"Hey," Brian snapped, and shot her a look.

"It's odd," Slater said. "I can't quite pin down your thing."

"What are you talking about?" Thorpe said.

"Were you two a couple before? I can't figure it out. Most lowlifes are a lot more transparent."

"I am not a lowlife," she said sharply.

"If you're in Memo's orbit, Miss Anne, the label applies."

"You don't get to call me that." She raised her voice. "You're the lowlife."

"You don't have to explain it to me," Slater said. "I know I'm trash. What exactly are you doing with Memo? Shilling his shoddy junk in this part of town? Washing his cash income for him?"

"Why would you care? And why do you just keep pressing?" She scoffed. "You already know way too much about us."

She wasn't going to squawk about the details, Slater knew, but she'd inadvertently confirmed that they were involved in Memo's business.

Thorpe eyed Brian. "Why would you bring this thug here? What is wrong with you?"

"It's my fricking house," Brian said.

Slater drained his glass and set it on the counter. "I'm out. Have a nice fight."

He stepped into his boots but didn't stop to squat and tie them until he was past the cars at the end of the driveway. It was dark out, and he checked the time on his phone. It was later than he thought.

———◆———

WHEN SLATER GOT TO his house he went upstairs and looked in the icebox, but there was really nothing to eat. It felt stupid to order food for himself, as he usually did that when Pike was around, but he did it anyway, and sat at the dining table munching on Thai.

Lenny was back in the high desert at Memo's compound, he saw, checking his phone, and both Thorpe's and Brian's wheels were at their house. Thorpe hadn't made any calls, but she'd exchanged a few texts. Most of them read as mundane, but a lone incoming message said, "I can stay Sunday night too."

Those idiots were involved with Memo, either peddling his dope or laundering his cash or both. But there was something different about them—they didn't quite fit the mold. Brian's business was a soft target to dig for more details, and nobody would be there at night.

When it got late enough, he went down to the garage. To get through the door at the truck-rental place he needed something stiff but flexible, and he scanned the tools hanging above the workbench, and rifled the shelves. This would work—he grabbed a flimsy black germinating pot and went after it with the pruning shears, cutting out a long strip of the plastic. He flexed it, and assessed the give, then slid it into his hip pocket.

Climbing into the Continental, he drove to Downey and rolled past Brian's business, scanning the place for signs of life. The gate was closed, with a chain and a padlock on the outside—no one was in there. Speeding up again, he parked a couple of blocks up the boulevard. The one downside of his whip was that it didn't blend in, and that made it hard to be stealthy. He was always at risk of some chump remembering this beautiful sleek machine.

He reached in the back seat for the box and pulled on a pair of the black latex gloves, then scrabbled in the glove box for a penlight. Climbing out, he walked back to Brian's place. This was a commercial stretch without nighttime retail, so there wasn't a lot of traffic—he could go over the gate rather than finding a less conspicuous route.

Waiting until a lone vehicle had rolled by on the boulevard, he grabbed the chain-link fence, notching his toe into the mesh, and started to climb. When he got to the top, he swung his leg over. It was awkward because of the sharp wire ends sticking up, but he managed not to get caught on them. It wasn't so high that he'd break anything, he decided, so once his other leg was on the inside, rather than climbing down, he jumped.

Slater hit the gritty asphalt on his feet but lost his balance and pitched forward. He had enough muscle memory from middle-school wrestling that he managed to avoid landing on his hands or doing a faceplant, instead twisting his torso to land on his thigh. It still hurt, and he sat there for a minute, massaging his leg and breathing hard from the exertion.

Eventually he got up and dusted himself off. Maybe the spike man was right—he wasn't getting any younger, and stuff like this wasn't getting any easier.

Walking the perimeter of the lot, he found only trucks and vans parked here. The dry Santa Ana wind from the desert had picked up, and out in the open it pestered, the relentlessness of it messing with his hair, chafing his skin, stoking his irritation. There was a lone windowless outbuilding here, probably for storing tools, with a padlock on the door. At the side of it a shop vacuum was mounted overhead, the nozzle gently swaying in the wind, and below it a coiled-up water hose.

At the main building he tried the handle. It was locked, and the lip of the door frame concealed the latch, but there was a bit of a gap. He pulled out the strip of flexible black plastic and pushed it between the door and the jamb. He could feel it curl around the right angle in the corner, but then it jammed. Pulling it out again, he shoved harder. This time it struck the latch, and overcame its spring, and the door swung open.

Stepping inside, he pulled it closed. Out of the wind it was dead quiet, and as he scanned the room, he could see no telltale glow of the infrared lamps of a camera. It was too risky to turn on the room lights, he decided—the window glass was frosted but it faced the boulevard. Instead he clicked on the penlight and sat at Brian's desk, holding the light in his teeth as he went through the drawers.

The bottom one held a few dozen file folders. Brian had it well organized, like his house, with each folder labeled. Most of his legit business was probably on the computer, as this just looked like legacy paperwork. There was no trace of Brian's relationship with Memo.

When he waggled the computer mouse, the monitor woke up and asked for a password. There was no point messing with that. He'd never get into it. The inner side of the counter had shelves under it, and a couple of drawers, and he went through them, rolling them out and rifling the contents. There were no drugs or guns or cash.

He swung the narrow little beam around the room one last time. Logically Brian wouldn't have that stuff here—he had workers that used this office, running the counter or cleaning the trucks, like the kid he'd called "dummy." Tucking the penlight in his pocket, he walked out, making sure the door latched behind him.

Climbing the gate felt harder this time, the wire mesh sharp on his fingers, the upward effort making his muscles burn. His toes didn't feel as secure in the narrow gaps either. Eventually he swung his legs over the top, and this time lowered his center of gravity by digging in with his boot, then dropped to the ground, landing in a crouch.

As he stood up, a guy stepped toward him on the sidewalk. The sight of him on the deserted street made Slater's heart pound as the sudden risk of getting busted flashed through his mind. But this was no cop—the guy was homeless, he decided, looking him over. Lanky, he was wearing a grubby winter overcoat, and had unkempt hair, a week's stubble on his face.

The guy stopped in front of him. "Yo, cholo—you can't break into stuff on my block."

"I'm not a cholo, you dipshit." Slater scoffed. "It's not your block either, even if you sleep here. This is my shop. I forgot my keys."

"Let's see some ID," he said, and jutted his chin.

Slater put his hands on his hips. "Why are you out here selling wolf tickets? Aren't things bad enough for you, sleeping rough?"

"You don't know me."

"I know that I really don't want to mess you up, but that's where we're headed."

"Give me twenty bucks and I won't call the cops."

"How about a sawbuck, and I don't give a fuck whether you call the cops or not?" Digging in his jeans, he pulled out his wad, and handed the guy a ten.

He stuffed the bill in his pocket. "Now I've got you for bribing a witness in a burglary. You're going down, motherfucker."

"Do you even know how stupid you are?" Slater demanded.

He jutted his chin. "That's what they all say."

No longer able to resist, Slater threw a fast right and connected with his jaw. "That's for calling me a cholo."

The guy spun sideways and stumbled a little. He looked dazed, and stood facing the street. "What the hell, man."

It had been a rabbit punch—no way should it have caused him that much disorientation. This guy was on something. Maybe Memo's substandard dope.

Slater scoffed and walked toward the Continental. How had it gotten this bad? There were tent encampments all over, and homeless people wandering around absolutely freaking everywhere now. It had become the background noise to everything.

FIFTEEN

I N THE MORNING SLATER took his time waking up. He'd gone easy on the sauce, so he felt lucid. Eventually he grabbed his phone and checked on his trackers. Brian's Rover was at his business in Downey, and Thorpe's vehicle was on the 405, headed south, well past Long Beach. Somebody had texted her yesterday about the weekend, and he found the message again: "I can stay Sunday night too." That was tomorrow. Maybe Thorpe would be out of town for a while. Unless she turned around soon, she'd be gone for the morning at least.

There were a few new texts, and someone had left her a voice mail. He tapped at the screen to play it. It was tinny through the phone's speakers, but he knew that voice.

"We need to talk," Memo said. "Brian's not answering me, and now neither are you. This is not a good look for you two."

Slater sent Max a text:

Do you have time for me this morning?

His reply came a moment later:

Affirmative. I'm at the office.

No way had Max typed that multisyllable response with those stubby thick fingers. The guy had discovered voice typing.

Forcing himself out of bed, he took a sniff of yesterday's jeans. It was time for another pair. Once he was dressed, he went upstairs, and grabbed an apple, and ate it on the way down to the garage.

From his gear cabinet he pulled out the signal jammer, and the lock-reading probe, and the heavy binder of ghost keys. In a plastic sandwich bag on the top shelf were some electric-socket cameras. A flat plate with the three prongs on the back, the front had the slots painted on in black to mimic the socket it was plugged into. If someone spotted it, they might assume it was a safety device to keep stupid rug rats from sticking a fork into the socket and getting fried. The switches and sockets in Brian's house were square and white, and he picked a camera to match.

Once he'd loaded it all into his canvas satchel, he backed the Continental out and drove to his office. Max had said he was here, but he couldn't see his car in the lot. He hustled across the street in a break in the traffic and went upstairs. The lights were on and Rey Pascual was still facing the front door. That meant Etta wasn't around, even though Saturday was a day off from her job. Whenever she used the front desk she turned Rey around to watch her work.

Max really was here, and Slater stepped into his office. Today he was wearing his gray grid-pattern suit with his shirt open at the collar.

"What's up?" Max said, and sat back.

"I need to keep somebody busy for half an hour or so. Have you got time for that?"

"Sure. Who's the pigeon?"

"He runs a truck-rental place. His name is Brian. I'll send you a headshot." Digging out his phone, he tapped at it. "I sent a link to his business too."

"That's a DMV photo," Max said. "They only give those to the cops, and maybe the DA."

"That's about Andy. I think he's got a source."

Max tapped at his phone. "It looks like Brian rents out cargo vans. I'll get him to show me a couple of those. It won't even be boring."

"I don't think there's any cameras inside his office, and I only spotted one outside. On the building aimed at the driveway. It looks like it's been there a long time, so it might not even be operating."

"Is he a lowlife, or just lazy?"

"He's definitely a lowlife," Slater said. "But I don't think he's hiding anything there. I wouldn't either. He's got workers."

"Got it."

"I'll be close to there," Slater said. "Let me know when you have eyes on him, and definitely let me know if he leaves."

Max sat up. "I need a couple minutes here, but I'll head out soon."

Walking out, Slater rode down to the street, and

drove to Brian's house. He parked in front of a yard a few doors down, out of view of the camera on Brian's garage and the one at the front door. By the time he'd pulled on his stealthy glasses, and a pair of latex gloves, and his blue ball cap, Max's text came:

With the pigeon now.

Once he'd switched on the signal jammer, activating its bright indicator light, he climbed out and slung the satchel on his shoulder. As he strode over to Brian's open gate, he scanned the block, but nobody was around to pay any attention to him.

As he stepped into the driveway, he saw that the camera on the eaves was strobing orange—it was offline. He stood with his back to the street and connected the lock reader to his phone. That launched Svetlana's app, with a black screen that said "готов." At the other end of the cable was a key-shaped probe, and he slid it into the deadbolt. The app flashed red, so he eased the probe out a little, and gently adjusted its position until the screen turned green and displayed a number.

Yanking the probe out, he knelt and lifted the heavy binder from his satchel, flipping through the pages of little pouches, looking for the right number. He could feel the sweat in his hair at the back of his neck. The side door wasn't in direct view of the street, but he'd be visible to anyone who glanced up the driveway. He needed to work faster.

When he found the right pouch he fished out the key, then lifted the binder back into his satchel, and stood up, glancing toward the street as he tried it in the deadbolt. It felt tight going in, and it wouldn't turn.

"Damn it," he muttered, and wiggled it around. But it was the right key, or close enough—finally the cylinder turned, and he felt the bolt retract.

Pulling open the door, he stepped into the house, and called "Hello," then stood listening. There was no sound, and he lifted the strap of the satchel onto his opposite shoulder, and twisted the heavy bag around onto his back.

In the hallway he went past Brian's bedroom and pushed open the next door. This one had to be Thorpe's. It was a lot messier, and the attached bathroom had an array of bottles crowded around the sink, soaps and skin care products and hair stuff. That meant Brian was the household neat freak.

Walking over to the office, it was immaculate, like most of the house, but one of the desks was messier than the other. He sat at Brian's first and went through the drawers. It took almost no time because there was next to nothing in it. Next he moved to Thorpe's. The drawers were more cluttered, but there was only civilian paperwork—stuff about her fugly car and her taxes and her banking.

He stood up, returning the desk chair to the position he'd found it in, and looked around the room. There was no safe, nowhere to store dope or weapons or cash. Striding out to the kitchen, he quickly opened the cupboards, one by one, but there was only pots and dishes and food.

When he tried the garage door, it was unlocked, and he stepped in and flicked on the lights, wincing at the harsh brightness. Brian's motorcycle was still parked in the middle of the space. Opening the cabinets in rapid succession, he found nothing but tools and cleaning products. Adjusting the weight of the satchel on his back, he stood for a minute on the pristine concrete, looking around the room.

That tool chest. Why did that snag his eye? It looked identical to his own, except that it was deeper. He'd noticed that yesterday. Why would it be just a few inches different? He stepped over and pulled on the sides. The unit was on wheels, like his was, and easily rolled away from the wall. It wasn't actually bigger than his, he saw, but the wallboard behind it stuck out several inches from the rest of the wall. Just below the built-in cabinets, the thicker part topped out in a narrow shelf, about the depth of a two-by-four. He could see that it was only as wide as the tool chest, as the cabinets on either side went back farther.

Slater squatted in front of the wall. Was this part of something in the next room? Sometimes they built boxes like this for oversize plumbing, or ductwork, or access to a sink cleanout. At the bottom there was a narrow gap above the floor, just an inch or so, and he probed it with his latex-clad fingers. This section of wallboard was loose, he realized, and it shifted upward when he bumped it. When he lifted from the bottom, he was able to pull it completely off. It was a discreet compartment, disguised to look like part of the wall.

He set the panel aside and studied the space behind it. The gap contained a heavy nylon bag, hung on a couple of hooks. It was the same height and width and depth, sized to fill the space completely.

Pulling it off the hooks, he set the bag flat on the floor and zipped it open. He already knew what was in it, based on the weight and the way the contents shifted in his hands. Inside was a fuck-ton of cash, mostly in elastic-bound racks, but there were also some bundles of twenties. None of the cash was new, he saw as he dug through it, and he did a quick count. It totaled somewhere north of nine hundred grand.

But that was only half the bag. He pulled open the zipper on the other side. This compartment was loaded with bright yellow bundles—stacks of banknotes emblazoned with 200 and EURO/EYPΩ/EBPO. They were also bound with elastic, and flipping through a couple of them, he saw that these weren't new or sequential either. Assuming the bundles were a hundred bills each, there was four hundred grand in euros.

Squatting there, Slater stared at it for a minute, the familiar muted green and the bright yellow, side by side. No one kept this much jack around if it was legit. But why the euros?

He needed to get out of here, he realized. He'd been radio jamming for way too long. He pulled a euro note from the middle of one of the bundles and pocketed it, then zipped up the bag, and hung it back on its hooks, and replaced the wallboard panel. Once he'd rolled the tool cabinet back into place, he hustled to the door and killed the lights.

The kitchen wasn't an optimal place for the camera, as the sockets were above the counter, making it too easy to spot. There was a socket near the floor facing the door to the driveway, and he crouched to press the camera into it, and looked it over as he stood up. It was obvious if you knew it was there, but the camera lens was subtle, a little pit in one of the painted-on holes. Svetlana's rationale was that it would only get discovered if someone was trying to use the socket, and most people wouldn't figure out what it was.

On the way out he used the ghost key in the lock, wiggling it around to get it to turn the cylinder, then strode down the driveway. He peeled off his gloves and tucked them in his hip pocket, and switched off the stealth glasses, and hung them on the front of his shirt.

In the car he fired up the engine and pulled into the street. Once he'd turned onto the boulevard, he dug out his phone to text Max. The screen said NO SERVICE.

"Fuck," he roared. He'd forgotten to switch off the jammer. Reaching into the satchel on the passenger seat, trying to keep one eye on the road, he found the switch and killed it. How fucking stupid was that? If Max had texted him that Brian was on his way home, he wouldn't even have got it. Why hadn't he thought of that? Brian could have walked in on him.

"Idiot," he said through his teeth. He sent Max a text:

You can cut him loose.

At least there hadn't been any angry zombies out in the street shouting about their lost connectivity. Pulling off his ball cap, he tossed it in the back seat, then dialed Etta.

"I need to talk to your friend the bank teller," he said when she picked up.

"Ray-*hee*-na," she said. He knew it was spelled Regina. "Good timing. I'm actually seeing her downtown later. We can come to the office."

"It's Saturday," Slater said. "I know you both have

the day off. Are you headed to some lesbian wood-working festival, or a sad folk singer with an acoustic guitar and facial paralysis?"

"We're having lunch, you dick." She scoffed. "You are such a wrong guy, you know that?"

"I know. I'm on my way there now."

When he got up to the office, Rey Pascual was turned to face the front desk, watching Etta, who was parked in the chair behind it.

"Where's the banker?" Slater said.

"She'll be here soon," Etta said. "Were you able to get into Thorpe's phone?"

"It worked great."

"I didn't actually talk to her, but she seemed like a real bear cat."

"I think Thorpe is probably AC-DC, if you're in the market. She's definitely shady as fuck, though."

She frowned. "No thanks. What do you need Regina for?"

Slater dug out the euro banknote and handed it over.

Peering at it, she rubbed it between her fingers. "It feels like plastic."

"I need her to tell me whether this is real or not," he said. "I might be dealing with a paperhanger."

"It can't be easy to pass counterfeit cash when it's foreign. Are you sure the guy isn't a scratch man?"

"Could be. Although he doesn't seem smart enough to be manufacturing it."

Etta handed it back. "Max says 'Never underestimate a lowlife.'"

"He's right about that."

Max really was an effective mentor for her, he

knew, and she learned fast. He wasn't crazy about everything Max did with her, like taking her to the range to get comfortable with handguns, but it was all more than Slater could do.

A knock came at the door, and he pulled it open. Regina was tall, with a mass of wild wavy hair, wearing jeans and a print top. He stepped back as she walked in. Etta rose, and they greeted each other at high volume, and then exchanged air kisses.

"You wanted to talk to me?" Regina said eventually, eyeing Slater.

"Can you tell me whether this is real?" He handed her the banknote.

"Where did you get it, if you're not sure?"

Etta waved a hand. "Don't ask."

"I actually work with these sometimes," Regina said. "People cash them in when they come back from a trip. We sell them too." She held it up to the light. "The watermark is there. When you tilt the bill, the hologram looks right."

"I didn't see a hologram," Etta said.

Regina handed it to her. "When you change the angle, the numbers change color. That's legit and hard to counterfeit, I'm told."

"Show me," Slater said, and took the bill. The effect was subtle, but it was there.

"When you hold it up to the light, the strip of foil looks dark," Regina said, "but it has lettering in it that lets the light through."

The tiny characters were there too, he saw. "It says 'euro' and 'two hundred.'"

He handed it back to Etta, and she held it up. "So it does."

"If you have a UV light, you can check for colored fibers in the paper," Regina said. "UV also makes some of the ink light up. But you don't have to bother. I'm sure this is real."

"I have a UV light." Slater pulled the stealth glasses off the front of his shirt and clicked on the power switch. He held the front of the frames close to the bill. "Check it out."

They both leaned in, and Etta said, "It's making little threads in the paper glow orange."

"Look at the signature under the flag in the corner," Regina said. "It went green." She stepped back and eyed Slater. "What the hell kind of glasses are those?"

"Expensive ones." He clicked off the power switch and hung them on his shirt.

"Why do they have UV light in them?"

"It's called avant-garde fashion," Slater said. "You should look into it."

"You know she knows how to keep her mouth shut," Etta said. "She got you that dye pack on the down-low."

Slater sighed. "The UV is supposed to mess with security cameras. The pattern on the frames is to confuse facial recognition software."

Regina threw up a hand and looked to Etta. "Tell me again why you want to be part of all this?"

"Because it's a blast." Etta jutted her chin at Slater. "You need to pay the woman for her time."

"How about two hundred euros?" He handed her the yellow bill.

"That's generous," Regina said, and pocketed it. "Is this serial number going to turn up on a bank robbery watchlist?"

"I'm not sure. If you're worried about it, swap it out with another one when someone brings in euros to exchange."

"That's not a bad idea," she said. "Devious, but it'll work. You definitely know how to be shady."

"It takes a chiseler to know a chiseler, toots," Slater said. "Remember that when you spend those euros."

Etta raised her voice. "Hey—like I tell my kids, be kind."

"Right." He put his hands on his hips. "I meant to say, your soul looks especially lovely today, Regina."

Regina frowned. "Can we go?"

Once Etta had shooed her out the door, she called back, "Later, Slater."

He flipped the bolt and went to sit in his office. Heaving his boots up on the desk, he laced his fingers behind his head and thought it through. If those were real euros, Brian and Thorpe weren't printing them or passing them. It didn't really fit with Memo's business either—his sordid skulduggery wouldn't extend across the Atlantic.

Brian had said they'd been in Paris recently. Had they brought all that jack back with them? Maybe they'd traded it there for Memo's dirty drug money in some laundering scheme. It was nervy to smuggle cash, especially through ports and airports, as it was so easy to get caught. They would have had to do that in both directions. That wasn't it. Something else was going on.

Looking at his trackers on his phone, Brian was still at his business. Thorpe's car had stopped moving, and he zoomed in on the map. She was in Orange County, at a community college. When he checked the precise location of her phone, it was inside a building on the campus. On the map it was labeled as the arts pavilion.

He dug through her recent texts, and one exchange stood out: "See you there at 1," someone had written, and Thorpe had replied "K." He couldn't see her contact list, only the number the text had come from. A search online didn't link it to a name, but it was in the 760 area code. That was basically all the deserts east of the cities, including Memo's part of the world. Tapping through the event history, he saw that it wasn't the same number Memo had called her from.

Somebody's area code wasn't a solid indicator of where they lived anymore. But even if it wasn't one of Memo's crew, it sounded like a meeting, and if it was in that part of the OC, he could go see for himself.

SIXTEEN

EAVING HIMSELF UP, SLATER flicked off the lights, and locked up, and went down to the street. The navigation sent him on the 5, and there was lots of traffic, but it was moving. As he turned into the lot at the college, he saw that it sprawled for acres around the buildings. It was always like this in the sticks, the structures an island surrounded by a sea of surface parking. Climbing out, he clicked the power switch on the stealthy glasses and pulled them on.

The location marker for Thorpe's phone showed that she was somewhere in this glass-fronted building. Stepping inside, he found a table set up next to big metal letters mounted on the wall that said THEATER.

The only person here was the woman seated

behind the table. With her blond hair tied back, she looked to be in her early twenties, and was currently absorbed in her phone. A cash box and rows of name tags were laid out in front of her, and tacked to the front of the table was a poster:

Lady Thibodeaux
in person
direct from New Orleans

It wasn't a concert, not with the prearranged name tags. Something else was going on. Glancing at his screen, he saw that Thorpe's phone was on the other side of this wall. That text might have been from her date for whatever this was. If it didn't have anything to do with her shady business dealings, it was pointless to go in. But he'd already driven all the way down here.

"Have you seen Lady Thibodeaux in person?" he said as he approached the table.

"I haven't." She smiled. "I like your glasses."

He gestured at the array of name tags. "I don't see my name on any of these."

She picked up a clipboard. It was a list, he saw, with most of the entries crossed through with green highlighter.

"What's your name?"

"I don't think I bought a ticket in advance," he said. "I had trouble with your website."

Her eyes narrowed. "They started a while ago, but I can sell you a ticket now. It's eighty dollars."

"Ouch. Lady Thibodeaux definitely gets paid."

"They say she's quite gifted. Admission covers all the events today."

"How many people are in there?"

"About a hundred and twenty. You won't bother anybody if you walk in. You can sit at the back."

Slater pulled out his wad of cash and peeled off the requisite twenties.

Once she'd tucked them into the cash box, she picked up a rubber stamp and flipped open the ink pad. "Show me your left hand."

She took hold of his wrist and carefully pressed the stamp onto his skin. It left a purple circle that enclosed a stylized big-eyed bird.

"Is that an owl?" Slater said.

"It's a symbol of Athena. She was the goddess of wisdom."

"I'd say she still is, if you chuckleheads are talking about her. She's also the goddess of violence. That's why she's always wearing a helmet and carrying a spear."

Her brow furrowed. "The entrance is around the side." She gestured to the broad hallway.

Walking around, Slater found the big double doors and stepped inside. It was a smallish theater with a steep rake and stairs in the aisle. Most of the spectators were in the lowest few rows, close to the stage.

He didn't have to look around for Thorpe—she was on the stage, sitting in one of the lounge chairs arranged in a semicircle, like it was somebody's living room. Thorpe and another woman and a guy with gray hair were in the chairs on the left side, and the lone chair on the right had to be Lady Thibodeaux. Wearing a long blue dress and a matching head wrap, she looked more West Africa than New Orleans.

Slater took a seat on the aisle a few rows down

from the doors. Scanning the backs of the spectators' heads, he saw that not all of them were college age, as there was lots of gray hair. He pulled out his phone and did a search for Lady Thibodeaux. She was a psychic medium and voodoo practitioner. He didn't need to read more than that, and stuffed the phone away. What the hell was she doing that was worth eighty clams?

The woman sitting next to Thorpe was talking into a handheld mike. Lady Thibodeaux had her own, mounted next to her cheek like a clerk at a late-night drive-through. The three on the left were all wearing name tags, and Thorpe's was written too small to read, like the guy's was, but this woman's would be legible from the other side of the freeway—in big thick letters it said JO.

"When you enter trance," Jo was saying, "is there any physical sensation?"

"It's more a mental feeling," Lady Thibodeaux said. "When I invite the spirits, they enter from above." From her dialect she definitely sounded Southern. She looked toward the ceiling and waved her hand above her head wrap. "They descend, and settle in, and get comfortable in my head."

The crowd tittered at that.

"We've probably heard enough from the panel," Jo said. "Let's turn it over to Lady Thibodeaux and her spirits for a few minutes."

Lady Thibodeaux smiled. "We call them my spirit guides."

Tilting her head back, she closed her eyes and took a slow breath. Silent and focused, the panelists sat watching her, along with everyone in the bleachers. Eventually she opened her eyes and spoke in a deeper voice.

"Good afternoon."

Her tone soft and breathy, Jo leaned into the mike. "Can you tell us your name?"

"I have many names. You may call me Hillah Bingels."

"Hilda?"

"It's Hill-*ah*."

Now she sounded like a limey, or maybe it was that transatlantic dialect, with the crisp enunciation, like they used in old movies.

"Hillah, can you tell us about the next few months?" Jo said. "The economy, and world affairs? What should we expect?"

The guy sitting next to Jo leaned toward the mike. "You can talk about more general things, if that works better."

"This is a strange place," Hillah said. "It's so bright outside, yet so dark in here."

"We call it Orange County," Jo said, and several people in the audience laughed.

Hillah lifted a hand. "You have a daughter. She's getting married."

"That's correct," Jo said. "The wedding is in mid-October."

"He is not a good man."

"I've sensed that myself. Why do you say that?"

"He's not what he seems. He's not what he says he is."

"You mean he's not ... human?"

There was a long pause before Hillah spoke. "There is much deception."

Slater sighed and folded his arms. This was run-of-the-mill stage magician stuff.

"And you." Hillah gestured to Thorpe. "You've been talking to those on my side of the veil."

Thorpe reached for the mike and took it from Jo. "That's true. I have. Do you know the entities that come to me?"

"I'm aware of them."

"Are they being honest with me?"

"On this side, things aren't so simple. It's not just good and bad, truth and lies."

"That's not really helpful," Thorpe said.

"I suppose you want the next lottery numbers, or where to look for a romantic partner."

"I'll take anything that sheds light on my life."

After a lengthy pause, Hillah finally spoke. "Someone is watching you closely."

"Who is it?"

"A dark presence. He is in your car, and he's in your pocket."

Hillah turned to look up at the audience. From this distance it was hard to tell, but it felt like she was looking right at Slater.

"Beware the wash-and-wear," Hillah said.

He sat up straighter, feeling the hair prickling on the back of his neck. Where had that come from?

"His motives are unclear," Hillah said, gazing at him a moment longer, then looked away.

"I know who it is," Thorpe said into the mike. "My business partner. He's a hot mess."

Someone in the audience laughed, and Hillah raised her voice.

"Take nothing for granted, woman. You're doing

things that can lead you down a dark path."

"You see trouble in my future?"

"The future is up to you. Every choice you make alters the path ahead. You're making choices that could abruptly end your life."

"I wish you could be more specific," Thorpe said.

Hillah tilted her head back and closed her eyes for a moment, then gestured to the man on the stage next to Thorpe. "You're in love."

That didn't seem especially insightful, Slater thought. Talking in such broad generalities was the technique any cheap floor-show psychic used. But that wash-and-wear crack was a lot harder to explain.

The guy took the mike from Thorpe. "In a way, yes, I am."

"You need to let go of it," Hillah said. "Unrequited love is pure, but it's pointless."

He sat up and eyed the audience. "Well, I see we're out of time. Thank you, Lady Thibodeaux, and thank you, Hillah Bingels. We'll break now for the individual sessions and small groups. There's coffee and snacks outside."

As the lights went up, Slater rose and walked out. He'd only taken a few steps toward the foyer when Thorpe appeared in the hallway ahead of him. He stopped short. That must be the stage door. She wasn't paying attention to the people streaming out of the theater with him, instead standing there talking to the gray-haired guy who'd been with her on the stage. No way could he walk out now without her spotting him, and if she did, she'd quickly figure out he was stalking her.

Turning on his heel, he walked the opposite

direction, farther into the hall. It was filling up as people drifted over to the snack tables, set up with trays of cookies and muffins and coffee urns. Glancing back, he saw that Thorpe was walking this way now, still in intent conversation with the gray-hair. But she hadn't made him yet.

A few paces past the snacks was a door hanging half open, and Slater stepped through, and closed it behind him. Compared to the theater it was a tight space, set up for meetings or maybe small classes, with a folding table and a few chairs, a whiteboard on the wall. Standing near the table was a woman wearing a gray suit jacket and jeans, a handbag over her shoulder, her blond hair bundled up.

"Thanks for being here," she said as he stepped in.

"I'm not here."

She raised her eyebrows. "You're already in trance?"

"I'm not working."

"I know I didn't sign up, but I thought you could squeeze me in before your first session."

He put his hands on his hips. "Listen, sister, I'm not the ghost guy."

"I know it's an imposition, but it's a simple question." She waved a hand. "I lost a piece of jewelry. A ring. It's an important family piece. I was wearing it, and then one day I noticed it was just gone. Do you think you could get any psychic insights about where it is? Where can I look for it?"

Slater took a breath. "In the trap under the bathroom sink. Get a plumber to pull it apart. It's not a lot of work. A handyman can do it."

Her brow furrowed. "That was fast. Communication with the unseen realm usually takes longer."

It was where people usually lost their rings, Slater knew. One night in a bar he'd helped a guy disassemble the trap under the restroom sink to retrieve one. They'd found it, and celebrated with a round of beer, no psychic power involved.

"What can I tell you?" he said. "It's a gift."

"Well, I won't take any more of your time. Thank you for seeing me."

As she walked out he looked into the hallway. It was full of people, their loud conversations fueled by caffeine and sugar. Maybe it was busy enough that he could leave without Thorpe spotting him.

He was still debating whether to go when the door swung open and a guy stepped in. Chubby, with luxy Latin hair and wispy sideburns, he was wearing a powder-blue dress shirt and black pants. Basically fuckable, Slater decided.

The guy greeted him, and stepped over to the table, and sat behind it. With a big dumb grin, he waved at the other chairs.

"Have a seat."

"I didn't actually sign up for a session with you," Slater said.

"You paid to attend the conference, though, didn't you? It's included. Why not find out what the spirits have to say?"

It would kill a few minutes until he could fade, he decided, and pulled out a chair. "Lay it on me, brother."

His brow furrowed. "Give me a moment."

"Are you going into trance right now? It would be more convincing if you had a head wrap like Lady Thibodeaux."

"I don't do trance. I'm clairaudient. I can hear the spirits talking." He raised his eyebrows. "But not when you're talking."

Slater folded his arms and glared at him, but the guy looked away. His eyes glazed over, and he squinted, and eventually spoke.

"You're not supposed to be here."

"I paid cash money to get in," Slater said, "just like everybody else."

"But you're not here to work on yourself."

"OK, that's accurate."

"At least you're honest about it. Sometimes people lie to us to try to debunk our powers. There's a poem that says, 'Beauty is truth, and truth is beauty.'"

"That makes absolutely no sense," Slater said. "The truth isn't usually beautiful, or even pretty. Not even a little. That's why nobody bothers with it."

His face contorted, like he was straining to hear something. "Odysseus."

Slater frowned. "Is that who's talking to you right now?"

He held up a hand. "What happened to Odysseus when he killed all the men who were after his wife?"

"That was basically the end of the story." He thought about it. "Their relatives came to murdertize Odysseus, and they all got into a brawl, but then Zeus intervened and gave everyone amnesia."

The guy was still staring into space.

"Did you hear me?" Slater demanded.

"The question was for you, not for me. Pipe down." He squinted a moment longer before he spoke. "Revenge."

"What about it?"

"They're telling me that revenge makes things worse. If someone goes after you, it's smarter just to let it go. Forget it."

"I've heard that one before." Slater scoffed. "The truth is pretty, and I should knuckle under. I think you're tuned in to the ghost of a shrink."

As he stood up, the guy met his gaze. "This session is covered in your admission, but we accept tips."

"That sounds shrewd." He stepped to the door, and eased it open a few inches, and peered out.

"Who's Odysseus, anyway?" the guy called after him.

The crowd had started to thin out, and there was no sign of Thorpe. He could leave. When he got to the foyer, he glanced over at the ticket table. The woman was still parked behind it, and standing in front was a guy wearing black compression shorts and a tight red athletic shirt. With thick brown hair, he looked to be around her age, in his early twenties, and he had a great body.

The guy picked up on Slater's gaze, and turned to look at him.

"What?" he demanded.

"I'm just admiring the merchandise." Slater paused and gestured at him. "You wear those shorts every day? You should—you've got the assets."

He frowned. "I wear them so I can clear the hurdles without knocking them down, you perv."

"Sure, I'm the pervert, when you're the one wearing the fuck-me fabrics."

"I'm an athlete," he said, raising his voice.

Slater matched his tone. "I can see your foreskin."

His mouth tightened into a thin line, and he stepped toward him, rapidly slapping Slater's face. His palm made a loud *smack,* and he definitely felt it, but it wasn't hard enough to turn his head or dislodge his glasses.

"Dude, stop it," the woman at the table said.

"I can't believe you just did that." Slater put his hands on his hips. "Did anyone ever tell you that you're a hothead?"

"Campus is supposed to be a safe space. This is harassment."

Slater looked to the woman at the table. "Is he juicing? It totally feels like roid rage."

"How would I know?" she said.

"You should report him to the hurdle-jumping authorities. Are you sleeping with him? You know you can do better."

"I'm not on steroids," the guy snapped.

"But you did hit me, toots, even though you weigh, what, a buck forty, and you're going to come at me? I know there's no heater concealed under those sweet little shorts, and if you're not packing, you're on a suicide mission."

"Asshole," he shouted.

Slater lunged at him and delivered a rapid kovac, slapping his face left and then right. "Why do you make me do this to you?" he growled, then planted a palm on his chest and shoved him away.

He stumbled back a few steps and held a palm to his cheek. "I'm calling security."

"You remember that you smacked me first, right? That means you're the one who'd get charged." He jabbed a finger at him. "Settle down." He turned to walk out, and called back, "And wear a damn jock-strap." As he stepped out into the daylight, he muttered, "Stupes."

SEVENTEEN

ONCE HE WAS BEHIND the wheel of the Continental, Slater pulled off the stealthy glasses and looked at his phone. Svetlana's software had a couple of video clips from the camera he'd put in the socket at Brian and Thorpe's place.

The first was Brian walking into the house. The camera angle was low and wide, so his shins were out of proportion to his upper body, but there was no mistaking it was him. The clip ended when he stepped out of frame. In the second clip the same pair of pants walked past, closer to the camera, then out of view. But the clip didn't end—he could hear Brian talking. He must have been in the front room, near the door, as the audio was clear.

"I was about to call you," Brian said.

A thin voice answered, at much lower volume—

Brian had the call on speaker. Even distorted through the chain of devices, he knew Memo's voice.

"You have to pay your bills, man," Memo said. "I gave you all that cash and product. Is the stuff not selling? What happened to those bored office drones? That city is full of them."

"There's no issues here. I'm just getting things organized."

"It's not like you're rebuilding a Twin Cam. It's money in and money out. Right now it's three thirty, and with the late fee it's three forty."

"Ten grand is a lot. Running it through the business is complicated. You know that. And I'm not that late."

"I can't figure out if you're intentionally trying to disrespect me," Memo said. "Do I need to come down there?"

"There's no disrespect," Brian said quickly. "It'll be there this week."

"You know I hate riding on the 10. And I really hate when people try to steal from me."

"There's nothing to worry about."

Brian's legs moved across the video frame again, and the clip ended.

Setting his phone in its dash mount, Slater fired up the engine and headed out onto the boulevard. There was no doubt about it now—Brian and Thorpe were shilling Memo's dope and doing his money laundering. If he'd been talking to anyone else, Brian would have been enraged and shouting, but he'd been compliant with Memo. Obviously he knew what the bikers were capable of.

Slater accelerated onto the freeway and gradually

merged left. Traffic was heavy, but it was still rolling, not yet stop-and-go. At this density the drive was meditative, as there was no advantage to changing lanes, and he could just follow the vehicle in front.

It gave him time to think about his next move. Pike would say just stay out of it, drop it, don't waste time on these knuckleheads. But that didn't feel quite right. Grabbing his phone from its mount, he found the number in his contacts for Jack. The guy was a club rat—he'd know where to get what he needed.

When Jack picked up, he said, "Urban Hair Events. To whom am I speaking?"

"It's Slater. Do you not have caller ID?"

"I never look at that."

"Listen—I need some lollipops."

"You mean GHB? I don't know anything about that. I don't do drugs."

"OK," Slater said, and waited.

Jack lowered his voice. "How much do you need?"

"Enough to get several people extremely fucked up."

"It sounds like somebody's having a party. Let me see what I can do."

The traffic around Downtown slowed his progress, and by the time he got to his house, the golden light of the end of the day was casting long shadows. Upstairs on the sofa he pulled off his boots, and felt the faux grass under his feet, and stretched out.

An alert had buzzed his phone a while ago, and he looked at it now; "распоз." That was Svetlana's face monitoring. When he pulled up the article, the headline said "19th-Century Adobe Restored to House Vernacular Art." It was a news release from a museum in Albuquerque. Scrolling through it, he came to the photos. The images were of a ribbon-cutting ceremony in front of a mud-walled building, with a dozen people standing around, some dressed like politicians, others in Western garb. And there was Pike.

Standing at the side, he was clean-shaven, that beautiful smile on his face, talking to a woman. Both of them looked to be spectators rather than participants. Pike looked so much younger. When he scrolled down to the date, the event had happened years ago, before they'd even met. The monitoring software must be scraping historical stuff, or maybe this had been reposted for some reason. When he looked at the museum on the map, it was less than a mile from Pike's house in Albuquerque. He'd been there because it was in his neighborhood.

Svetlana had dialed him in to an impressive system, but the implications were a little worrying. What if somebody like Memo had access to this, and ran Seth Pine's face through it, and found a picture of Pike with a badge on his hip?

Sometime later he woke with a start. Pike was standing in front of him, wearing his sloppy biker shirt and jeans, a sweet smile on his face.

"You were at the museum," Slater said.

"What are you talking about?"

Slater sat up, and rubbed his eyes, trying to clear his head. "Lo, the man with a million volts in his pants. You're really here. I thought I was dreaming."

"It's all for you, baby." Pike sat next to him, and leaned in to kiss him, mouthing his jaw and his neck. He felt warm, and a little sweaty, and perfect.

Eventually Pike pulled back and took a breath. He tapped the stamp on the back of Slater's hand. "What's this?"

"An owl. I went to an event behind the Orange Curtain today. For work."

"It looks like a nightclub stamp."

"I didn't think I'd see you for a while."

"I've got nothing to lose now," Pike said. "Memo and his crew know that I come around here."

"I thought maybe something had gone down with Memo and Lenny."

"Like what?"

"Like you'd seduced them, and you had them both in your thrall. The way you did with me, overpowering me with your mutant pheromones. And then you were going to forget all about me. One day some biker would show up here with a cube van, and tell me 'Seth Pine wants his stuff, so step aside, bucko.'" Slater frowned and raised his voice. "How could you do that? Not even tell me you got into a three-way with those gonifs, and make a patsy out of me?"

Pike chuckled as he put a hand on his neck, and stroked his jaw with his thumb. "I didn't tell you any of that because none of it ever happened. Except in your overly vivid imagination."

"I know they'll give you the big eye, and the sweet words, but you don't need to be sleeping with any of those guys."

"I'll take that under advisement." He sat back. "Listen, were you hanging out with Lenny?"

"For a hot minute," Slater said. "I went with him to make a cash pickup."

"Why would you do that?"

"He asked for my help. I couldn't really say no."

"Actually, you could. You do not want to mess with these people. Lenny is not a right guy."

"You know, I like this man." Slater swirled a palm at him. "The bossy biker. I'm thinking he needs to get physical with me. Show me what's what."

Pike sighed and pushed his hair back. "Do you want to eat first?"

"We can walk down to Sunset."

"Fine, but nothing grilled or fried. I need fresh food."

Once Slater had pulled on his boots, they trudged down to the street.

Walking abreast on the sidewalk, Slater said, "Lenny's father was the first human in space."

"The first person in space was a Soviet named Gagarin. I doubt they're related."

"Actually his father was sent up a few months before that." He explained the story about Project Mercury and Lenny's father getting swapped out for the chimp.

Pike laughed. "A child astronaut. That is straight-up absurd."

"I think Lenny sort of believes it. He sounded resentful that the chimp got all the publicity while his father was left in obscurity."

"I wonder if maybe Lenny hasn't done a whole bunch of acid over the years? It sounds like his brain isn't firing on all its cylinders."

"I know he doesn't drink," Slater said. "He told me he's in program."

Pike eyed him sidelong. "That's actually good intel."

"Who's working for you, babe?" He wrapped an arm around his shoulder.

"You know damn well you shouldn't be."

They found a place to eat on the boulevard, and sat outside, and Pike ordered a salad.

The server nodded as he tapped it into the device he was holding. "Do you want avocado on it?"

"Nothing would make me happier right now, Steven," Pike said.

The guy met his gaze and smiled. "Got it."

Once he'd stepped away, Slater eyed him. "Flirt much?"

"I read his name tag," Pike said.

"I'm not complaining. Watching you do it is a turn-on."

"I still have white privilege, but when I'm dressed like this, I have to reach farther to connect."

"People definitely look at you differently with the hair and the beard. They give you more space. I think you make them nervous."

"I don't look like an office guy anymore." Pike folded his arms. "I miss you. I miss this. It's Saturday night—I wish I could take you to some hotcha place, and catch a band, or learn to dance the shimmy. But none of that fits with Seth's background."

"I don't need to go groove with the hep cats. I know your job has to take priority right now. It won't be forever. The most important thing is that I get to hold you in my arms tonight." He raised his eyebrows. "And I know exactly how to make you shimmy."

The server stepped over and set down their plates. "I told the kitchen lots of avocado. It appears that they went all out."

"Looks good to me," Pike said.

"I never really got into them. Lots of times you buy them and they're mushy and blotchy inside."

Pike looked up at him. "The ones from the supermarket aren't very good. You have to find somebody with a backyard tree. Those are always way better."

"Good to know," he said, and walked away.

Slater gestured with his fork. "You're a local now. You know that, don't you?"

"You mean chatting with the guy?"

"You were actually flirting, not chatting. But it's not about that. If you know the esoteric dope about avocados, you're as much an Angeleno as you're going to get."

"Even with the long hair?"

"This town is for everybody. Even you, you big hippie."

"How's the pupusa?" Pike said.

"These people are not Honduran. It tastes like the kind of stuff you get out of town—like, way out. On a back road in Arizona. A roadside diner next to a gas station. They're Latin, and you order the pupusa, but what comes out of the kitchen is something completely different. It has some bizarre salsa on it, but it's the best thing you've eaten in months."

Pike chuckled as he jabbed at his salad. "I know exactly what you mean."

After they'd eaten, walking back to the house, Pike pointed out one of the street trees, with pale trumpet-shaped flowers amid the foliage.

"It seems late in the year for that to be blooming."

"They do that right into October. It's called a *Chitalpa*. They're not native but the city plants them nowadays because they're drought-tolerant."

"Where are they from?"

"It's a hybrid of a tree from the Southeast and one from Asia."

He looped his arm around Slater's waist as they walked. "It's such a complicated field."

"Plants are pretty straightforward," Slater said. "They tell you what they need. It's people you have to watch out for. Most of the time I feel like I never know what the hell is going on. So do you know Lenny's last name?"

Pike eyed him sidelong. "Why?"

"We're tight now. I bought him some gold lamé booty shorts, and a hoochie-daddy crop top, and a leopard-print cowboy hat. I need to ship it all to him."

"Bullshit. I'm not even going to imagine him wearing that outfit. Try again."

"I want to calculate his Kabbalah bubble quotient. It needs to use all the letters in his name."

Pike chuckled. "I know you just made that up. It's not something you need to know. You have no idea how many people have been working on taking down these knuckleheads. You can't be meddling in this."

"Sure thing, Pops," Slater said, and frowned.

"I'm not being patronizing. It's the rules. I cannot discuss my work."

He wanted to say *That ship has sailed,* but he held his tongue. "I heard some other stuff you might want to know about. Brian and his business partner are selling for Memo, and probably laundering cash through Brian's business."

Pike looked at him. "How do you know that?"

"I overheard Brian on the phone. He had Memo

on speaker. Memo said, 'You're late with the three hundred and forty grand,' and Brian said he'd deliver it next week. Memo told him specifically he should be marketing to office workers."

"Brian must be a distributor. For the meth alone that's a huge number. It has to be about more than sales."

"Money laundering," Slater said.

"Who's his business partner?"

"A woman named Thorpe. She might be his ex. They live together."

"Write down everything you know about them," Pike said, "and text it to my regular number. When were you listening to Brian's phone calls?"

"I cannot discuss my work."

Stepping up to the front door, Slater twisted his key and pushed it open. He felt a little bad ratting them out, as Brian and Thorpe's business was none of his concern, but in this situation it might benefit Slater—it might bring Pike back to him sooner. That made it worth being a snitch.

"If we use that information," Pike said, "you know you're going to have to sign a statement explaining how you heard it."

"You could just say it was an anonymous source. Either way, it's valid dope." Slater paused on the landing at the bedrooms. "So are you going to fuck me like a biker?"

"Biker-style. Does that mean you want me to get all cranked up on meth first?"

"No way. We'd be here all weekend. I need an end point."

Pike chuckled, and followed him into the bedroom, then jabbed a finger at him. "Clothes off."

He stood watching as Slater pulled off his boots, then ditched his jeans and his shirt. Pulling off his leather vest, Pike left his shirt on as he stepped up to Slater and pushed him onto the bed. Straddling him, he grabbed his head with both hands and mashed their mouths together.

Leaning back, he unbuckled his belt and unzipped his pants. Slater reached for his cock. The guy was already hard.

"Do bikers leave their jeans on?" Slater said.

"Shut the fuck up." Pike grabbed the lube, and pushed his knees apart, and eased his way into him. Starting gently, he worked up to pounding him, his hands on Slater's shoulders.

"Biker trash," Slater said through his teeth, holding his gaze.

Pike grimaced and strained into him as he came, then sank onto his sweaty body. Eventually Pike pulled away, then moved down to take him into his mouth. It was an odd sensation with all the whiskers, but Slater was already revved up, and he soon came, running a hand into his hair to get him to stop.

"That was so fucking hot," Pike said, and rolled onto his side, and leaned in to meet his mouth.

Sometime later, in the night, Slater woke. He wasn't sure why, but then in the faint light filtering in from the street, he saw that Pike was awake, his head off the pillow.

"Where are we?" Pike said, his voice hoarse.

"At the house." He could see his chest heaving. "You're safe."

"Are you sure?"

"It's late." He shifted closer and wrapped an arm around his belly. "Go back to sleep."

EIGHTEEN

W HEN SLATER WOKE, HE saw that Pike was getting dressed. It was early—outside it was still gray with the light of dawn.

"You're leaving," Slater said.

"I've got stuff to do in the city before I head out." He stepped over and kissed him. "I'm going to miss you, forty-niner."

"Me too." Slater pulled him down and kissed him again.

Eventually Pike pulled back. "Don't get me started."

"I love you, you big mook."

Listening to the sound of Pike's footfalls on the stairs, then the rumble of his motorcycle engine fading as he rode down the street, he forced himself to sit up, then went to shower and get dressed. Upstairs he found coffee in the pot, still hot, and poured himself a mug.

There was a bag of bagels in the Frigidaire, he saw, and pulled it out. Pike must have brought these. He'd sliced them too. Even working his undercover identity, and staying way out of town, he managed to do this. The guy was so competent, so good at this regular-life thing. He knew how to make coffee and freeze bagels and talk to the neighbors. To Slater all that stuff felt like trying to balance spinning plates on sticks.

He dropped half a bagel into the toaster, then took it to sit at the dining table. It was too cold to be on the deck, based on how dewy and gray it looked outside. The Santa Anas were done for now—the haze out there was the cold damp air blowing in from the Pacific.

Chewing on the bread and slurping java, he spent a minute texting Pike the details about Brian and Thorpe, their names and addresses and phone numbers. Since Pike wouldn't come across with Lenny's surname, he'd have to figure it out himself. He texted Andy:

Can I come by?

His reply buzzed his phone a minute later:

It's Sunday.

Slater wrote back:

I know you're not a Jesus freak. It won't take you long, and it needs doing now.

Andy's response came soon after:

You can come over, but golden time pricing is in effect.

"Idiot," Slater muttered, and tucked his phone away as he hustled down to his garage.

This early in the day the surface lot behind Andy's loft was mostly empty. When he walked around to the entrance, he spotted Andy ahead of him, on his red mobility scooter, riding into the building. Slater caught up to him in the lobby.

"You were over at that gunsel's lair," he said.

Andy scoffed as he rolled into the elevator car. "Usually I just call him my husband. And it's more of an ... apartment than a lair. I came back here for you. That means I'm missing out on ... French toast. You'd better be worth it."

Following him on, Slater stood next to him, and pressed the button for his floor. Once the doors rolled closed, Andy beeped the scooter's horn. It was obnoxiously loud in the enclosed space.

"It sounds great in here, doesn't it? It's the echo." He beeped again.

"Knock it off," Slater said, raising his voice. He had to chuckle. "You're quite the handful, you know that?"

Inside his loft, Andy parked the scooter near the door, and walked to his desk. Slater stood watching him. He was such a beautiful man. It made his stomach ache.

"So what are we doing?" Andy said.

"I know a guy's first name, not his surname, and I know he has an empty twenty-acre parcel out in the Mojave. I need to know where the land is."

"He owns it?"

"That's what he told me."

"If it's in his own name, I know ... where to look,"

Andy said. "The city's or the county's land-use map."

"It's in the middle of nowhere. It's going to be unincorporated."

"So that means county. Sometimes people put … real estate in a trust or an LLC. Then it's … harder to find the connection."

"I don't think this guy is organized enough to be concerned about tax ramifications."

"What county is it?"

"It has to be San Bernardino."

Andy swiveled to his computer, and pulled on his gauntlets, and soon brought up a map. "Show me where."

He pointed out the general area, and watched as Andy zoomed in. "He said it was away from the paved roads."

"What's the guy's name?"

"Lenny, so probably Leonard."

Andy started rapidly clicking around the map. "Not many of these lots are twenty acres. Most of them are five or ten. That makes it faster."

As he worked, Slater looked out the window at the square. The haze was starting to burn off.

"This might be the one," Andy said.

"Show me."

"I'm going to check a few more first to … make sure there aren't other possibilities." A minute later, Andy glanced up at him. "Take a look. There's another parcel owned by … a trust, but it's close to the highway. This is the only one in that area that … fits all your criteria."

Leaning in, Slater scanned the property record on the screen. "Leonard W. Garvin."

"The previous owner was Louis Garvin," Andy said, clicking to that record. "It changed hands nine years ago."

"I know he got it from his parents. Can you show me the satellite image?"

From the overhead view, he could see that there wasn't even a dirt road that far out, just a double-track in the sand along the property boundary. The track ran half a mile or so from the closest road, he saw as Andy zoomed out, and even that was several miles off the pavement.

"All this aligns with what he told me," Slater said. "Can we find out anything else about the owner?"

He watched as Andy pulled up a browser and logged into a site.

"Is that a banking database?" Slater said.

"Bank stuff might be part of it. This is a ... data broker. They vacuum up details about everyone. I'm sure we're both in here somewhere." A minute later he glanced up. "This is probably the same Leonard Garvin. His legal address is in Landers. Age forty-three. Does that fit?"

"That's totally Lenny. That has to be his land. Send me the location."

As he swiveled toward him, Andy pulled his arms out of his gauntlets. "I'm still working on that company you wanted me to track down."

"Lau Skilled Importers."

"Right. I'll add today's job to your cumulative bill."

"I know how long it took you, so don't try to chisel me."

"If you could do it yourself, you would," Andy

said. "You're paying for my … expertise, not just my time."

"It still feels like a racket." He raised his eyebrows. "Bye, beautiful."

———·———

ONCE SLATER WAS ROLLING east on the 10, and settled in for the long drive, he checked the socket camera. There were a couple of new recordings this morning, but they were pointless, just Brian walking through the frame.

When he got through the Gorgonio Pass into the Coachella Valley, the sun felt stronger, and he pulled on his sunglasses as he drove up into the high desert.

When he got close to Lenny's land, a few miles off the pavement, he pulled over where two of the dirt roads met. It was already desolate, with no structures in view. The map showed he was maybe half a mile from where the double-track started—far enough away that Lenny wouldn't see the Continental if he happened to be around. The tracker showed his bike wasn't here, but if they were using the remote land to store stuff, he wouldn't be moving it by motorcycle.

It was plenty warm here, and the sun felt strong. Once he'd climbed out and stretched, he opened the trunk and grabbed his straw gardener's hat, tying it under his chin so it wouldn't blow off. He set off for the double-track, filling his lungs with the clean dry air, then followed it toward Lenny's land.

There were no Joshua trees here. They weren't ubiquitous in the Mojave, only growing where the conditions were right, and this was likely too low in elevation. The pinky-tan earth was stark and dry, populated by the creosote bushes that Memo was so resentful of, along with the short-lived forbs and a few sparse grasses. The little leaves on the creosotes were dark green, but not the near-black color they took on in times of drought. They'd had some rain this summer. It wasn't lush here like farther south at the national park, but it was beautiful, and he could feel the light and the air recharging him as he walked.

He'd reached Lenny's land, he saw, looking at the map on his phone. The double-track ran along the edge of the plot, and he stepped away from it, into the untrammeled landscape, the gritty earth crunching under his boots. The satellite view showed an arroyo running diagonally through the twenty acres, not far away, and he headed toward it.

As he walked, off to the side a silvery glint caught his eye, next to a creosote bush, and he altered his path toward it. When he got closer he saw that it was a mylar balloon, deflated and with the pink plastic string still attached, snagged on a cholla cactus. That had come from one of the millions of backyards in the coastal cities, carried here by the prevailing westerlies until it had lost its helium. He gently extracted it from the spines and crumpled it up, wrapping the string around it, and stuffed it in his hip pocket.

Eventually he got to the arroyo, the lowest path through the gently rolling landscape. It was sand and fine gravel, with nothing growing on it, which meant it regularly saw running water. As he walked along it for a while, deeper into Lenny's land, there were no signs of boots or tires. But then, a few minutes later, he spotted evidence that someone had been here recently—a gentle mound in the surface of the arroyo. The disturbance was subtle, but the soil was darker than its surroundings. Wind and water hadn't done this. It had been dug up from below.

The footprints or tire marks had weathered away, but not the spot where they'd been digging, not yet. It was oval-shaped and maybe two feet by four. A little farther along, he found three more of them, all close together, all the same size. He walked another few minutes up the arroyo, and climbed a rise at one side to scan the land, but apart from those mounds, the desert looked pristine.

He walked back and looked them over. This is where he would have dug too, in an arroyo, where it was less rocky and there were no plant roots to go through. It had likely rained over the summer with the monsoon, and the running water would have disguised the work, but it took time for something this big to weather away to invisibility.

There were no human-made structures in sight, just the distant mountains all around. Memo and his crew couldn't have come in here on those road bikes, but it would be easy on a dirt bike or a quad. It was possible they'd stashed something here like weapons crates, or ammo boxes, but the size of the disturbed plots would definitely fit a corpse. The thought of what might be buried under his feet made him a little queasy, and he took a deep breath to dispel it.

With his phone he took some photos of the ground, and made a note with the latitude and longitude of the site, then headed back toward the double-track. Looking at his own footprints, they were pretty obvious right now, but the wind would obscure them in a day or two. Once he was on the double-track, he followed it to the road, and headed back toward the Continental.

As he was trudging up the dirt road, he heard tires on the gritty earth behind him, then the sound of the vehicle slowing down. He paused to look as it pulled up alongside him and stopped. It was a dark-red SUV. The driver's window rolled down, and then the one for the back seat. Behind the wheel was a college-age woman, wearing dark sunglasses, her hair tied back. Another woman of the same age sat in the back, and a third leaned over the driver to gawk at him.

"I love your look," the driver said.

He waved an arm. "What look?"

"The straw hat and the jeans. It's so desert. I really love the local color out here."

"All you need is a horse," the woman in the back seat said.

"No—a burro," the driver said. "I can see you walking with a burro. That's totally desert."

Slater wanted to snap back, to ask them whether they knew they were idiots, but he couldn't afford to draw attention to himself right now. "I'll bring my burro next time."

"Are you a prospector?" the one in the passenger seat called to him.

"Something like that."

"Is there gold in the Mojave?"

"Probably. Personally I haven't found any."

"Well, good luck," the driver said, and they waved as the car rolled off in front of him, kicking up dust. It had Cali plates—they were likely from LA, on an adventure to explore the desert, in the mind-set that they were in a foreign land.

When he got to the Continental he ditched his hat in the trunk and drove toward the pavement, taking it slow on the washboarded dirt. His phone buzzed in its dash mount. The caller was labeled UNKNOWN, but it was a 760 number. That was around here. He picked up and said, "Ibáñez."

"I know you helped Lenny with a pickup."

"Memo?"

"I'm happy you're getting into the spirit of the business."

"Thanks, baby," Slater said. "I still don't want to work for you."

"How did it go with Brian?"

"Hasn't he filled you in?"

"We don't talk all that much," Memo said.

"I did a small-potatoes type job for him."

"So when's the last time you saw Lenny?"

"Last week, when he was in LA," Slater said. "It must have been Thursday."

"Have you heard from him since then?"

"We don't actually hang out."

"Well, I can't get a bead on him," Memo said, "and that's making me nervous."

"Maybe he needed the weekend off. Doesn't he have a girlfriend?"

"If you hear from him, he needs to check in."

"He's not going to call me, man. If he comes by my place to tase me again, I'll pass that along."

NINETEEN

ONCE HE'D ENDED THE call, Slater pulled up the tracker on Lenny's bike. A few hours ago he'd checked to make sure it wasn't out near his twenty acres, and he'd noticed that it was nearby, but it wasn't at Memo's compound. Looking at the location history, he saw that it had been in the same spot since late yesterday. It was just a few miles away. He tapped the screen to navigate to it.

It was still rural here, he saw as he got close, but it wasn't desolate. Houses with outbuildings were scattered around, and the marker was less than a mile off the pavement. He pulled up on the only house that was within the tracker's location circle. The yard had a low fence made of corrugated steel. It actually looked good—rustic but not grubby. Inside the fence was a well-established palo verde, shading the patio furniture that was arranged on the sandy bare ground. A sign on the fence said SUNSET HOUSE.

When he tried the gate, it was open, and he stepped inside. Lenny's bike was parked near the fence. He stepped over to the house, to the wide sliders next to the patio furniture. The curtains were open, and Slater pushed his sunglasses up into his hair, then leaned in to peer into the dark interior, cupping his hands to the glass. Next to the sofa a human form was sprawled out, facedown, wearing worn jeans and no shirt. Lenny.

The sliders were locked, but when he went around to the front door, it wasn't bolted, and he stepped inside. It smelled like a dive bar at closing time, the unmistakable odor of booze by-products percolating through skin. It wasn't a very big place, with a kitchen at one side of the little living room, a bedroom farther back.

Crouching next to Lenny, he pressed a couple of fingers to his neck. He felt warm, and had a pulse, and stirred at Slater's touch.

Rising, Slater looked around. On the sofa was a nearly empty fifth of bourbon. It wasn't enough to kill him if he got into it again, and he was already lying prone, so he wouldn't choke on his own vomit. He should probably just leave the guy. Rubbing his eyes, he tried to will himself to walk out. But he just couldn't do it.

"Fuck," he muttered, and squatted next to Lenny, and rolled him onto his back. He groaned but didn't open his eyes. Slater slapped his face, right and left, a firm kovac. "Snap out of it."

Lenny halfheartedly pawed at his arm, then

squinted at him. "Quit your slapping."

"You'll take it and you'll like it," Slater said through his teeth, and slapped him again, harder this time.

Rolling away, Lenny struggled to sit up, and eventually leaned back against the sofa. Slater stood erect and stepped back. He had some definition in his pecs, and stretched out like that had revealed he had a sweet caboose. This guy was definitely a Mojave 9. Meeting Slater's gaze, he scowled at him.

Slater waved at the room. "It smells like a dive-bar latrine in here. Why are you playing the wastoid?"

He groaned and pulled himself up onto the sofa. He was breathing hard. "I needed to get away."

"This place is a rental?"

"I told Memo I'd been working on my engine." He pushed his hand through his long hair, moving the unkempt mess away from his face. "I needed to give it a Mojave tune-up."

"The fuck is that?" Slater demanded.

"You let her rip on the open road. Make sure everything's working right." Lenny gestured vaguely. "If nothing falls off, you're golden." He started to laugh, and it turned into a bout of coughing.

Slater went into the kitchen and found a glass, then filled it from the tap. Walking back, he handed it to Lenny.

"Drink this."

Grabbing the bourbon bottle next to him on the sofa cushions, he took it back to the kitchen and dumped what was left down the sink. There was a coffee machine on the counter, with those stupid little instant pods, and he set a mug under it and got it working.

He pulled open the cupboards to find nothing but dishes and condiments, but loose in a drawer he found a stray oatmeal bar. Carrying the mug back to the living room, he set the coffee on the table next to Lenny.

"When's the last time you ate?"

"I don't know, man. Yesterday."

Slater handed him the oatmeal bar. "Eat that."

Reaching for the coffee, he slurped at it. "What are you doing here anyway, besides telling me what to do?"

"Who's your sponsor in program?"

"I don't need to talk to him."

He put his hands on his hips. "That's exactly what you need right now. Program doesn't work if you're not honest about your stuff. You have to ask for help when you need it."

"The fuck would you know?" Lenny said. "You're not a twelve-stepper."

"Lots of people in my life think I should be."

He slurped at the java. "I got sober when I was at summer camp. It's a lot harder on the outside."

"Where did they put you?"

"Chuckwalla. It's in the low desert out by Blythe. Have you been in?"

"Not really," Slater said. "Short visits to the local hoosegow."

"So you know what it's like to be considered garbage."

"People who think like that don't matter. We're on the margins, man. Outside all that stuff. Desk jobs and golf games and grating cheese onto your lunch."

"It sucks to be on the outside," Lenny said. "I have nothing."

"I don't see it that way. It's more like you're liberated. Most people spend the whole day grinding to keep all this going." He waved his arm. "We're part of it too, but you've got a lot more freedom than the bankers and the lawyers. You don't need to drown yourself in fricking applejack."

"Tell that to my parole officer."

"Are you still reporting?"

Lenny looked away. "Not anymore."

"So you've paid your debt. You're not worthless, Lenny. No one is beyond redemption."

"You sound like the Jesus types in stir."

"It's not about that. I'm just saying you can leave your past in the past."

Slater sat in the armchair, and they talked for a while. Lenny ate a few bites of the oatmeal bar and finished the java. Eventually he sat up.

"You need to leave. I have to get out of here, but first I need to shower."

As he stood up, Slater raised his eyebrows. "You need a hand with that?"

"No," he said flatly.

"You have to call Memo. He called me today."

"Damn it. What the fuck am I supposed to tell him?"

"How should I know? Why are you even stooging for him anyway?"

"I'm not a stooge," Lenny said, raising his voice. "The club is a brotherhood."

"So tell him the truth. He'll respect that. Tell him you needed a day off to get fucked up after your Mojave tune-up. Tell him you're coming off the jag now, so you won't be doing it again anytime soon."

"Are you going to call him?"

"Fuck no," Slater said. "The more distance between me and that guy, the better."

"How did you find me, anyway?"

"I was driving by, and I saw your bike."

His eyes narrowed. "Bullshit. You live in LA."

Slater jabbed a finger at him. "Call Memo."

"Don't tell me what to do."

He scoffed and walked toward the door. On the way out, he called back, "Namaste, motherfucker."

At the gate in the fence, he stepped out to find a kid straddling a bicycle. Around ten, maybe, she had a long braid down her back, and was watching Slater as he walked out.

"How you doing?" Slater said.

"Is the other guy still in there?"

"What's it to you?"

"My mom takes care of this place."

"He's checking out soon," Slater said.

"There's only supposed to be one person staying here."

He put his hands on his hips. "You should think about a career in law enforcement, princess."

"I'm a boy."

"My mistake."

"It's because of my hair, isn't it," he said. "My people wear braids. It's our cultural heritage."

"You're Native American?"

The kid nodded and shifted his handlebars.

Slater dug out his wad of cash and folded up a fin. "I wonder if President Lincoln would help you forget that you saw me breaking the rules."

"Five dollars isn't a lot of money anymore."

Slater chuckled. "How about President Hamilton then?" He pulled out a ten.

"That guy wasn't the president."

"Are you sure about that? It seems odd that they put his picture on the sawbuck if he was just a regular schmo."

"Maybe you missed school the day they taught that," the kid said. "A hundred years ago when you were in third grade. Did you even finish third grade?"

"Knock it off with the static, kid. Just take the sawbuck." He handed it over and walked away.

———◆———

ONCE SLATER WAS ON the highway, he texted Pike's regular number:

> Lenny owns a plot of land not far from Memo's place.
> You need to check on it.

He sent a second text with the coordinates of the disturbed earth in the arroyo, and a couple of photos of the mounds he'd found.

As he merged onto the 10 heading west, he gunned it to match the speed of the traffic climbing out of the Coachella Valley. A while later he saw a text from Jack:

> Momma's got lollipops.

Slater texted him back:

> Your place in a couple hours.

The vehicle trackers showed that Thorpe's G-Wagen was in Laguna Beach. Maybe the psychic channeling event had stretched into a second day, or maybe she was down there with the baldy. Brian's ride was at his house. That made sense if his business was closed on Sunday. Slater sent him a text:

Can I see you tonight? I've got an itch I need to scratch.

An hour later, when he was close to the city, he heard back from Brian:

I'm out riding today. Come by later.

The daylight was fading to twilight when he pulled up at Jack's place in Los Feliz. It was over an Italian restaurant, busy with evening diners, and it took him a minute to find street parking. As he climbed the stairs, he could smell tomato sauce and grease. Jack's was the door on the left, he remembered, painted with a faded B, and he rapped on it with a knuckle.

Jack cracked a smile as he pulled it open and waved him in. With his dark hair short and in a natty cut, he was wearing subtle eye makeup and lip gloss, and had stubble on his face. It was warm up here over the kitchen, and he was dressed in a T-shirt and cargo shorts.

The dominant feature of the studio apartment was clothes. They were jammed on a pair of rolling garment racks, and piled on the credenza, even draped on the back of the sofa. By volume it looked like the dead-stock collection that Cassidy had taken them to.

"What's with the whiskers?" Slater said. "Are you not performing these days?"

"I can't shave every day. I have extremely sensitive skin, so I save it for days when Miss Mercy Days is on stage. I have a gig later in the week. You should come."

He gestured to the garment racks. "At least you'll have something to wear."

"You can never have too many clothes."

Jack waved him to the little round kitchen table, its pair of folding chairs the only viable place in the room to sit. Slater took one of them and watched as Jack dug in his little backpack, then sat down, and handed him a plastic snack bag with white powder in the bottom.

"I thought it would be in a bottle," Slater said. "I've only seen it as a liquid."

"Dealers mix this into water to make the liquid. It's much easier to know how much you're taking when it's the powder."

"That sounds like a very good idea."

Jack slapped his forearm. "I know what I'm doing."

"So what's the dosage?"

"To have a good time, one or two grams. The absolute max is three grams, and that's only for people who do it a lot."

"What does that look like?"

"Five grams is a teaspoon."

"I don't really cook."

Jack huffed and got up, stepping over to dig in a drawer next to the kitchen sink. He brought back a little measuring spoon, and pulled open the bag, and dug into the powder. Pulling out a level spoonful, he dumped it into his palm.

"That's half a teaspoon, so two and a half grams," Jack said. "That amount will knock you on your ass.

You should start with a lot less."

He poured it back into the bag, and sealed the zip top, and held his hand open to examine the powdery residue. Slater took hold of his wrist and licked it off his palm.

"Fresh," Jack said.

"It's kind of salty."

"That's not enough to get you high."

"I just wanted to taste it," Slater said. "How long does it take to hit you?"

"Twenty or thirty minutes, I'd say. It makes you hornier and super chatty. You'll know you're high when you notice that happening." He raised his eyebrows. "Don't mix it with booze or you'll die."

"Junkies always say that," Slater said. "One drug at a time."

"Words to live by."

"What do I owe you?"

"Three hundred."

He dug out his wad and peeled off the C-notes, then set them on the table. Once Jack pocketed them, he met Slater's gaze.

"We could sample this now, if you want. Do a quality verification check."

"No," he said flatly. "It better not be baking soda."

Jack frowned. "I wouldn't do that to you." Reaching for his hand, he took hold of it, and tapped Slater's ring with his thumb. "So does this mean you're off limits?"

"Not really. But I have to fuck a guy later, so I can't really get into it."

"That makes me sad, Slater. You're sitting right here."

Slater pursed his lips for a moment. "I suppose I could smoke you. But no backsies."

His eyebrows shot up. "You'd do that?"

"Why not? When a man is tired of blow jobs, he's tired of life. And like you said, you're sitting right here."

"I love that I won't have to reapply my lip gloss. Pike won't mind?"

It was surprising that the guy remembered his name. They'd only met once.

"Don't talk about him," Slater said.

Jack rose and went to the sofa, shifting a pile of sweaters on top of another. "How about here?"

He sat down and unbuckled his belt as Slater tucked the bag into his pocket.

"Let me do that," he said, and knelt in front of him, and unzipped his fly. Jack was already getting hard. Pulling out his junk, he went down on him.

"Oh, yeah, do it," Jack said, quickly getting into it. He put a hand on Slater's head. "Suck it, you piece of trash."

Slater looked up at him as he worked him, making his eyes wide.

A minute later, as he came, straining into him, Jack growled, "Suck my dick, you fucking hoodlum."

Rising, Slater adjusted his crotch, then went to the kitchen sink to wash his hands.

"No offense with the mean talk," Jack said, still breathing hard. "I got caught up in the moment."

Slater shrugged. "With sex, there's no accounting."

"You're sure you don't want to do anything about you?"

"Later, Jack," he said, and walked toward the door.

TWENTY

THERE HAD TO BE a liquor store around here, and Slater checked his phone as he trotted down the stairs. Sure enough, there was one right up the block. He could walk.

When he stepped in, there was no one inside but the clerk at the counter.

"Nonalcoholic tequila?" Slater said.

He pointed to a shelf at the back, and Slater looked over the options, then bought a fifth of it, plus a bottle of real tequila. Out on the sidewalk again he turned onto the residential side street, where there wasn't a lot of traffic, and scanned for a sewer grate as he walked. He spotted one at the next cross street and squatted next to it. Breaking the seal on the real tequila, he poured it into the storm drain.

Next he opened the bottle of fake stuff and

poured it into the empty bottle, then capped it and put it back in the paper bag. Retracing his steps to the boulevard, he pitched the empty into a trash can, then headed back to the Continental.

Thorpe's ride was still in Laguna, he saw, once he was behind the wheel, and Brian's was still at his place. He fired up the engine and got on the 5, heading south toward Brian's house. When he got to his neighborhood he detoured to a supermarket, and went in to buy a little bag of limes.

At Brian's place he parked on the street out front, and grabbed the paper bag, and walked up the driveway to the side door. When Brian pulled it open, he was dressed for a day off, in jeans and a gray polo shirt, a smirk on his face.

"You can't stay away, huh. What's in the bag?"

"Tequila and limes," Slater said.

"I don't know if I need to be doing that."

"Let me get my boots off." He handed him the bag, then sat on the ottoman near the socket camera to untie them. As he got up again, he pried his camera out of the socket and pocketed it. It was unlikely anyone but him would be able to get at the footage, but he didn't need to be creating evidence of what he was up to.

When he stepped into the kitchen, Brian had set the tequila bottle and the limes on the counter, and was carefully folding the grocery bag. Slater started pulling open drawers.

"Make yourself at home," Brian said, and frowned. "What do you need?"

"A knife. To cut up the limes."

He rolled open a drawer in the island, revealing

a set of chef's knives neatly arranged in a wooden block. Of course the guy would have them all sorted and organized like this.

"Can you wash your hands first?" Brian said.

Slater scoffed but stepped over to the sink, and washed, then grabbed the tequila bottle. "We'll need shot glasses."

"So we're doing this, huh." He laughed and went to open a cupboard.

"Get a spoon," Slater said, and cut a couple of the limes into quarters. He pulled out the bag of GHB and set it on the counter.

Brian poured two shot glasses. "You brought your own salt?"

"It's bar salt."

Digging into it, he spooned some onto his hand, between his thumb and forefinger, then picked up a lime wedge.

"You first," Slater said, and held out his hand.

His brow furrowed. "You want me to lick you?"

"It's hot, don't you think? I just washed. Get your shot ready."

Brian picked up the shot glass. "That seems like a lot of salt."

"It's actually not. Bar salt is low sodium. You never worked in a bar?"

"I've been to bars."

Taking hold of Slater's hand, he drew it close, and licked the powder, then slammed the shot. Slater shoved the lime wedge into his mouth. Brian recoiled, but let him do it, and bit down on it.

"That's strange tequila," he said, and coughed. "It doesn't taste very strong."

Slater slammed the contents of the other shot glass, then bit into a lime wedge. He was right—this stuff didn't have the vapor that real booze did, or the bite of the alcohol, but the taste was close.

"You forgot the salt," Brian said.

"Next round. Come on—one more."

Brian filled the glasses again, and Slater spooned more of the powder onto his hand. Holding his gaze, Brian licked his hand, then slammed the shot. He grimaced as he bit into the lime. As he slammed the other shot and bit into a lime wedge, Slater wondered if the guy would notice he hadn't ingested any of the powder. But Brian was already distracted, over at the island, where he rolled open a drawer, and pulled out a paper napkin, and wiped his mouth.

"You're a lot of man, Ibáñez."

"A little tequila will get you in the mood."

"I was already in the mood." Brian raised his eyebrows. "From the moment you texted me. Come on." He led Slater to his bedroom and started to unbutton his shirt. "I've been riding around all day with that twelve hundred between my legs. Now I want you between my legs."

Slater ditched his jeans, and soon they were both undressed.

"Can I fuck you this time?" Brian said.

"Works for me."

He sat on the bed, and Brian embraced him, kissing his neck, then stretched out next to him, exploring his skin. He ran his hands over his pecs and his arms.

"I really dig your body."

Slater squeezed his cock. He wanted to get this

rolling before the drug kicked in. "Where's the lube?"

Once he'd grabbed it, Slater mouthed his jaw, and massaged his pecs, and pulled him down on top of him. Brian moved close, pushing his knees apart, and penetrated him. Moving slowly, he sighed and closed his eyes.

It felt like he was more into it than he would have been without the dope, but it was hard to tell. He gradually built up the pace, pounding hard, and Slater gritted his teeth. It felt wilder than last time. Brian took hold of Slater's cock as he thrust, stroking him, and with his other hand wound up and slapped Slater's face.

Baring his teeth, Slater roared at him, a guttural cry that emptied his lungs. Brian slapped him again, and that sent Slater over.

"Man, did you just come?" Brian said. His voice was breathy. "That's so intense. I fucking love this."

A moment later he grunted and strained into him, his face contorting, then sank on top of him, pressing his warm skin against Slater's torso.

"Where did you learn to do that?" Brian said. "That's so fricking hot." As Slater ran his hands over his back, he added, "You have a great touch."

The guy was definitely getting chattier. Sitting up, he shifted Brian onto his back, lying on his side to massage his chest. He looked a little amped up now, Slater decided, studying his face. It was more than just the sex. The drug was hitting him.

Brian grinned and reached for his cheek. "That face."

"How are you doing, Brian?"

"I love the feeling of your hands."

"You were in Paris this summer."

"Not really." His expression didn't change as he ran his fingers into Slater's hair. "Why do you care about that?"

He caressed his neck, and his arm, and squeezed his bicep. "You told me you were over there."

Brian closed his eyes, savoring Slater's touch. "I was at the airport in Paris. Actually I went to Orléans. They pronounce it or-lee-*on*."

"Why were you in Orléans?"

"To pick up the euros."

"Where did the euros come from?" Slater said.

His brow furrowed as he worked to focus on him. "What do you know about the euros?"

"Nothing. You said euros. I didn't."

"You're so curious." Brian smirked again. "I really like your body." He ran his hand along Slater's arm and his shoulder.

"Everybody loves Paris," Slater said.

"It was Orléans. The cash was all about Thorpe. It's her side hustle."

"How does she hustle in euros?"

He groaned. "It's so complicated."

"I get it," Slater said. "You don't really understand what she does."

"Fuck that. I understand plenty." Brian leaned in and mouthed his clavicle. When he rolled back, he met his gaze. "Her company is Swiss, right, so lots of their transactions are in Europe. She figured out a way to shave a tiny amount off the euro transactions. Something about rounding decimals. Fractions of a cent. But with enough transactions it starts to add up. You can see why I can't extricate myself from her.

She makes me crazy, but she's really good at making money."

Slater caressed his chest. "The fractions start to add up. Where did that happen?"

"In Europe. In a bank account. She had to go there to get into it." His expression clouded. "Then we had to trade it with some dirtbag so the cash wouldn't be traceable. That fucker kept twenty percent."

He clicked his tongue. "The world is full of thieves."

"Tell me about it."

Brian reached for his chest, and squeezed his nipple. Taking hold of his hand, Slater interlaced their fingers.

"So you can't extricate yourself from Thorpe. How did it start with her?"

"We were sleeping together." He paused and blinked a few times. "She got tired of me. Why do you even care about her?" He heaved a sigh. His eyes looked a little glassy now. "You know, I need to be with better people."

"What kind of people?"

Brian closed his eyes and didn't answer. After a minute Slater squeezed his hand.

"What kind of better people?"

Opening his eyes, Brian struggled to focus on him. "You know—the A-listers."

"The A-listers in the truck-rental business?"

"I mean celebrities. Like those housewife shows, and the bachelors." His brow furrowed in concentration as he reached for Slater's face.

"Those are some lofty aspirations," Slater said.

Suddenly Brian's eyes grew wide, and he twisted

away, leaning over the side of the bed. His body tensed up and he retched. But nothing came up, and he took a breath, then dry-heaved again. Had he overdosed the guy? Slater rubbed his back with his palm.

"Take deep breaths."

When Brian rolled onto his back again, his face was red.

"Tell me about Memo," Slater said.

"Memo's kind of a dick. The guy scares me."

"You're handling product for him," Slater said.

"I'm not a street drone. I don't even deal with street drones." He closed his eyes.

Slater waited a minute before he spoke. "You're not a street drone."

Brian looked at him as if he was startled to find him there. "Of course I'm not. I'm wholesaling to dealers. It's hard fricking work. So many people to deal with. And then inflating the sales numbers at my company to account for Memo's income. Memo only lets us keep a little of it for taking all that risk." He rubbed his forehead. "I feel kind of weird."

"You drank a lot of tequila."

It seemed like the guy was starting to fade out. But at least he was breathing. Slater put a hand on his cheek.

"Yeah, it's weird," Brian mumbled.

"How are you doing?"

Brian just moaned and didn't open his eyes.

He wasn't going to get anything more. Sitting up, Slater rolled him into the crash position, pulling his top knee forward. He pulled the covers over him and sat to watch him for a while. His breathing seemed regular enough, he decided. He really hoped he hadn't overdone it. If he had to call an ambulance for the guy, there'd be a lot of explaining to do.

Rising, he pulled his clothes on, then went to the kitchen. Once he'd sealed the bag of GHB, he stuffed it in his pocket, then washed the shot glasses and left them in the drying rack, and used soap to wash the spoon, just in case somebody decided to test it for drugs. Tossing the bag of limes into the icebox, he wiped down the counter.

At the door to the driveway he pulled on his boots, then put the little camera back in its socket, and went to check on Brian again. He sat next to him on the bed for a few minutes. The guy was totally out, but his breathing wasn't labored.

On the way out he glanced into the kitchen. He'd almost missed the tequila bottle. That would have been an egregious error. Grabbing it, he walked out to the driveway, and climbed in the Continental, and flicked on the headlights.

When he pulled into his garage, he opened the gear cabinet and put the little bag of dope on the top shelf. It was a useful tool—Brian had talked a lot, and he'd been totally disinhibited.

Trudging upstairs, he poured out his ration of bourbon, and slammed it, closing his eyes to savor the burn. He eyed the empty tumbler. How could it be gone already, in the blink of an eye? He poured a little more—he deserved it, as he'd been on the road half the fricking day, and then worked late. With the glass in hand he went out to the deck and stood looking at the glittering lights of the Financial District in the distance.

He felt a little queasy about Brian. It didn't seem

like the guy was going to overdose, but not everybody could handle their drugs. He slurped at the heady golden elixir. Slater was definitely on his security cameras this time. If anything went wrong, there'd be questions. There was nothing he could do about that.

The things he did—spying on people, poking around their private spaces, drugging the guy. He took another mouthful and savored the burn. They merited the scrutiny, of course, as Slater needed to know what they were up to. But it definitely meant he was every bit the lowlife that they were.

TWENTY-ONE

❧❧❧❧❧❧❧❧❧❧

SLATER WOKE TO THE buzzing of his phone on the bedside table. When he grabbed it, the caller ID said REDDY KILOWATT.

"Are you in town?" Slater said as he picked up.

"Not really," Pike said. "You texted about Lenny."

"You know that guy is a rum-dumb."

"You said he was in program."

"That's what he told me," Slater said. "But I also saw him blackout drunk."

"Maybe he had a relapse."

"Did you check out the land he owns?"

"I just saw your message," Pike said. "Why do you think that's important?"

"It's valid intel. Lenny said Memo was interested in his land. It's big, and isolated, and there's no structures on it. You saw those photos—somebody's been digging along the arroyo."

"So you went out there."

"Just to have a look around."

"Is that where you saw Lenny?"

"Nobody saw me on his land," Slater said. "It's pretty remote."

"You're acting like this is your case. It's not. You need to keep your distance."

"You said that already, Seth. Listen, if people around Memo have gone missing, I'd bet cash money they're planted on Lenny's land."

Once he'd ended the call, he saw there was a text from Andy:

I got something for you.

Forcing himself out of bed, he pulled on his jeans, and felt a lump in the back pocket. A balled-up wad of silvery plastic with a pink string around it, he saw, digging it out. He'd found this on Lenny's land just yesterday. It felt like that had happened weeks ago, and on another planet.

In the kitchen he ditched the balloon in the trash, and grabbed an apple, and ate it on the way down the stairs. He backed the Continental into the street and drove to Andy's. Once he'd parked behind his building, he walked up the block to get java.

When Andy pulled open his door, Slater gestured with the two little paper cups. "Greek coffee."

"You know what I like." Andy waved him in. "Can you pull the lid off?"

Once he'd settled into his gaming chair, Slater handed it to him, and Andy took a sip.

"So what's the dope on Lau Skilled Importers?"

"The company seems to be about … one guy. Raymond Lau. On that business networking site he calls himself Ray Lau. He imports … chemicals from Red China. That address in Vernon is a … warehouse. It's not very big."

"What kind of stuff does he import?"

"I'm not a chemist, but you … mentioned the drug trade," Andy said. "Some of the stuff listed for him could be … used to make fentanyl."

"What about meth?"

"Probably. I'd have to check. Take a look."

He drained his cup, then swiveled toward his desk and pulled up a website. Slater stepped closer to look at his screens.

"This is his B2B pitch," Andy said, and scrolled through it, pausing at a text box with big letters: *Highly skilled at clearing Mexican customs.*

"A legit business wouldn't care about that," Slater said. "He's appealing to people who need precursor chemicals to make dope."

"All that stuff is produced in … China, so it's definitely possible."

"I'm glad you found this. What do I owe you?"

"For this one and the last two, eight dollars."

Slater drained his cup, and dug out his wad, and started to peel off the C-notes.

"You're not complaining about my rates," Andy said. "Are you … feeling OK?"

"You know you're chiseling me, and I know you're chiseling me." Slater folded the sheaf of bills lengthwise and set them on his desk. "I know I just have to accept that, the same way I have to accept you cutting off my sex supply."

"You get more sex than ... anyone I know. You don't need it from me."

"But you're like the vegan macarons from that bougie bakery on Sixth Street. Everybody else is just dried-out gas-station mini doughnuts."

"You're calling me a snack," Andy said.

"You're a total snack."

"What about that slab of cream cheese who ... actually sleeps in your bed?"

"He's been away."

Andy threw up a hand. "So find somebody else. You're an addict—addicts always find a way."

He frowned. "Stale doughnuts, son. And they've been sitting on the snack-treat delivery truck all week."

When he got downstairs, he nosed the Continental out of the parking lot and headed to Vernon. Not far from Downtown, it was all industrial spaces and warehouses, the wide boulevards clogged with slow-moving semitrucks. He navigated around them until he came to the address for Lau Skilled Importers.

The fence fronting the street concealed the yard, but he could see the building above it in the distance. It was a lot smaller than the sprawling white monolith of a warehouse next to it. Lau's looked to have two floors, with windows on the upper level.

Slater pulled into the driveway for the neighboring warehouse. Lining the side of the building was a long row of numbered truck docks. Trailers were parked at some of them. Farther along was the gate for Lau's place, and it was rolled open.

There was lots of room on this side for semitrucks to maneuver, and he turned around, and parked just past Lau's gate, tight to the outside of the fence. Mounted next to the gate, he saw as he climbed out, was the hazardous materials diamond. This was a real one, with numbers on it, not a stealthy cipher for an artist's studio. He couldn't remember what each color meant, but the 3s and 4s meant Lau had seriously dangerous chemicals here.

Walking in through the gate, he saw the structure had a lone loading dock. There was probably room for a semitruck to back in, but it would be tight. The steel shutter on the dock was rolled halfway up.

Parked at the side of the yard was the Lexus with the Taiwan bumper sticker, and next to it was a Ranger. It was at least twenty years old, from when that model still looked like a pickup and not an open-back sedan.

He tried the regular door at the side of the building, but it was locked, and it didn't have a bell. Walking over to the loading dock, he looked it over. Sometimes they had levelers that folded down, but this was an old building, with just the grimy concrete lip. Attached below it was a strip of black rubber. It had tread on it, like somebody had nailed up hunks of an old heavy-equipment tire.

A seam in the wall below the bumper gave him a foothold, and he climbed up, and heaved himself inside on his belly. Nobody was in sight as he got to his feet. A sweet little forklift was parked nearby. Farther back were rows of blue and green barrels on pallets, stacked two and three high, and some pallets of square-shaped stuff wrapped tightly in plastic.

At the side of the space was a doorway, and Slater went over and pushed it open. A few steps led down to the front door, and a flight of stairs led upward. He climbed it and stepped into the room at the top. It was an office, with a couple of desks, and file cabinets, and piles of paper. Behind the desk was the guy Lenny had met at the central market. He was wearing a white dress shirt, and up close he could see the guy's haircut was utilitarian.

"Ray Lau," Slater said.

Lau scowled at him. "How did you get in here?"

"The door was open."

"No, it wasn't."

"I wanted to talk to you about some of your products," Slater said.

He sat back. "You can set up a meeting through the website. That way I can vet you before we actually meet."

"Well, I'm here now."

Picking up a walkie-talkie from his desk, Lau spoke into it. "Where the hell are you?"

A deep voice gave a curt response, but Slater couldn't parse the words, as they were garbled with static.

"I know you can get pretty much anything from Red China," Slater said. "Does it all come through Mexico?"

"Who are you working for?" Lau demanded.

"I work for myself. Can you get the precursors for opioids like fentanyl, or only for meth?"

Lau shook his head. "We're not having this conversation."

The sound of footfalls came from the stairs behind him, and a big guy in navy-blue work clothes stepped in. With his black hair slicked back, his bulk looked to be muscle, not flab. This guy was a bruiser, and he was totally fuckable.

"Get him out of here," Lau said.

The guy stepped up to Slater and reached for his shoulder. Throwing up his arm, Slater shoved off his hands, but the bruiser reacted fast, with a solid left to his cheekbone. Slater tried to punch back, but the guy was on him, and grabbed him bodily, and threw him into the stairwell. Slater managed to stay on his feet, his back slamming against the far wall.

This guy knew what he was doing. He studied Slater for a moment, then stomped toward him.

Slater's back hurt, but he needed to move, and he groaned with the effort as he started down the stairs. The idiot was trudging down after him, he realized, and he trotted faster. When he got to the door at the bottom, it was bolted, and there was no thumb turn, just a keyhole.

The bruiser stopped just above him, on the landing with the door to the warehouse, his fists balled.

"Who locks an exit door from the inside?" Slater demanded. "The fire marshal would not be happy with you." As the guy took a step down, Slater showed his palms. "Listen, I know I'm outgunned here. Just let me walk out."

As he mounted the steps, the guy let him pass, and Slater pulled open the door to the warehouse. Once he was through the doorway, the bruiser grabbed him and shoved him toward the loading dock. Losing his footing, Slater tumbled on the concrete floor, managing to roll onto his side as he landed.

"I get it, man," he shouted, looking back at him. "I'm leaving. Can you not see that?"

He sat up, and the guy was on him again. As he leaned in to reach for his arms, Slater kicked up at him. He felt his boot connect with his face. The guy shouted as his head snapped with the impact, but it didn't slow him down, and he threw Slater hard toward the edge of the loading dock.

Slater went over the edge on his side, airborne for a second, and swung his legs around to land on the gritty asphalt on his butt. He roared with the impact—that really hurt.

Inside, the bruiser rolled up the shutter on the dock, and then stood at the edge, breathing hard. A trickle of bright red was on his upper lip, and his nose looked messed up. That was mollifying. At least he'd got in one decent blow. Getting to his feet, Slater rotated his back, then rolled his neck. His whole body hurt, but nothing was broken.

"Why don't you try using your words, you damn bully?"

He started toward the gate, limping a little, and massaged his thigh. "Walk it off," he muttered.

When he got to the Continental, he paused to swat the dust off his butt and his legs, then climbed in and drove out to the street. Once he was around the corner on the boulevard, he pulled over to catch his breath and clear his head.

His cheek was red, he saw, pulling at the rearview mirror to study his face, and it looked swollen, but maybe it wouldn't bruise. He was definitely going to be sore tomorrow. Digging out his phone, he texted Pike's regular cell number:

> Do you know about a guy named Raymond Lau, at
> Lau Skilled Importers? Has a warehouse in Vernon.

Lenny met with him in LA on Thursday at the central market and gave Lau a package. I can sign a statement to that. I've got another witness who can attest to it too.

He knew that would piss him off, that Slater was still involved when he'd told him repeatedly to butt out, but nobody else had seen that meeting, and now it seemed significant—Lau was a patent lowlife.

A while ago there'd been an alert from the socket camera at Brian's house, and when he checked it, he saw Thorpe walk in the door, then step out of frame, and the clip ended. At the same moment his phone buzzed with an incoming call—that was her number.

"Who's this?" he said as he picked up.

"Janine Thorpe, you thug. We need to talk."

"Why would I talk to you when you just insulted me?" Slater demanded.

"It's about Brian. I know you were here last night. You need to come over."

"That's a pass, sister."

She raised her voice. "I know what you did. Get your ass over here."

Pulling the phone away from his ear, he looked at the screen. She'd hung up on him. That queasy feeling stirred his gut again, amplified by the residual adrenaline rush of getting beat down. Thinking about it, though, if Brian had croaked last night, or wound up in the ER, it would be the cops after him, not her. But he did need to find out what they knew.

TWENTY-TWO

PULLING INTO THE STREET, Slater got on the 710 and headed south. Once he was on the block with Brian's house he parked a few doors down, and walked back, and rapped on the side door.

When Thorpe pulled it open, she scowled at him. "What happened here last night?"

"You said you knew about that."

"I want specifics."

"A play-by-play?" Slater said. "That's a little kinky. You should have told me in advance. I could have made a video."

Brian's voice called from the kitchen: "Let him in."

Thorpe stepped back, and Slater paused inside the door to pull his boots off. Brian was perched on a stool at the island in the kitchen, and he sat up straighter when Slater walked in. He had dark circles under his eyes, and they looked bloodshot. As he stepped closer, he saw that it was only on one side, a red blotch in the white part of Brian's eye.

Slater leaned in and peered at his face. "What happened to you?"

"You look like I feel," Brian said. "Like somebody worked you over."

Behind him, Thorpe spoke. "The only reason the cops aren't here right now is that the web says those happen naturally. It's a busted blood vessel. You can't do anything about it."

He frowned at her. "OK."

It was an empty threat—no way would they ever invite the cops here, or swear out any kind of complaint. Despite the veneer of suburban affluence, they were still drug dealers, with too much to hide, too much to lose.

"I'm so hung over," Brian said. "My head is pounding. I can't really remember what we did, Slater. I kind of remember talking to you. I think something messed up happened."

"You were slamming the tequila shots, if that counts as messed up. It's pretty strong stuff. Even so, you managed a happy ending."

"How much did I drink? I only remember a couple."

"I don't know," Slater said, and put his hands on his hips. "Five or six, maybe? You were enjoying them."

"The spirits said you were unpredictable," Thorpe said. "They told me your motives were convoluted and concealed."

"Tell your spirits that if they want to throw down with the ten-dollar words, they can come haunt my house. If they've got something to say, say it to my face."

She scoffed. "Like they'd talk to you."

"I'm pretty tits-out about my motives, woman. Last night they were to get fucked up on tequila and get into his pants. Evidence from this plane of reality suggests that your not-husband just drank too much."

"You are an emotional wreck," Thorpe said intently.

He waved a hand. "I get that a lot."

She eyed Brian. "What do you think?"

Brian gestured helplessly.

"Fuck it," Thorpe said. "I don't trust you, but we need you to do something else."

"You mean a job? So chasing you last week was just a test of my skills? Did I pass?" Slater scoffed. "It doesn't even matter. I'm not going to work for you losers again."

"I am not a loser," Brian said, raising his voice.

"A booze hag, then."

Thorpe shot Brian a look, then eyed Slater. "The gig is easy. You just have to take something out to Memo, and make sure he's the one who gets it. Put it in his hands."

"I don't do courier work," Slater said, "and I'm not going to drive around with felony amounts of your dope in my car."

Brian frowned. "We don't do that. If you think about it, you're already participating in Memo's business. Memo might insist."

"Fuck Memo. What do you need to send to him?

He doesn't need dope since he's making it. That means cash or weapons. There's nothing else he's interested in."

"It's cash," Brian said.

Thorpe glared at him. "What the hell?"

"He's not going to do it unless he knows what it is," Brian said.

"You think I'd jack Memo?" Slater demanded. "Big mistake. He'd grease me in a heartbeat. Don't kid yourself—he'd come for you too if you crossed him."

"So you'll do it?" Brian said.

Slater pursed his lips for a moment. "I'll do it for five grand."

Thorpe scoffed. "Are you high right now? You need to stop using Memo's product. You're supposed to sell it to the dopers, not become one."

"Take it or leave it."

"Come on, Slater," Brian said. "You have to negotiate. That's part of the deal. We'll pay you three."

"Cash up front," Slater said.

"I'll get the briefcase." Thorpe stepped into the hallway.

Slater jutted his chin at Brian. "You think the tequila did that to your eye?"

"Apparently it's caused by straining. Like when you upchuck. I don't remember doing that, but if I was blotto, I probably did. I don't think I ate much yesterday."

When Thorpe returned, she handed him a sheaf of C-notes. Slater held them up to the light from the window.

"These look real. Where did you get them?"

Ignoring that, Thorpe set a boxy black briefcase on

the kitchen island. "Can you drive this out tonight?"

"That's not going to happen." He tucked the cash away. "I'll go tomorrow."

"Don't try to open the case," Brian said. "It's booby-trapped. Only Memo's key can get into it without destroying the contents and blowing up in your face."

He frowned. "At least you trust me."

"We can't trust anyone. You know that."

"You already told me what's in it," Slater said. "Why would you booby-trap it?"

Thorpe raised her eyebrows. "In case someone intercepts it."

It didn't wash. Slater looked to Brian, then back to her. "You two are idiots. Did you know that?"

"Fuck you," Thorpe snapped.

"No thanks."

He grabbed the handle of the briefcase, and lifted it off the island, then went to step into his boots. Once he was behind the wheel of the Continental, he drove a few blocks, and turned onto a quiet side street, and pulled over to think it through.

His head was starting to hurt, undoubtedly the result of Raymond Lau's goon tossing him around like a dog with a chew toy. He dug in the glove box for the little bottle of ibuprofen and shook a couple into his mouth.

Brian knew what his car looked like—he'd commented on it. No way could he take the risk of driving it right now, when he didn't actually know what he was carrying. He could cold-plate the Continental, even swipe a set from one of the cars on this street, but it was still risky. There was an easier way. He dialed Max's number, glad that he picked up.

"I've been asking you for a lot lately," Slater said.

"The safe in our office is stuffed with cash these days," Max said. "I'd say whatever we're doing is worth it. What's up?"

"I need to switch cars. I think my client might have set me up to get pulled over with a hot briefcase."

"What's in it?"

"I'm not sure. It could be a fuck-ton of meth, or handguns, or cash."

"So you're working for a drug dealer," Max said.

"I'm thinking it might be a way to wipe out their obligation to their upstream supplier and leave me holding the bag. They want to put me in the frame as the patsy who got caught."

"I get it. All it would take is to call in your tags. You'd definitely get stopped."

"Can you come to where I am? In South Gate."

"Send me your location," Max said. "I'm near Downtown. It won't take me long."

While he waited he checked the vehicle trackers. Both Thorpe's and Brian's cars were still at their place. On the socket camera the most recent clip was from a minute ago, of him stepping into his boots and then walking out, briefcase in hand.

He eyed the side mirror to watch a vehicle roll by, relieved it wasn't the cops. If his tag was on the BOLO list, there was an automated plate reader on every prowl car that would tell them to stop him.

Before long a charcoal-gray vehicle pulled up behind him, and Max climbed out, wearing one of the new jackets they'd bought with Cassidy, the blue and white plaid.

"You look sharp," Slater said, as he stepped out of

the Continental.

Max gave him the once-over. "You don't. Did you get hit by a bus?"

"Some meathead worked me over. It was my own fault. I went in without an invitation." He waved at the car. "What happened to the Challenger? I saw it at the office last week."

"I sold it. I actually wanted another one, but they don't make them anymore. The Charger is close. This one's a hybrid."

"I guess it still has some personality," he said, looking it over. "They're starting to look like every other car out there."

"I hate that too," Max said. "You have to walk over and read the badge to tell who made it."

"Thanks for doing this. I'm pretty sure my client is running a gimmick on me."

"If you're working for a drug dealer, I know you've got your hands full." He gestured to the Continental. "If I get pulled over, is there anything in the vehicle that doesn't need to get found?"

"Good thinking."

Opening the trunk, he retrieved the vehicle tracker that was tucked down beside the spare tire, then slammed the lid and grabbed the briefcase from the front seat. Once he'd switched keys with Max, he put the briefcase on the passenger seat of the Charger.

"There's aspirin in the console, if you need it," Max said. "You can plug in your phone. You'll be able to call and text hands-free."

"Sweet."

"I know the Continental has AM radio, at least." Slater frowned. "And FM. It's not 1940."

"True." He gestured to the big vehicle. "Up in here it's more like 1970. But I'm not complaining. I'm happy to drive it. It feels real."

When he climbed into the Charger and pulled the door closed, it suddenly got oddly quiet. It smelled like a new car, and it felt confining, molded to his body, more like a space capsule than his classic ride. Like Lenny's pop blasting into orbit instead of that chimp. As he adjusted the seat, he saw the Continental pull away. Once he'd plugged in his phone, and figured out where the starter was, he nosed into the street.

The controls felt responsive, and the ride was smooth and quiet. He clicked his tongue. These new cars weren't completely unseductive. Talking to the vehicle's software, he managed to send Svetlana a text:

Can I come by today?

As he turned onto the freeway ramp, the car's screen dinged with her reply, but it didn't display the words. Instead he had to tap it to get it to read it aloud. It was surreal to hear Svetlana's words spoken in the perfunctory flat Midwestern accent of the software voice through the car's surround-sound speakers:

I am always here for you.

Traffic on the freeway slowed as he got close to Downtown. His phone buzzed, but nothing showed up on the car's screen except the map. Picking up the device, he saw that it was Svetlana's app, reporting it had recorded a new call on Thorpe's phone. He tapped at it to play the conversation, and it came through the car's sound system.

"We put three forty in a briefcase and gave it to that grunt you sent to Brian," Thorpe said.

"You mean Ibáñez?" That was Memo's voice.

"That's the one. He's driving up there with it tomorrow."

"Finally," Memo said. "You know you can't do business this way."

"Your money is literally on its way to you."

After the recording ended, as he braked in the sea of stop-and-go traffic, he thought about it. Maybe getting him felony-stopped in the Continental wasn't their plan. Maybe they really did want the briefcase to get to Memo. Still, something hinky was going on. He could feel it in his gut.

TWENTY-THREE

VENTUALLY HE WAS IN Glendale, and pulled up in front of Svetlana's building, and grabbed the briefcase as he climbed out. His back still hurt, and he took a second to swing his arms to move the muscles and get the blood pumping. Walking around to the alley, he looked up into the camera over the back door. Almost instantly the lock snapped open. It seemed ironic that Svetlana had automated it with facial recognition, and then sold him tech to confuse other people's facial recognition systems.

With the briefcase dangling from one hand, he stood waiting in the little chamber between the doors. The only sound was the high-pitched whir of a fan. He knew it was pulling air through the chemical detectors she had in here while the other sensors scanned him with who knows what kind of radiation.

The inner door unlocked. That meant her tech hadn't picked up anything suspicious from the briefcase. When he stepped into the workshop, Svetlana was standing near her computer, wearing a blouse in a pink and orange print, cut low to show her ample cleavage. She gestured to the briefcase.

"You're driving a new car, and carrying this briefcase. Have you decided to become an office worker?"

"Not yet. The car is borrowed, and I was told this case has a booby trap in it."

"And you want to open it," she said.

"Unless that's a bad idea."

As he stepped closer, she peered at him and frowned. "Someone has punched you in the face."

"It comes with the job."

She nodded. "This case has no explosives. My sensors would have detected the chemicals in the air. But I can scan the contents. Come with me."

Svetlana led him through the door at the side of the workshop, briefly holding her wrist to the keypad to unlock it. It seemed hard-core to have your card key implanted under your skin, but it probably saved her a lot of time. From the hallway she stepped into a small windowless room. Cluttered storage shelves lined one wall, and on the opposite side was a work table.

"This is an ultrasound machine." She gestured to the boxy device on the table. "It's used to examine your organs."

With beige housing and an LED readout, it did look like a medical device. Sitting next to it was a computer monitor, and tethered to the box with a cable was a wand that looked like a flattened computer mouse.

Waving for him to set the briefcase on the table, Svetlana turned on the machine, and pressed some buttons on the front panel, then took the wand, and pressed it onto the briefcase. They both watched the screen as bright angular shapes loomed and faded among the hazy shades of gray.

"This is the locking mechanism," she said, moving the wand over one of the hasps. She drew it along the sides, then under the handle, gazing at the shadowy grainy images. "All simple mechanical parts. I can see no electronics inside."

Eventually she set the wand down. "No explosive chemicals, no liquid, no wires, no radios, no triggers. I think there is no booby trap."

"Is it empty?" Slater said.

"There's something inside. Those square shapes we saw on the screen. But it's not very dense. Not enough to be plastic explosive."

"Could it be cash?"

She raised her eyebrows. "Shall we open it?"

He chuckled. "Let's do it."

"Bring the briefcase," she said, and switched off the machine.

Slater followed her out to the main workshop, and set the case flat on the stretch of workbench she pointed out. She stepped up to it and touched the hasp.

"It's locked," she said. "Do you care if the mechanism is broken?"

"It doesn't matter."

Walking farther along the workbench, she grabbed a tool. It looked like a mini pry bar, he saw when she returned. Svetlana deftly hooked it under the hasp on the left side and lifted it. The lock popped open with a metallic *snap*. Once she'd made the same maneuver on the other side, she lifted the lid.

Slater leaned in to look. Inside were a jumble of paperback books. He picked up a few of them to find more underneath. *Death Comes to Modesto, The Melted Pineapple, Murder at the Wig Store,* and a couple with the covers ripped off. He pulled open the top pocket to peer inside. It was empty.

"This is not what you expected?" Svetlana said.

"There's supposed to be three hundred and forty thousand dollars in here."

"You have been cheated."

"Not just yet." He closed the top and folded down the hasps. They didn't latch anymore, but when he lifted the handle they still held it shut, even with the weight of the books inside. "I appreciate your help. What do I owe you?"

"This work took me almost no time, so I will charge you zero. Consider it repayment for your advice on my jury duty problem."

He lifted the briefcase off the workbench. "*Spasiba bolshoye.*"

She cackled at that. "*Ni problyema.*"

Out on the street, he climbed into the Charger, and set the briefcase on the passenger seat, then started the engine to get the air blowing.

The actual gimmick was starting to come into focus. Brian and Thorpe were setting him up to fumble the cash delivery to Memo. Of course Memo would think Slater stole the dough. They could keep the three forty, but that would only work if Slater couldn't come back to argue about it—they were counting on Memo not hesitating to grease him.

After that, Memo would write it off, at least as far as they were concerned. It wasn't their fault because Memo had sent Slater to them. But Memo would look for the cash even after he iced Slater. That meant he'd go after Pike and probably ice him too.

"Mother fucker," he muttered.

He'd underestimated those grifters. Brian and Thorpe weren't angling to get him arrested to solve some of their problems. They were trying to get him murdertized. He took a breath and willed his heart to stop pounding.

At least he finally had the truth. It stood out because it was so rare. Like the silvery glint of mylar in the muted Mojave landscape. This truth wasn't pretty, like in the psychic's wide-eyed poem, but it was elegant in its inherent lack of distortion, making sense of all the other parts, patiently knitting the world together.

He sent Max a text:

Where you at? Nobody's looking for the Continental.

A moment later came his terse reply:

My pad.

Pulling into the street, he drove downtown, to Max's apartment, and stopped in the driveway of the garage while he looked around for the opener. Once he'd found it, and the gate started to roll open, he looked over at the street trees in front of the building. Laurel figs. They used to plant those things everywhere, even though the roots busted up the sidewalks. There were so many of them that a symbiotic fig wasp was thriving in Southern California, even though it didn't belong here either.

Chara at the yoga studio had said that—her yoga business and the drug trade were symbiotic. "That's the way the economy works." Like shilling meth to tweakers was a reasonable business. Like she was just making money that was lying around to be made. But she was no symbiont. Her and Brian and Thorpe and Memo—they were all fricking parasites.

Rolling into the garage, he pulled into the stall next to the Continental, then grabbed the briefcase and climbed out. Max was walking over from the stairwell.

"Did you manage to scratch it?" Max said, a dumb grin on his face. "It's brand-new."

"There's not a mark on it." He handed him the keys. "There is a little bit of vibration when you get up around one forty. You might want to have that checked."

"Good to know. Although I don't think there's anywhere within a hundred miles where the traffic would let you drive that fast."

"It works great for drifting too," Slater said. "I did a couple of street takeovers, and made some tire smoke."

Max chuckled. "I'm so glad you're not that guy. So what's up with the briefcase?"

"The Russian got it open." He lifted the case and pulled open the lid.

"Books?" Max said. "I guess that's better than twenty pounds of meth."

"I'm being set up." He folded it closed, and told him about the gimmick, outlining it in broad strokes.

Max furrowed his brow. "You know, the manufacturer might not blame you, especially if he opens this while you're there, and you play dumb."

"But he might," Slater said. "I probably would. He's basically a gangster—shoot first and ask questions later. I can't take that risk."

"So what's your plan?"

"I'm still working on it."

Max handed him his keys and took his own. "Stay safe, at least."

"Always, brother."

Pulling out of the garage, Slater headed toward his house, sticking to the surface streets. The freeway was always jammed at this time of day. When he got upstairs, he pulled his boots off, and scrunched the faux grass between his toes. He stretched out on the sofa and thought about Brian and Thorpe. Which one of them had come up with the plan to put him in the frame? In the end it didn't matter, he decided. Both of those lowlifes were in on it.

He was hungry, he realized. He should have eaten when he was out. On his phone he ordered a tlayuda from a place nearby, then trotted down to the front door when the driver rang. It was starting to get dark out.

Eating it at the dining table, he got up after and threw out the wrappers, then pulled open the cupboard to look at the fifth of bourbon. It was sitting there waiting for him. But not yet. He needed to do things in the right order—work, then guys, then booze.

Once he'd turned on the radio, and found the station that had decent music in the evening, he stretched out on the sofa again. He was in it now—he'd taken possession of the briefcase, and he needed to get himself out of it. Saving his own skin came first. That was the straightforward part. But maybe he could mess with Thorpe and Brian at the same time. He thought it through, trying to foresee all the contingencies, then went over the plan again. If everything went right, he knew it would work.

Digging out his phone, he opened the hookup app, and scrolled through the images of torsos and the dick pics. Why did he do this when he knew Pike hated it, and when he needed to get up early? Before he could force himself to kill the app, he got a message:

Yer hawt. Can I come over?

The direct approach was invaluable, like a gold nugget in a streambed of dull rocks that just wrote "Hey" and "Sup." The app said the guy was a hundred feet away. Not bad looking, he decided, going through his profile. A little square, and a bad haircut, but basically fuckable. Slater messaged back:

Are you homeless? Not a dealbreaker, but I need to prep for that.

His response came a moment later:

I'm staying in the neighborhood.

Slater sent him his address, and added, "No drugs."

He barely had time to get up off the sofa when the bell rang, and he trotted down and pulled open the door.

The guy beamed. "You look like your profile pic."

"Back at you," Slater said, although he was a little

chunkier than his photos implied. "Where are you staying that you could get here that fast?"

He gestured across the street. "With Tilly. Do you know her? She's my sister."

"We've met. Come on up."

"I'm Rodney."

"Slater," he said, glancing back at him, and stepped into the hall between the bedrooms.

"It's just you?" Rodney said. "Tilly told me two guys live here."

Slater groaned. "I fricking hate this stuff."

"What stuff?"

"Neighbors, and gossip, and bullshit." He waved an arm. "If I fuck you, the next time Pike sees Tilly, she's going to tell him, 'oh, hey, your boyfriend fucked my brother.'"

Rodney frowned. "You're sneaking around on your boyfriend?"

"I have a permission slip for when he's out of town. But I don't need to be on Tilly's sucker list."

"I told Tilly I was going to walk down to a pub on Sunset. She doesn't need to hear about you."

He raised his eyebrows. "Loose lips sink ships."

"I can keep my mouth shut for you." Rodney dropped his chin and held his gaze. "Unless I'm on my knees, that is."

"Good answer."

Stepping up to him, Slater put a hand on his neck, and leaned in to kiss him. His mouth was warm and firm and intent. The guy ran his hands over his back and his butt, then grabbed his belt, pulling him close, grinding his woody into his crotch. Eventually he pulled back.

"Do you want to fuck me?" Rodney said.

"I can definitely do that."

Following him into the bedroom, he pulled off his shirt. "I'm going to lie on my belly, and you're going to pound me."

Slater unbuckled his belt. "A man who knows what he wants. I like it."

Once he was naked, he straddled the guy, and massaged his shoulders, and his torso. He was getting hard, and pressed his woody against him.

"Yeah," Rodney said. "That's it. Do it."

Reaching for the lube in the bedside drawer, he pushed into him, gently at first, and lowered his weight onto him.

With his face buried in the crook of his arm, Rodney whimpered as he got into it. Slater mouthed his neck and his shoulders, and started thrusting into him, building up speed. He shoved his arms under Rodney's, and pulled himself tight to his body as he climaxed, inhaling the scent of his sweaty hair.

When he pulled back, Rodney shifted onto his side.

"That was amazing."

Slater grabbed his cock, rock-hard now. "What are we going to do with this?"

"Do you want to ride me?"

Pushing the guy onto his back, he straddled his hips, and lowered himself onto him. Once he'd eased his way into it, he kneaded his chest, and worked him, rocking back and forth. When Rodney came he groaned and thrust into him.

Slater climbed off and moved up the bed, stretching out on his back, and folded his arm over his eyes.

Rodney's breathing gradually slowed.

"I wish I was around longer," he said finally. "I'd come back for that every night of the week."

Slater stirred, moving his arm. "Where are you from?"

"Milwaukee."

"I thought Tilly was Latin. You don't seem Latin at all."

"That whole thing is totally an affectation with her. She's as white-bread as I am. I bet she never met anyone who spoke Spanish until she went to college. She claims she's just reinventing herself, but you could argue it's cultural appropriation." He reached for Slater's face and gently touched his cheek. "Did someone take a poke at you?"

"I walked into a door," Slater said.

The guy kept talking, and Slater grunted acknowledgment, and tuned him out. Eventually he woke when Rodney got up and started to get dressed, and mercifully soon left.

Not bothering to put clothes on, Slater went upstairs and pulled out the bourbon, and sloshed his ration into a tumbler, and stepped over to the French doors, looking out at the city.

It looked so innocuous from this vantage. You couldn't see the rackets and the frame-ups. The bruisers, and the punch dummies, and all the chiselers. Just the bright lights of the buildings. All the grit and the grime was invisible until you had to slog into it.

TWENTY-FOUR

E HADN'T OVERDONE IT, Slater decided, when he woke to his alarm. His back and his legs still ached from the tune-up he'd had, but his head felt clear. That was a relief. Scrabbling for his phone on the bedside table, he checked the vehicle trackers. Thorpe was still at home, and Brian was at the truck-rental place. There was nothing new from the socket camera or from her phone.

Pushing himself out of bed, Slater went to shower. In the bathroom mirror his cheek was still a little red, but the swelling had gone down, and it wasn't going to bruise. Once he'd toweled off he got dressed and headed upstairs. He toasted a bagel and took it out to the patio table on the deck. It was cold out but the bright sun felt good.

Thorpe was moving now, he saw, looking at his

phone. The circle for the location of the G-Wagen was hopping along Alameda. She was headed to that standing appointment with her trainer at the gym.

After he'd finished the bagel, he trotted down to the garage, where he opened the gear cabinet and loaded the signal jammer into his satchel. He wouldn't need the lock reader—he already had the key to the place.

Driving to South Gate, he parked up the block from Brian's house, then checked the tracking app to make sure his Rover was still at his business. The tracker on the G-Wagen was grayed out, last seen at the office building where Thorpe's gym was.

He pulled on his stealthy glasses, and the blue ball cap, and a pair of black latex gloves. Climbing out, he flipped on the signal jammer, and slung his satchel over his shoulder, and walked to the driveway.

At the side door he used the ghost key, wiggling it around until it turned the cylinder. As he stepped inside he called out "gas company." Standing there listening, there was no response, no sound in the house. Nobody was here.

Walking through the kitchen, he opened the garage door and flipped on the bright lights. He strode over to the tool cabinet and pulled it out from the wall, then lifted the wallboard cover off the hidden compartment. Taking the bag of cash off its hooks, he set it on the floor and squatted next to it. He winced at the sudden pain in his thigh, a remnant of yesterday's dustup, and shifted onto one knee to ease it.

The bag felt heavy, like it had before, and when he zipped it open, it didn't look like they'd taken anything out since he'd first seen it. He quickly counted out thirty-four racks, tossing the twenties back. Once he'd loaded them into his satchel, he stared at the cash. They had so much more dough here—another half million or so. It wasn't like they were setting him up because they were desperate. They were just greedy, and saw an opportunity, and tried to throw him under the bus.

He unzipped the other compartment to reveal the bright-yellow euros. It didn't even look like money. More like the play money in a board game. But it had value somewhere.

Taking this would be flat-out thievery. They didn't owe him anything. Taking it would make him just as much a grifter as they were. But these people were trying to get him killed. There had to be a cost for that. Unlike the greenbacks, he knew the provenance of this lode, knew that Memo or some other drug-industry lowlife wouldn't be looking for it. Fuck it, he decided. When you robbed a thief, maybe it wasn't even thievery. Lifting out the bundles in big handfuls, he loaded them into his satchel on top of the dollars.

Slater zipped the bag closed and lifted it back onto its hooks. It was a lot lighter now. He replaced the wallboard cover and rolled the tool cabinet back into place. As he walked out, he locked the door behind him, and shifted the satchel around to his back.

When he stepped past the gate at the end of the driveway, a woman appeared on the sidewalk, her eyes locked on him. With her dark hair styled back, she was wearing a silk print blouse and gold jewelry at her neck, and incongruously, gray sweatpants and clunky tennis shoes.

"Can I help you?" She stopped in front of him, her brow furrowed.

Slater paused on the sidewalk. She'd already confronted him—walking away would only up the likelihood that she'd call the cops.

"I doubt it," he said.

"Are you a handyman or something?"

"Brian wanted me to stop by and pick up some tools."

"They're not home."

"I'm aware of that," Slater said. "Brian's tied up at work. He gave me the key and asked me to come over."

"You work together? With the rental cars?"

"Brian rents trucks and cube vans. I work for him sometimes."

"OK." She looked him over. "What's with the gloves?"

Slater looked at his hands as if he'd forgotten he was wearing them. "The guy is a clean freak. He asked me to wear them so that I wouldn't mess up his stuff." He forced a laugh and peeled the gloves off. "I should get him to come over to my place and tidy things up."

She'd bought his story, he realized, as she looked around the street and pushed her hand into her hair, no longer interested in him.

"Are you getting cell service?" she said. "I live next door. My internet went out, and now my phone is offline too. I'm supposed to be in a video meeting right now."

He pulled out his phone and glanced at the screen, even though he knew it would say NO SERVICE—the jammer in his satchel was still on.

"I've got a good connection," he said, and tucked it away.

"I don't know what to do. I can't call the cable company because my phone's not working."

"Those outages are usually pretty brief," Slater said. "I'd go try again."

She headed back to her yard, and Slater walked the opposite direction, toward the Continental. Once he was out of the range of the cameras on Brian's house, he pulled his satchel around and killed the signal jammer. The nosy neighbor would be in her meeting soon, and she'd forget all about him.

The morning traffic was thinning out as he drove to his office, and parked across the street, and carried the satchel and the briefcase upstairs. As he flicked on the lights he eyed the statue on the front desk.

"How you doing, Rey?"

Briefly checking Max's office, he strode over to his own desk, setting the bags on the floor as he squatted next to the safe.

Dating to the same era as this building, it was an old-school black metal box, bolted to the floor and inscribed MONTCLAIR SECURITY in faded gold leaf. Slater dialed in the combination and heaved open the heavy door.

From his satchel, he loaded the bundles of euros onto the shelves. It was getting crowded in here. Like Max said, there was lots of cash from other jobs. They were trying to smurf it into their bank accounts, but it was a slow process, depositing small amounts at irregular intervals to avoid scrutiny. Looking at it now, he wasn't sure what he was going to do with the big pile of yellow plastic. Maybe Max would come up with a plan.

Closing the door, he twisted the handle, then spun the dial to zero out the wheels. He lifted the briefcase onto his desktop and pulled it open, then scooped up the paperbacks, and piled them on the desk in the front office. Maybe Etta could donate them to some lesbian free library.

Once he'd lifted his satchel off the floor, he started to transfer the greenbacks. The racks filled about half the space in the briefcase. He closed the hasps and then flicked off the room lights, carrying the briefcase down to his car. Setting it in the trunk, he threw a tarp over it.

When he got on the freeway he merged left, and stayed in the middle lanes, rolling at the speed of the traffic. With all that cash on board he did not want to get stopped. It was a long drive, and he periodically checked his phone. The tracker on Lenny's bike had returned to Memo's place after Slater had seen him, then late yesterday it had moved again and stopped.

Slater zoomed in on the location circle. It was at a place in the desert labeled SOLID WASTE FACILITY. Lenny wasn't on another bender—he'd found the tracker and thrown it in the trash. Maybe the guy wasn't as dumb as he thought. He'd figured out how Slater had shagged him to that rental.

He had to stop for gas, but the traffic was moving, and a couple of hours later he pulled up at Memo's compound. The gate was closed, and a metal sign wired to it said HONK in spray-painted black letters. Once he'd given the horn a couple of blasts, he climbed out of the Continental, and looked up into the camera, and waved at it.

It felt dry out here, but the air was clean, and he turned his face to the sun to soak up its warmth. Before long the gate started to roll open. Climbing in behind the wheel, he drove inside.

A guy strode toward him from the direction of the big shed. Like the rest of them he had too much hair, and was wearing jeans and a leather vest. As Slater got out, the guy stopped and jutted his chin.

"What do you need?"

"From you, nothing," Slater said. "Where's Memo?"

"That's not how this works." He gestured to the Continental. "You don't ride. The fuck are you?"

He knew it was a mistake, but he couldn't help himself, couldn't suppress it. Slater threw a fast right, and caught the guy off guard, landing the punch on his chin and snapping his head.

The guy knew how to brawl, and instantly swung at him with both fists, hitting him hard in the ribs, and a glancing blow to his hip. Slater grabbed him around the torso and threw his weight sideways. The guy managed to hold on to him, and dragged him down too, and they both hit the dirt.

Nearby, he heard someone shout, "Break it up."

The best solution in a grapple was to hold on to the guy and look for an opportunity to knee him in the nards. Slater tried to flip him over, but then he felt hands on his arms pulling him off. It was Lenny, he saw, and he let himself be hauled back.

Once Slater was on his feet, Lenny eyed the other guy. "Knock it off."

Lenny was the punch dummy, the enforcer, and the guy knew better than to challenge him. Instead he got to his feet, and spat in the dirt, and jabbed a finger at Slater.

"You are a fucking psycho."

"You kiss your mother with that mouth?" Slater demanded.

"Just settle down," Lenny said. He jutted his chin at the other guy. "You don't need to be here."

He scoffed and walked back toward the production shed.

"Get a horse," Slater shouted after him.

The guy didn't look back, but raised his arm to flip the bird at him. Lenny finally released his grip on Slater's bicep and stepped back.

"What is wrong with you?" he demanded.

"I don't know, man. It's a long drive." Slater swatted the dust off his shirt and his jeans.

Memo was here, he saw, walking over from the office trailer. "Are you tweaking right now?"

"I'm not."

"Of course you'd say that." He chuckled and looked him over. "You have something for me."

"It's in my car."

Slater stepped over to the Continental and opened the trunk, lifting out the briefcase. When he turned back to them, Lenny had his handgun drawn and aimed at his gut. With the briefcase hanging from his thumb, Slater flashed his palms.

"I'm not armed."

"Check him out," Memo said.

Lenny tucked his weapon away, and Slater set the briefcase on the dirt and spread his arms so that Lenny could pat him down.

Eventually Lenny stepped back. "He's clean."

As Lenny headed for the production shed, Memo gestured for Slater to come with him, and walked toward the trailer. When he stepped inside, Memo went over to the credenza next to his desk.

"Do you want a drink?"

"It depends on what you've got." He set the briefcase on the floor. It didn't matter, not really, but he didn't need to advertise that he'd drink just about anything.

"What I've got is bourbon."

"Set me up," Slater said.

Memo poured from a bottle into two glasses and handed him one. There was a generous slug in it, Slater saw, and tapped his glass to Memo's, then took a sip. This was quality stuff, rich and nutty, not the rotgut he bought for himself. He savored another mouthful.

Setting his glass down, Memo lifted the briefcase and laid it flat on the desk. He touched the hasps, then looked up to meet Slater's gaze.

"The locks are broken."

"I needed to make sure the cash was inside," Slater said. "You know how it is. I couldn't really show up here empty-handed."

Memo flipped open the case and took out one of the racks. He riffled through it, seemingly satisfied that it was all C-notes, then lifted out the others, counting them under his breath.

"It's all here," he said. "Good man."

He didn't seem surprised, Slater decided. That meant he hadn't been expecting it to be loaded with books. Memo wasn't in on the gimmick. Like Slater, he was just one of the moving parts in somebody else's scheme.

Once he'd loaded the racks back into the brief-case, Memo closed the top, and looked up. "Do you need some scratch?"

"Brian and Thorpe paid me already." Slater frowned. "Why does it feel like I'm working for you now? A week ago I'd never heard of you."

Memo laughed and picked up his glass, tipping it toward him. "There's plenty of room here, brother. We can all make some money."

"I know those two are making serious bank."

"They're definitely flashy. The cars they drive, and the way they dress."

"I saw the production space in Commerce," Slater said. "The lease on that must be insane. Or did you buy the building?"

His eyes narrowed. "The production space."

"Setting up right in town seems riskier than working out here, but I guess you all know what you're doing."

"Production for what?" Memo said, raising his voice.

"Aren't you part of that?" Slater waved his glass. "I'm thinking they're making the same thing you make. They were talking to a supplier about the inputs. A guy named Ray Lau."

Memo set down his glass. "When did you see this place?"

"When I was working for Brian." Slater raised his eyebrows. "Did I say something wrong? I thought you were part of their business. Nobody told me any different."

"What were they talking to Lau about?"

"I don't want to get anyone in trouble."

"Talk," Memo demanded.

"Chemicals. I don't remember the names of them. Do you know that guy? Brian said Lau sells all kinds of stuff to all kinds of people. Maybe they're planning on making fetty, not meth."

"Where is this production space?"

Slater slurped at his glass, relishing the heady burn, and affected nonchalance. "In Commerce somewhere. By the tracks. They're just starting up, so there's no equipment in there yet. I don't know anything else. You should really talk to those two about it."

Stepping over to the door, he pulled it open and shouted, "Lenny."

Back at his desk, Memo slammed the rest of the bourbon in his glass. When Lenny stepped in, he pushed his sunglasses up onto his forehead. "What's going on?"

"We're riding tomorrow."

Lenny eyed Slater. "Did you skim from the cash? How stupid can you be?"

"I didn't touch your goddamn money," Slater snapped.

"Tweakers are chatty," Memo said, looking at Slater. "It's a thing. Speed freaks and dusters are different. They're unpredictable. Fetty and GI gin just make them sleep. But meth is pretty reliable." He eyed Lenny. "We're going to visit Brian and Thorpe in the city. Ibáñez is not going to mention that."

"They're not my people," Slater said, "and I'm not working for them anymore. I'm not going to be talking to them."

"A minute ago you said that it feels like you're working for me now," Memo said. "Remember that.

If you do give them a heads up, I'll take you out too."

"I believe you, brother." Slater flashed his palms. "I'm not an idiot."

"You need to tell Lenny what you know. Specifically addresses. Where they live, where they work, and where they're setting up production."

"Sure."

Memo stared at him absently for a moment longer. His chest was heaving, and he was working his jaw, almost like he was chewing something. He strode out and slammed the door behind him.

TWENTY-FIVE

"**M**EMO'S PISSED," LENNY SAID.

"I can see that."

"What did you do?"

"Nothing." Slater frowned. "I gave him some intel. I thought he was starting a production project with Brian and Thorpe, but it turns out those knuckleheads are setting up their own factory."

"OK, that would definitely piss him off. What did he want you to tell me?"

"Addresses. Are you going to write this down?"

Lenny sat at the desk, and Slater dug out his phone. He recited the address of the house, and Brian's truck-rental business, and Thorpe's office in the Financial District, even though that was useless, as she was rarely there. He omitted any mention of the fictional production space. Lenny didn't ask, as he hadn't heard him describe it. Hopefully it would get forgotten in the shuffle. They had all the details they needed to track down Brian and Thorpe and ambush them.

"That's all I've got," Slater said. "I guess Memo's done with me for today."

"If he's not around, that's a safe bet. I'll walk you out."

Lenny followed him into the yard, closing the office door behind him.

"I found your little black box on my bike," Lenny said as they walked toward the Continental.

"I don't know what you're talking about."

"Don't bullshit me. I know that's how you tailed me to that rental." When they got to the car, he stood to face him. "I guess it's only fair. I was shagging Pine, and I worked you over."

"Memo asked me where you were," Slater said.

"I get it, man. He wasn't even pissed at me. I think telling him the truth actually worked."

He nodded. "Like they say, progress not perfection."

Slater climbed into the Continental, and drove back to the pavement, and down the hill to the 10. Late afternoon was the wrong time of day for this drive. There was lots of traffic, and some serious slowdowns in the Inland Empire. When the sun went down he flicked on the headlights, and farther west he was able to make better time in the toll lanes.

Once he was in East LA, he checked the vehicle trackers. The one for Lenny was offline now, likely compressed under a mountain of garbage at the landfill, but the ones on the G-Wagen and the

Land Rover were still active, even though it had been nearly a week. Svetlana had said she'd improved the battery life, and they were living up to her word.

Both vehicles were in the same place, in Downtown, the circles tightly overlapping at the corner of Seventh and Broadway. Slater tried to picture that intersection in his mind. He knew there was a parking structure, as he used it sometimes. The only destination he could think of right near there that someone as bougie as Thorpe would go to was a nightclub. When he checked the location of her phone, sure enough it was there, across the street from the cars, at Greenleaf.

Pike loved that place, and they'd been a few times for the band and the floor show. It had a dress code—he couldn't walk in there in denim. It would be faster to stop at his office than to go to his house.

Twilight had faded to night by the time he pulled up at his building. He parked at the curb in front and left the flashers on. It was long enough after business hours that he'd get away with it for a minute. Upstairs he found the lights on, and stepped over to Max's office.

Sitting at his desk, Max leaned back. "How did it go with the briefcase?"

"I think I figured it out. I'll tell you about it, but not now. I'm kind of in a rush." He pulled open the wardrobe in the corner, still jammed with the vintage clothes they'd bought upstairs, and pulled out the red-and-purple suit. "I'm glad these are still here."

"What's with all the euros in the safe?" Max said. "It looks like a bottle of mustard exploded in there. It's a lot of jack."

"That's business income. I'm pretty sure it's clean."

"Good to know, but we still can't put that in a bank. Do you have any idea how difficult it's going to be to get rid of those?"

"We'll figure it out," Slater said. "Maybe you and Vanessa need a few days on the Riviera. Does she like museums? Europe's full of them. You can wear your groovy new threads."

Stepping over to his office, he hung the suit on the door and pulled his boots and jeans off. He could keep his shirt, he decided. It was a solid dark color so it worked with the plaid. When he stepped into the pants, they fit his waist, and they were the right length, but the legs flared toward the bottom. Was it too odd? Maybe it didn't matter. As long as they let him into Greenleaf.

He pulled on his boots and went over to Max's doorway.

"Whoa," Max said, and sat back. "Speaking of groovy."

"Cassidy said these were the best clothes in all of human history."

"I think she might be a little biased."

"Is it too much?" Slater said.

"As long as you're home by midnight."

"What about the boots?"

"You look fine."

"I'll take it, even though that sounds a lot like a lie."

Slater hustled out and went down to his car. Cruising up Broadway, he found an open meter and pulled in. As he walked back to the place, he stuck a hand down his pants to reposition his junk in the unfamiliar trousers, and shrugged his shoulders to adjust the jacket. The lapels were so damn wide.

Greenleaf was upstairs above Sackett's, a cafeteria that had been here forever. The place had been updated, but it was still slinging hash, even at this hour. He climbed the stairs from the dining room up to the nightclub.

At the top was the bouncer, a thick guy with a shaved head, wearing a dark suit and perched on a stool. He gave Slater the once-over and carded him. Once he'd glanced at his ID, he handed it back and looked away.

Slater stepped past him and stood surveying the room. Nobody was up on the dance floor, but the tables around the sides were mostly occupied, and the stools along the bar flanking the far wall were crowded with bodies. Some of them were watching the band on the stage.

Wearing the dark-green velour jackets of the house band, there were seven of them, a drum kit and a keyboard plus a lot of brass. He didn't know the slow and sentimental song they were playing, but they sounded great.

A woman stepped toward him, wearing a chic blue dress, her dark hair styled to tumble on her shoulders, her lipstick bright red. It took him a second, but he remembered her name—Les James. She owned the place.

Les paused next to him and leaned in. "I love that suit."

"I think I do too."

"You look familiar," Les said. "Why do I know you?"

"I came in here when you were getting set up. Before you opened. You had your sleeves rolled up that day." He looked over her dress. "You certainly clean up nicely."

She chuckled and held his gaze for a moment. He knew that look: not quite flirty, but open to it if he went there. It was way more interesting when guys did it.

"Of course. I remember now. You're a friend of Woody's."

"The tired canary. My name is Ibáñez." He nodded toward the stage. "The band sounds sweet tonight."

"Sweet for now. They'll get hard later on to get people up dancing. After the floor show."

"Well, mazel on your success here," Slater said. "This place is top-shelf."

"Thanks. Are you meeting someone?"

He jutted his chin. "They're right over there."

"Have fun," she said, and briefly touched his arm before she stepped away.

Thorpe and Brian hadn't noticed him, and he stood watching them for a minute. They were sitting at a table, side by side, looking at the stage. Brian was wearing a dress shirt open at the collar, and Thorpe was in a shimmery gold top, the fabric bundled at the shoulders. It showed some cleavage, and the color suited her. Despite being a damn grifter she knew how to dress—it was an elegant outfit for a night out. Between them was a bottle in an ice bucket stand, and two champagne glasses sat on the table.

They didn't notice him approach. For one, they'd never seen him in a suit, and he was probably the last person they were expecting to see. He walked behind them, and grabbed a chair from an empty table, and swung it around to sit next to Thorpe.

"What are we celebrating?" Slater said.

Thorpe sat up straighter, and Brian's eyes grew wide.

"What's your damage, Brian?" Slater pointed a thumb at Thorpe. "You look like you've seen one of her ghosts."

"You were supposed to go out to the desert today," Thorpe said, her brow furrowing.

"You seem surprised that I made it back." He gestured to her top. "What are you wearing?"

"It's couture."

"If you say so." He looked her up and down. "It just looks a little …" he paused for effect—"cheap."

"Fuck you," Thorpe spat. "What's with that suit? It looks like you robbed somebody's grandfather's attic. Or were you digging up bodies in the clown graveyard?"

"It's wash-and-wear," Slater said. "You've heard that expression, haven't you? Beware the wash-and-wear."

She recoiled. "What did you just say?"

Brian held up a palm. "You took the briefcase to Memo?"

"I put it right into his hot little hands." He mimed shoving the case.

"You saw him open it?" Brian raised his eyebrows.

That look. The guy was trying to come off as guile-less. It took all his strength not to leap over the table and punch him in the face. Leaning toward Brian, Slater jabbed a finger at him. "You tried to put the skids under me, chump, and you're going over for it."

"You went to the police?" Thorpe demanded. "Why the hell would you do that?"

"There's no cops, you moron." He scoffed. "You know, I'm really hoping your number is up."

He got up and walked away, taking deep breaths to dispel the red mist. Brian followed him to the stairs, and trotted down after him.

"Hold up," Brian said. "What are you talking about? What happened with Memo?"

Turning back, Slater grabbed him by the throat and slammed him against the wall. Brian took hold of his arm with both hands and tried to pull it away. They always did that, and it was completely ineffectual. With his free hand Slater delivered a rapid kovac, slapping him left and then right, and spoke through his teeth.

"Why do you make me do this to you?" He slapped him again. "You really want me to crack you, don't you?"

The bouncer was on him now, his big hands on his shoulders, and pulled him off. Eyes wide, massaging his throat, Brian stood there with his back to the wall. At the same moment Les James appeared at the top of the staircase and came down a few steps.

"I'm just taking out the trash," the bouncer said, looking up at her. "They won't be causing any more *desmadre.*"

"Let go of him," Les said.

The guy frowned but stepped back.

"You're the only *desmadre* in here, pal," Slater said, adjusting his jacket. "So you can spare me the chin music."

"We can't have fisticuffs in here," Les said.

"Tell that to your ape." Slater frowned at the guy. "He's the one manhandling the merchandise."

"Well, it looks like it's over now. You can come back in if you promise to behave."

"I was actually on my way out." He jutted his chin toward Brian. "Keep an eye on this one. He's the dine-and-dash type."

"Hey," Brian snapped. "It's you. You're the low-life." He jabbed a finger at him and raised his voice. "You."

Looking pointedly at Brian's chest, Slater tapped the wide lapel of his own jacket. "You spilled something greasy on yourself."

Brian quickly pulled at his shirt and looked down at it. Slater scoffed and trotted down the stairs.

It was stupid to go talk to them. He knew that. He should have just stood back and let things unfold. Let Memo take them by surprise. Now he'd warned them that their gimmick hadn't gone to plan, and he'd given them a chance to skip town. But he just couldn't resist. He climbed into the Continental and eyed himself in the rearview.

"What is wrong with you?" he demanded.

Nosing into the street, he stopped at his office. Max was gone, and he flicked on the lights, and changed out of the suit. He could take all this stuff to his house, he decided, looking into the little wardrobe. His car was right at the curb. Loading his arms with the yards of polyester, he carried it down and dumped it in the passenger seat.

When he got back to his place, once he'd carried all the clothes up to his bedroom, he ditched his boots, and turned on the radio, and stretched out on the sofa. He really wanted to talk to Pike. It sucked so hard that he was unreachable.

———⋅———

WAKING SOMETIME LATER, STILL on the sofa, Slater felt cold. He looked at his phone. It was late. He checked on the vehicle trackers. The G-Wagen and the Rover were both back at their house.

There was a new clip from the socket camera. It started with the door opening, and the pair of them walking in, Thorpe in her shiny couture. They stepped out of frame, toward the kitchen, but their voices continued.

"If you call him, it just looks suspicious," Thorpe said. "If he didn't get the money, he's going to call us. We'll go from there."

"What if he comes looking for me?" Brian said. "I don't get why he let that hothead just walk out."

"Memo didn't open the briefcase. It's the only explanation. If that thug hadn't delivered it, he would have called already."

"Then what was Ibáñez talking about?"

"There's a product shipment Thursday, isn't there?" Thorpe said. "You can talk to Memo then."

The voices faded, maybe as they moved to a different part of the house. He could hear them indistinctly for a few seconds, and then the clip ended.

Pushing himself off the sofa, Slater went over to the kitchen and poured his ration. It had been a long day, so he went heavy, and added another couple of fingers. Stepping onto the patio, the night air felt cold, and he shivered as he looked out at the city.

At least those two weren't going to fade. Memo was coming for them, and they'd be there. He took a slurp from the glass. The cold air made the city lights look brighter. It was completely misleading, like costume jewelry, or those guys with padding built into their skivvies, or Dutch courage from a bottle. It made the place look sharp, and upbeat, and noble, even. It was anything but. Everybody out there was either a grifter or a mark.

TWENTY-SIX

〰〰〰〰〰〰〰〰〰

I N THE MORNING SLATER heard a dull chirp, and it pulled him up to consciousness. There was daylight outside, gray through the sheers, but it was still early. He grabbed his phone from the bedside table.

Several alerts had come from Svetlana's software. The first one was a while ago, early this morning, notifying him of a new video clip from the socket camera. He tapped the screen to play it. As he watched, he sat up, and his heart started to pound.

With a loud *bang*, the door from the driveway flew open. They'd used a ram, and the guy wielding it quickly stepped to the side. Four bodies hustled in, wearing jeans and T-shirts marked POLICE in bright yellow, their sidearms strapped to their thighs. Those were the ones who came to make felony arrests, not to ask questions or make notes or poke around.

A minute later Brian and Thorpe were both frog-marched out the door. It looked like Thorpe was wearing stretchy gym clothes, and Brian was in a T-shirt and sweatpants. As they went out, Slater caught the glint of metal in the small of Brian's back—they were handcuffed.

He sat there staring at the screen after the clip ended. Had they gone after Memo too, or was this about some separate shady enterprise these two were involved in? When they went after coconspirators, they hit them all at the same time, so that nobody could tip off anybody else. They usually did it early, like this with Brian and Thorpe, when people were most likely to be home.

Right now his priority had to be to wipe his tracking software from Thorpe's phone. It shouldn't be traceable to Svetlana or to him, but the cops were canny. He opened the tracking app, relieved that the phone was still online, and tapped through the menus to find the command. Eventually a bubble appeared that asked, "For sure erasing all?" He tapped YES, and it disappeared.

Next he spent a minute on the vehicle trackers. They still had battery power, and he knew there was a command he could send to wipe them, leaving no software on board. Once he'd found it, and nuked them both, they disappeared from the list of devices. The physical boxes were still attached to the vehi-cles, but Svetlana assured him those would be next to impossible to trace.

There'd been another alert from her software. That was the sound that had woken him. The message said "распоз"—the web face monitoring. Slater clicked through to the source. This alert was about Pike. The software had picked up his face in a news article, with the headline "Meth Gang Arrests." Time-stamped this morning, it was short on detail, and felt like it had been generated by a bot, pulling the basics from a just-the-facts law-enforcement media release. But it included a string of booking photos.

The first mug shot was Lenny, looking tired and resigned, and then Memo, with a scowl on his face. The guy he'd scuffled with yesterday was next, and then the hot one who'd called Pike "Yella." Up close he wasn't actually so hot—in the mug shot he was half smiling, half wincing, showing that his teeth were all stained and messed up. There were photos of a couple of other bikers, and finally Seth Pine.

He studied Pike's mug shot. The guy had the look of a hardened lowlife. His expression was bored, but with a challenge in his eyes, a tacit "fuck you" and "bring it." Even with all the hair, the guy was so damn hot.

Looking up at the hazy daylight filtering in through the sheers, he took a breath. It was over. Pike could come back, and maybe get a damn haircut. The downside was now that Memo had legal problems, he wasn't going to go after Brian and Thorpe. Looking at his phone again, he texted Hopkins:

> Can you meet me at the coffee joint near your office? It's important.

His response came soon after:

> I'm not in the office until later. Meet me for lunch? That falafel place on Spring.

"Idiot," he muttered. Being a desk jockey must be a sweet deal if you could just show up whenever you wanted.

Pushing himself out of bed, he got dressed and went upstairs, and ate half a bagel and an apple. It was a while until he had to leave, so he fired up the coffee machine, even though it was a pain.

At the table, slurping his java, he checked for other news stories about the bust. A couple of articles came up, but they were all just a few sentences, likely written by bots repeating the same basic facts the cops released before the journalists could ask all the questions and flesh out the details.

Eventually he trotted down to the garage and backed the Continental into the street. It was too early for the lunch rush, and the falafel place was quiet when he walked in. Hopkins was at a table next to the window and waved to him. At the counter Slater bought a coffee, and carried it over, and took the chair opposite the guy.

"I assume you know what happened this morning," Slater said.

He set down his pita sandwich and wiped his mouth with a napkin. "Oh, yeah. All my people are talking about it."

On his phone Slater pulled up the article with the booking photos and handed it to Hopkins. "Pike got benched along with all the dirtbags. Is somebody going to reach out to the sheriff over there?"

Studying the screen, Hopkins chuckled. "The look on his face. He's really in character." He handed the phone back. "He'll get sprung when they separate them all. That might happen after he's arraigned.

If it's out in the country, that might take a day or two. Until then he'll be maintaining his cover. Since the feds are the ones who orchestrated the bust, they might have brought them all to the city. In that case, things will happen faster."

"How can you not know whether they transported them or not?" Slater demanded.

"I haven't been to the office yet. I was at the doctor." Hopkins sat up straighter. "Holy balls, there he is. He must have just got out. I bet he's on his way to the office."

Slater followed his gaze, and saw Pike stride past the window, a red bandana tied in a loop around his head. He jumped up and hustled out to the sidewalk.

"Yo, jailbird," he shouted, but Pike kept walking. Slater cupped his hands around his mouth. "Reddy Kilowatt."

Pike finally turned around, and flashed that beautiful smile. Walking back to him, he put his arms around his waist. Slater grabbed his neck and kissed him. He nibbled his jaw, and his ear, inhaling the heady scent of his skin.

"I knew you'd come back," Slater said under his breath. "Punk."

Pulling away, Pike met his gaze. "You know I'm going to destroy you later."

"Bring it. I like the bandana, by the way. It keeps your hair out of your face."

He chuckled. "What are you doing here?"

"You should come inside. I've got Hopkins in there."

Pike followed him in and greeted Hopkins in a loud bro exchange. He sat where Slater had been, so

Slater took the chair between them, and reached for his coffee.

"I saw they took you in this morning," Hopkins said. "You were at the production site?"

Pike nodded. "I thought it would look better if I got pinched too. I got drunk there last night so I had an excuse to stay over. I figured the arrests would go smoother if everybody was hungover."

"Smart."

"I'm actually glad you're here," Pike said, eyeing Slater. "We need to debrief you."

Slater slurped at his java. "I'm not ready for that. I'm still processing the shock of seeing your mug shot. It's left me feeling quite vulnerable. I'll come in another day once my nerves have stabilized."

"He needs time to get his story straight," Pike said, eyeing Hopkins. "At least tell me how you wound up as the courier yesterday." He waved a hand. "Off the record."

"Did you know Memo was planning to go after Brian and Thorpe?"

"I heard," Pike said. "That's one of the reasons things got accelerated to hit them this morning."

"I'm glad you picked up those deadbeats too," Slater said.

Hopkins frowned. "Was that in the media?"

It hadn't been, not that Slater had seen—that was a slip. This guy was such a damn cop. He'd picked up on it right away. He frowned thoughtfully. "It must have been, Hopkins. How else would I have heard about it? Do you know what they're charged with?"

"Felony distribution and money laundering, at least," Pike said. "They were one of Memo's fronts in the city."

"If they got busted," Hopkins said, "there must have been solid evidence against them."

"I got nervy and asked Memo about Brian. He explained that him and Thorpe were moving way more product than Seth Pine was."

"That is nervy." Hopkins chuckled. "It sounds like Memo wanted you to get competitive."

"That's the only reason he'd tell me something like that. He also told me how he'd entrusted them with laundering some of his money. The material evidence for that was the cash delivery from Brian and Thorpe." Pike looked at Slater and furrowed his brow. "Again, why were you running cash for them when I told you to stay out of it?"

"I had no choice. Brian said he'd get Memo to take me out if I didn't play ball. These are dangerous people. As you know, they assaulted me with a stun gun and illegally detained me."

Pike held his gaze. "You know that was an empty threat. Memo didn't owe Brian or Thorpe anything."

He shifted in his chair and wrapped a hand around his cup. "Openness is such a lofty goal."

"It is, Slater. In our narrative complex, and in whatever you did for Brian and Thorpe."

He took a breath. "They tried to set things up so that I'd deliver an empty briefcase to Memo. They figured Memo would assume I stole the dough and then croak me, so they could keep it all. Memo would have gone looking for Seth Pine too since he knew we were sleeping together."

"It wasn't empty," Pike said. "Memo told me you made the delivery yesterday before I got there. I know you brought cash."

"If they gave it to you empty," Hopkins said, "where did the cash come from?"

"Does that matter?"

"A lot," Pike said intently. "It's going to come up."

"It was in their house," Slater said. "I was invited inside to pick up the shipment, and I saw all that lettuce. I made sure it got into the case."

"They just let you take it?"

"So many questions." Slater huffed. "Honesty and openness, right?"

"You shouldn't have to think about it," Pike said.

"I figured out what Brian and Thorpe were up to." He raised his eyebrows. "They were planning my demise. So I tried to arrange it so that Memo would go after them instead of me."

Hopkins frowned. "You tried to get them rubbed out? How?"

"I might have told Memo that they were going into production themselves to undercut him. That was a fabrication."

"Oh, forty-niner." Pike winced and massaged his forehead with his fingers.

"Hey, they put me in the frame. They tried to get me planted out in the desert. It's only fair."

Pike looked tired now, and folded his arms. "Do you remember what happened to Electra and Orestes when they took their revenge?"

"Didn't the Furies eat them?"

"They ate Orestes," Pike said. "Electra had to live with her own guilt."

"I don't think the Furies will come for me," Slater said. "My plan for those lowlifes backfired."

"What the hell are you two talking about?" Hopkins demanded.

"We've been reading the classics," Pike said. "It's kind of our thing. The Furies were the goddesses of retribution. They hunted down Orestes after he killed his mother."

"You are so fucking weird," Hopkins said.

Pike just laughed, and reached for Slater's cup, and sipped at his coffee.

"In the official debrief," Hopkins said, eyeing Slater, "you should gloss over the Furies, and also your revenge plan for Brian and Thorpe, considering that's hella illegal."

"He's right," Pike said. "Just say Brian coerced you to take the briefcase to Memo. You opened it to check and the cash was inside. Nobody will question that, since the money arrived at the other end, and you say it came from their house."

"I'm not just saying that it did," Slater said. "It really did."

"Omitting that part isn't lying," Hopkins said. "It's just to simplify the details a little. Smooth out the rough parts."

"I'll do that." Slater met his gaze. The guy was overestimating him. He had absolutely no problem distorting the story to protect himself. But he didn't need to point that out.

"And emphasize the thing about them coercing you," Hopkins said. "You don't want it to look like you were working for these people voluntarily."

"Guys, I get it," he said.

Pike was watching him, his brow furrowed.

"What?" Slater demanded, and threw up his hands.

"I'm just going through it. I guess it all washes."

"You don't need to treat me like one of your perps."

"It's the way we do things," Hopkins said. "You never take anything as the truth unless you can verify it. You know the drill."

Slater picked up the java and sipped at it. "It's really grating that Brian and Thorpe are sleeping in warm taxpayer-funded beds tonight instead of taking the long dirt nap out in the Mojave."

"Jail isn't actually all that comfortable," Hopkins said, and frowned.

"Based on the amount of meth and cash involved," Pike said, "they're going to be in for a while. Apparently the team that served the search warrant this morning found half a million bucks hidden in their garage."

Slater raised his eyebrows. "Interesting."

"You seem surprised," Pike said. "The three forty that you found in the house wasn't with the half million?"

"If I'm not going to be explaining that part, what difference does it make? I didn't coerce anybody." He waved a hand. "Knowing Brian and Thorpe are locked up isn't nearly as satisfying as if they were planted, but I guess it's better than if they were walking the streets and eating bonbons. What happens to Memo?"

"For Memo there's the manufacturing and distribution," Pike said. "That involves serious prison time. And we sent a crew to look at Lenny's land. They said there's definitely been digging recently along the arroyo, so that was good dope."

"You can leave my name off that part. Just say Lenny told you what he told me."

"No way." Pike chuckled. "You're already deep in this. That was your choice. You went out there to poke around, and you're going to have to include that in your statement."

"There can't be any unexplained leads," Hopkins said. "The prosecutors need to know why we looked at that place."

"Lenny told me that Memo was interested in his land, and he wished he'd never mentioned it to him."

"So it's simple," Hopkins said. "Just say that."

"Anyway," Pike said, "the crew that went out there thought it warranted a closer look. They requested a forensics team. If it turns out to be buried bodies, Memo is going away for life. Even if he wasn't the trigger man, he was calling the shots."

Slater nodded. "That suits me. I really don't want to be working for that lowlife anymore. What about Lenny?"

"I'm not sure where he'll land," Pike said. "Maybe he'll get smart and turn witness. He could make a deal to minimize his sentence."

"I don't think he's actually that smart," Slater said. "I feel a little bad for the guy."

"He's the one who decked you and zip-tied you to a patio chair."

"You don't need to have sympathy for these knuckleheads," Hopkins said. "They're not good people."

"I know that," Slater said. "but Lenny was the only one who never lied to me."

———•———

www.ingramcontent.com/pod-product-compliance
Lightning Source LLC
Chambersburg PA
CBHW011850300726
48970CB00009B/2729